SPIRAL WINDS

GARRY KILWORTH

SPIRAL
WINDS

THE BODLEY HEAD
LONDON

Acknowledgements: for permission to use two paragraphs
from the Penguin edition of the Koran translated by N. J.
Dawood.

The connection between this novel and my short story, also
entitled 'Spiral Winds', which was published in Interzone 9,
Autumn 1984, is merely the setting and general location.

British Library Cataloguing in Publication Data
Kilworth, Garry
Spiral winds
I. Title
823'.914 [F] PR6061.I39

British Library Cataloguing in Publication Data

ISBN 0 370 31112 4

Phototypeset by Falcon Graphic Art Ltd
Wallington, Surrey
Printed in Great Britain for
The Bodley Head Ltd
32 Bedford Square, London WC1B 3EL
by St Edmundsbury Press Ltd
Bury St Edmunds, Suffolk

For Andrew and Cheryl

AUTHOR'S NOTE

In May, 1935, T. E. Lawrence, the Arabian adventurer, was killed in a motorcycle accident involving two boys on bicycles. The idea for this novel has come from that incident, but I wish to point out that all characters are fictitious and are in no way intended to resemble known people. I have deliberately avoided research into the lives of the two youths who witnessed Lawrence's accident, so that no unconscious representation should appear in these pages. The geographical area covered in the novel is South West Arabia, where I spent some of my adolescent years and where I was sent for the final withdrawal of the British in 1966/67.

Garry Kilworth, 1985

The following phonetically spelt Arabic words, followed by a translation, may prevent frustration:

Aqabat – mountain pass
Jabal– mountain
Hayt – escarpment, hill
Hisn – fort
Sangar – ancient stone firing position
Ra's – headland, point
Wadi – dry watercourse, river, valley
Jambia – broad-bladed Arab dagger
Futa – cotton kilt
Wabar – coney
Simoom – hot suffocating wind.

Remember Charlie,
Remember Baker,
They left their childhood
On every acre.

'Goodnight Saigon'
Billy Joel

PLACE

They were playing a game of alternate questions and answers, only in this game one not only had to find the answer, but also the question.

"Listen," she said. "The sky is a deep blue, moving down to the horizon, until the rippled edge of the land accepts the task of filling the vacuum. Since it is morning, the east is lighter in tone, gradually, imperceptibly, growing darker as the eye travels westward.

"There is sand, occasionally broken by a range of volcanic hills rising like flames out of the dust, as far as you can see. Ribbed sand and barren, red rock. Here and there the topography is grooved by the track of an invisible, giant snake. Small cones of dust, whirlwinds, appear and disappear like phantom spinning tops.

"The heat is like an immense weight, that lies on the chest of the earth, heavier than an inquisitor's pressing-stone, yet no confession of heresy is forthcoming from the tortured landscape. Only the brooding silence of an eternal martyr.

"Over an area of bare rock the colour of coagulated blood, sliding upwards on a spiral thermal, a kite finds its lazy way to heaven, until its cross-shape becomes a speck. Tiny creatures scuttle between rare islands of shade and a wheatear rests on a ridge of yellow-ochre ironstone, which contrasts sharply with his black-and-white colours. Here, grows *shersher* and *ribla*, and coarse stiff grasses – *sherh* and *thumam*. Where water appears at the surface, tamarisk may be found, with its feathery clusters of pink or white flowers, and *samr*, with its down-soft blossoms.

"You stand in the centre of this vast, open place and you know that a single step will serve you no better as a means of escape than twice a thousand thousand. Even if your stride took you, magically, from horizon to horizon, you would die before you reached the safety of its borders.

"When darkness falls, the stars appear, closer to you than

9

you have ever seen them before: they seem almost within reach, and so coldly bright they would burn your hand like dry ice. The air freezes beneath them and the weight of heat is replaced by the weight of intense cold. The last vestiges of warm air, clinging to the earth, are sucked away by the great mouth of the night, and with them your own warmth, leaving your limbs like blocks, unwieldy, numb to the touch.

"What is my question and what is the answer?"

He said, "Your question is *where?* and the answer is *the desert.*"

"Wrong. My question is *when?* and the answer is *then, now* and *always.*"

ALAN

Alan leaned against the rail of the ship and stared across the smalt-blue waters of the bay with a feeling of disappointment in his breast. For a start, the ship had arrived in Aden three days late, due to storms, and though he had no appointment to keep he liked to be on time. It threw out his whole personal system if he was not in a place just when he expected to be. Secondly, one of the reasons he had chosen a sea voyage, in preference to air, was in order to experience the slow approach to Steamer Point, the main town. Now, because of a recent terrorist rocket attack on the oil refinery at Little Aden, ships' captains were cautiously mooring well outside the harbour. All he could see was a haze of brown rock – that would be the extinct volcano known as Crater, with the original town of Aden inside it – and a smudge of ochre beyond. It was bitterly disappointing. Not even the bum boats selling trash, or the boys who dived for coins, were willing to come out this far from shore.

The sea voyage itself had been typically unexciting, apart from the passage through the Suez Canal. The canal had been a place of activity, with feluccas struggling in the water like wounded butterflies and the banks bustling with energetic natives. He had always believed that hot countries engendered idleness, but having seen the brown and black figures, swathed in white, labouring in the fields alongside the canal, this myth was quickly dispelled.

The Red Sea had been a stretch of sweltering, seemingly unending, blueness. Only the occasional shark or shoal of flying fish broke the monotony of the long days. Alan was not a good sailor and the constant hammering of the ship's engines gave him a headache which found relief only in sleep. He was sick of deck quoits and bridge, and after the first week had attempted to keep away from the rest of the passengers, though he found that privacy on a ship was something of a luxury. On one occasion only he had been

11

invited to dine at the captain's table and though he enjoyed the privilege immensely, it was very brief and he had been sitting next to a colonial matron bound for India, who insisted on telling him repeatedly that independence had made no difference to the way she was treated in that country. She was so thick-skinned he doubted she would notice if they booted her up the backside, as he himself felt inclined to do halfway through the meal. She insisted, too, on using antiquated words like *steamer* and they grated on his nerves.

"What time does the steamer dock in Aden?"

"I'm sorry, I don't have my fob watch," he had replied, he thought with acidity, but she had smiled and given a tinkling laugh.

The British were in the process of withdrawing from Aden and by all accounts they were not getting off lightly for their years of occupation. Two terrorist groups were in main contention for power in 1966 – the National Liberation Front (NLF) and the Front for the Liberation of South Yemen (FLOSY) – and though these groups fought amongst themselves, the British were also prime targets. The Egyptians under Nasser supplied arms to the insurgents, mostly of British manufacture, a not uncommon irony, but there were also some Russian weapons. Incidents were on the rise and Alan was passing through at a bad time.

He leaned on the rail and watched the sun drop swiftly below the horizon. Soon the lights on the distant shore gave it a jewelled appearance. The air became no cooler: in fact the humidity, in the nineties, rose slightly. He felt limp and wet in his cotton shirt. The smells from the distant shore drifted across – not unpleasant, but certainly different.

A boat arrived alongside and passengers were ordered to gather their luggage together ready for disembarkation.

He awoke the next morning in the Red Sea Hotel to the sound of bagpipes playing 'The Barren Rocks of Aden'. Going to the open window he looked down to see a parade in progress on the nearby hard-packed red-earth square known as the *maidan*. Immediately below him were armed guards, presumably protecting the hotel. Limbs burned almost black by exposure to the sun hugged SLRs, the common British

Forces weapon, as innocuously as babes.

Steamer Point itself was a crescent of shanties and shops nestling in the crook between two spurs of Crater. Immediately facing the harbour, the buildings of the main street were protected by a large statue of Queen Victoria, who looked out upon her lost maritime empire with a tight expression. She was separated from the waterfront by the *maidan* and some precious grassy areas sprinkled with oleander shrubs, pinking the area beneath some royal palms. The latter were normally planted around the tombs of kings, since they were magnificent trees, twenty times the height of a man, and Alan thought it appropriate that they should shade the statue of a queen he admired.

From the main street, back to the gradual ascent of Crater, before it rose to sheer and jagged heights, the dwellings became progressively worse in appearance, culminating in hovels made of sandfilled biscuit tins covered in rags. Jabal Sham-san, the topmost point of the volcanic lip, was a pinnacle of red, igneous rock: a fairytale tower on which should have been perched the castle of Oberon. There were also fortifications of a bygone era, walls and keeps, that followed the line of the lower rim of rock. Dozens of kite hawks, brown scavengers of the skies, circled endlessly, effortlessly above, their keen eyes attentive for offal. Below them, in the safety of the rocks, pi-dogs wandered – lean, tic-infested and timid.

The bay itself was full of bum boats, dhows, and in the distance, liners like sleek racehorses, ready for the start. Alan watched a dhow pass close to the shore, could hear the creaking of its timbers and the crack of its sail as it changed tack.

He dressed quickly, eager to meet this land that had for so long been on his conscience, since he had once helped to rob it of one of its sons. It was right that he should be here. He could smell its unusual medley of odours: dust, fish, camphorwood, leather, sweat. He could hear the creaking of camel-drawn carts, the occasional rattling acceleration of an overheated engine. His perceptions were sharp and keen, honed by his excitement at the prospect of meeting an alien culture head on. Moments later came the call to prayer from

13

the muezzins, high in the minarets, and he felt that at last he had arrived. The sound floated over the town like the hollow, mooning note of an English owl over woodland.

Breakfast was being served on the veranda, behind a street-screen of anti-grenade fencing. He sat at a corner table, his eyes on the roadway outside. On the far pavement a beggar lay slumped against a wall like a badly filled sack of straw. Ancient and creased on every part of her exposed skin, she had no legs and the stumps were black with busy flies. Alan changed his seat.

A Somali waiter gave him orange juice followed by bacon and eggs. He thought they must be Christian caterers to serve bacon and enquired about a 'local' breakfast. The question received a blank stare for an answer, and the plate was pushed closer to his hands.

At precisely eight-thirty, his contact arrived. Alan approved of punctuality and said so.

Trevellian was young – possibly in his late twenties – but confident, and obviously used to dealing with older men. A thick gold wristwatch over a white sweatband was consulted immediately after they had shaken hands.

"Time for a coffee. Have you had one yet? Good, then I'll join you," Trevellian said. "After which we can get you fixed up. I understand your paper wants you to go up country – the Radfan and perhaps Yemen?"

"Yes that's right. I . . ."

"Ah, the coffee," interrupted the silk-haired Trevellian. A brass tray with coffee cups and pot was placed before them. The Somali waiter smiled. "Local," he said.

Trevellian stared at him in amazement, then laughed as he walked away.

"Good God, I think the fellow's having you on. Not often they joke, you know. Nothing's local here, except the bloody heat and the dust. Everything else is imported. Milk? I'm afraid it's condensed."

"No thanks. I'll have mine black, but with sugar."

He watched the bronzed arm with its fine blond hairs as it poured out the coffee. Trevellian was dressed in brilliant white shirt and shorts – these and his teeth set off his tan to great effect. Blue eyes suddenly fixed on his.

"If you don't mind," said Trevellian, "I think I'll have something with this. Waiter," he called, "a slice of lemon cake, when you're ready." A nod from the Somali who was serving an elderly couple due out with the tide on the same ship Alan had arrived on. The woman smiled and waved and he nodded curtly. The pair of them were dressed in faded colonial outfits, and looked a little shabby to Alan's thinking.

Cleanness, thought Alan. It was important. He was conscious of the beggar at his back and of the pristine skin of his near neighbour. Such a contrast. His new acquaintance wore his whites like a suit of polished armour, sparkling with inlaid sunlight; the blond body hair glinting like fine gold wire. A Christian armour, forged with purity, worn with *trawthe*. Admirable.

"Ah, the lemon cake. Local, I presume, waiter? Ha, ha. Grow them in the cellar, don't they?"

Both men seemed to appreciate the quip, the ebony and the teak. Only the pine, unseasoned and unfinished, did not share in the fun. He was conscious of being made to look a fool.

"Can you get me a guide?" he said, to change the subject.

"Good Lord, yes, but you'll need some guns too, to get you over a sticky patch just beyond Aden. I've got just the men for you. Rough types, but you'll need someone who can handle himself. The tribes out there can be pretty fierce. Got your goolie chit?"

"My what?"

"A joke, sorry. We usually tell moonies – new people – that they need a chit to go up country if they don't want to be castrated."

"That isn't funny," said Alan, going white at the thought.

"Well it is if you're not going up country."

The white teeth nibbled the edge of the lemon cake.

"Are you kitted out, by the way?" asked Trevellian.

"No. I was hoping I might get some khakis here."

Trevellian passed him a card.

"Use my tailor – he's good. It's in the backstreets but it's worth the risk. Makes a nice sharkskin evening shirt, if you're going to have time to be a little social while you're here. Just be careful. Keep your eyes skinned. The buggers are cowards really – hit you when you're not looking. Did you hear the incident last night?"

"What?"

"About three o'clock. Couple of Yemenis in a small car. Someone threw a grenade through the back quarterlight – vehicle looks like a balloon now. A very messy balloon, on the inside. A Russian job – detonator makes a noise like a pistol shot, just before it goes up. Remember that. If you hear a shot, hit the deck."

"No, I didn't hear it."

An army landrover passed by the hotel at that moment, bristling with tense-looking riflemen. The vehicle had an iron fencepost welded to its front bumper, which stuck out like a giant rhinoceros horn.

Alan said, "What's that for? The metal snout?"

"What? Oh, that. Cheesewire. The beggars stretch it across the road to try and decapitate motorcyclists – and people in open cars. It's not worked yet, to my knowledge. Not seen any headless riders, have you?" He laughed, breathing sweet lemon breath into Alan's face.

No, thought Alan, but I've seen someone without legs. The sooner he got out of Aden, the better. It was sordid. There was nothing romantic about a military machine defending itself against ragamuffin terrorists in dirty backstreets.

Alan noticed the black pips on Trevellian's epaulettes for the first time.

"You're a captain," he said.

"Shortly to be a major, if I keep my nose clean. That's one thing about being in a place like this – quicker promotion. Look, I'll have to leave you now. I'll drop by later to pick you up and introduce you to a few people. Don't forget – watch yourself. You're not safe anywhere at the moment – even where you see soldiers. The beggars are getting bolder all the time. Would have bought it myself if the golly had remembered to pull the pin out of the grenade. That's one thing in our favour. They're not very well trained – not yet. So, keep your eyes in the back of your head and you'll be all right. Cheers."

He rose, shook hands, and left.

Later, Alan went for a walk along the crescent. A group of children followed at his heels, incessantly murmuring "*Baksheesh.*" Shop owners, Indians, Arabs, Africans, accosted him at almost every step. They told him, as he walked away, that he was starving their children. Why didn't he do them a kindness, they said, and cut their throats if he wasn't going to buy? Rugs were thrust into his face, and watches, wallets, camel saddles, even bullwhips. What on earth did anyone want with a bullwhip? he thought. Presumably some people bought them, or the shops wouldn't stock them. He purchased a cigarette case which played 'Clementine', after a lot of haggling, though he really didn't want the thing. The shopkeeper had had breath like a gorilla's armpit fumes.

He had begun the walk in ease, but very soon afterwards the tenseness of the atmosphere filled him with apprehension. He became alert, alive to the fact that at any time a shot might electrify the already expectant population and there would be a burning sensation in his body, a pain of fire, and he would fall before smug onlookers. His eyes. How inadequate they seemed now. He needed more than just two, more than the narrow angle of vision they offered him. How difficult it was to carry fear casually, while inspecting stools and coffee pots! How difficult it was to fight down that feeling that had his nerves like stretched wires, his muscles so taut they ached, yet still nod and smile. And those damned children. If he gave them money, they would never go away. If he didn't give them money, they would follow him until he did. And if he was shot, would they rob him before the soldiers arrived? Why not? It wouldn't matter to him then.

Gradually, the fear left him. It was a bright day. Hot, but bright. His sweat dried in his shirt, leaving it stiff and uncomfortable. He passed a nurse, a European, in the street – starched, white and clean. Very, very clean. He leaned on a wooden stall, watching the clip-clopping of her shoes along the road. The shop fronts, dripping with leather and brass, produced no beseeching sales talk. How did she do it? Perhaps one had to be clean, spotless, like Trevellian and the nurse? Then they couldn't touch you.

He went into the backstreets, while his courage was high, and found – after asking a policeman in a black fez – the tailor

17

recommended by Trevellian. He was a smooth, over-polite Indian who ran his hands over sensitive areas when measuring Alan's waist and inside leg. Alan bore this with patience. He had agonised over the correct thing to wear in the desert and this man seemed to know exactly what was appropriate. He would thank Trevellian later.

The smell of the backstreets wafted into the open shop doorway. The owner had a small fan, but it seemed to make little difference to the air inside the shop. Flies flew in and out, with impunity, as if they too had been recommended this particular tailor. Across the street, directly opposite the shop, was a tandoori oven. The baker was skilfully swirling dough into pancakes and slapping them on the inside walls of the clay beehive shape. Next door to him was an ironsmith's, where two men worked, a forge between them, hammering out unidentifiable shapes from an old anchor chain. Occasionally they applied some ancient-looking bellows to the forge and filled the tailor's shop with waves of added heat and the smell of charcoal, as the fire flared white and intense. The tailor himself also sold silver filigree work and he persuaded Alan to buy a delicate little butterfly brooch.

He left the shop and on walking back to the crescent heard a loud explosion, which seemed to come from within Crater, behind the lip of the cone. There was a lot of shouting, the sound of running feet wearing boots, and then the noise level reduced again to the normal bustle of the backstreets.

The sound had stunned him into immobility and the tremor left his legs boneless. He hurried with a thumping heart until he could see the oleander bushes and then made his way towards the hotel. Life seemed to be going on as if nothing had happened. He collected more children. Out in the shallower waters of the bay he could see fishermen swirling circular nets above their heads and tossing them like gossamer pancakes on to the blue sea. The violence and the following indifference were incongruous. As he crossed the street to the hotel, he tossed the cigarette case and butterfly into the legless beggar's hands. She stared at him in disbelief, before they disappeared, as if by magic, into the folds of her rags. He wondered why he didn't feel any better for his generosity. The Somali waiter grinned as he passed.

18

In the afternoon, Trevellian called to take him to RAF Khormaksar, where he was to have tea with the Commanding Officer and his wife. On the way they passed 376 Signal's Unit watchtower, where a lonely-looking RAF corporal was silhouetted against the blue sky, no doubt wishing he were at home in England with his family, instead of presenting himself as a target for some terrified Arab ex-clerk told to go out and shoot someone with a white face.

They skirted Crater, passing the entrance: a mere slit in the cone, wide enough for a single car, where at a future date a 'mad' colonel, beloved of his troops and disliked by his superiors, would lead the Argyll and Sutherland Highlanders into the enclosed town, to retake it after terrorists had enjoyed a brief spell of unchallenged occupation.

On arrival at Khormaksar, Alan was introduced to various people, who looked at him rather strangely when he enquired as to the correct form of address one should adopt when meeting a sheik or sultan.

From there he was taken to Shaikh Othman Gardens, where he met his first desert Arab. His guide was tall and arrogant-looking, with a short beard, coal-black like his eyes. Over a dirty shirt, he wore two crossed bandoliers of bullets, the leather stained with sweat and berry juice. He had a dusty cloth wrapped around his head in the semblance of a turban and he cradled the inevitable rifle. One of his eyes had a slight squint to it, which gave him a faintly wild, unstable look and gave Alan the uncomfortable task of wondering where to look himself and in which eye to place his confidence.

Alan inwardly quailed at meeting this imposing man. How was he to command such a warrior? How had Lawrence and Philby impressed such impressive men? He seemed to be staring at Alan the way one would inspect a *chit-chat* house lizard that was incapable of catching flies.

Though the man said little himself, Trevellian introduced him as Yussuf, the son of a local sheik. While this introduction was being carried out, a look passed between the captain and the Arab, which Alan was too slow to interpret. It seemed that a private joke was taking place, but about what

Alan had no idea. He shrugged it off as another imponderable facet of this strange land to which he had been sent.

Trevellian then asked Alan if he wished to see the flamingoes, out on the salt flats, before he went up country.

"Not much wild life up there," he said. "A few hyenas and hawks – not much more."

Alan declined. He wasn't interested in bird watching.

As they drove out of Shaikh Othman, he asked Trevellian who had found this awful heap of stones and dust in the back-end of nowhere.

"The Portugese were here for a long time – most of the fortifications you see were built by them. The Turks too. Then in 1839 a British sea captain called Haines hove in with the Indian Navy and we've had it ever since . . ."

"Until now."

"Yes, as you say, until now."

On the way back to Steamer Point they passed through Murder Mile, the strip of road that split the district of Maala into two malevolent halves. Because of the tight-fitting, interlocking Arab dwellings it was difficult to chase a terrorist in this part of town and more incidents took place here than in any other area, except possibly Crater. A recent rocket attack on one of the servicemen's flats which lined the road had resulted in a missile passing through one wall, piercing a newspaper being scanned before its reader retired for the night, and out through the opposite wall, without exploding. The newspaper now formed part of the ever-growing museum of artefacts connected with the troubles.

All Alan saw were women in dark purdah: black masks made of insulating tape and cardboard. It made them look terribly sinister and he could imagine them swooping down from the hills like Harpies, driving the fear of death into ordinary mortals like himself, with their hawk-like features and destructive eyes.

Trevellian dropped him at the hotel and he went immediately to bed.

When he woke the following morning there was a large, oily-black cockroach floating in a glass of water by his elbow. It was quite dead – drowned. Its legs stuck out from the yellowish underside of the carapace, giving it a claw-like appearance, while its antennae drooped into the water. The water itself was slightly discoloured around the creature.

He stared at the thing in disgust. It could not have scaled the outward-sloping walls of the glass, so it must have dropped into the water from the ceiling. The horrible thought that he was left with was that he had taken a drink in the early hours, from that very glass, without switching on the light.

Had it fallen in before, or after he had quenched his thirst? These creatures infested drains and sewers – God knows what. When had it fallen?

He had dropped off to sleep at two-fifteen. He had been reading about biblical Yemen, when the Queen of Sheba had ruled the region. The book lay open by the bed, where he had dropped it. It must have been about an hour later that he woke to take a drink.

He examined the wall.

How long would it have taken the foul creature to climb that? Presumably it could not move fast over a gloss-painted surface, could it? On the floor they scuttled rapidly, but on a vertical surface? Doubtful. Then there was the ceiling.

He paced the distance between the wall and the position of the glass. About five feet. How fast could a cockroach travel upside down? Surely it could not have navigated the wall and ceiling in a single hour? Yet, when one thought about it, an hour was a long time.

He considered going to the hospital for an injection, or whatever they thought fit, but decided he might be laughed at, so discarded this notion. Instead, he found some TCP in his luggage and took several gargles, swallowing a little in the process. He tried to recall if he had heard a splash during his half-awake state, but could not remember. In future he would cover the glass and, of course, the bottle of water. The next time he saw a cockroach, he would wait to see if it climbed the wall, and if it did, he would time its progress. Then he could put it out of his mind.

After breakfast he sat down and wrote a letter to Jim, telling him about his progress so far. Then he wrote a piece for his paper. At ten o'clock there was a mortar attack on the Seamen's Mission, not far from the hotel. Alan ran to the window at the first explosion and saw the last of the mortars fall, mostly in the sea. The gunner had overshot. There was a scream from the depths of the hotel during the attack, but Alan learned later that the first bomb had frightened the cook into spilling boiling soup on his foot and that it was not, as he thought at the time, a simultaneous attack on the hotel itself. He went out afterwards, when it was deemed safe, to inspect the damage to the mission, but all he found were some small potholes on the beach. It was hardly worth a couple of lines in his column. A nervous sentry called out, "Halt – *waqaaf*," as he passed the mission on his way back, but apologised when he saw that he was addressing a European. Out in the water, where the bombs had fallen just thirty minutes earlier, some young Arab boys were setting lines for catfish.

When Trevellian called for him at twelve, he asked if mortar attacks were common. It seemed to him that they were far more dangerous than the odd hand grenade tossed by a nervous runner.

"Not an everyday occurrence, certainly. They usually do it from the back of a lorry and drive the thing into the backstreets. I doubt you'll see another one while you're here. There's a rather droll story about an attack on the hospital. Some chap was working on the engine of his car when the mortars began falling around him. Afterwards, when they went out to look for him, he was nowhere to be found. 'Blown to bits' some fool said, but mortars are only antipersonnel – they're not high explosives – so they kept on searching. Finally, one of them heard a knocking from the bonnet of the car the chap had been working on and when they opened it, there he was, tucked inside, wrapped around the engine. He'd jumped inside and pulled down the lid.

"Now under normal circumstances, you couldn't stuff a cat in the space that chap managed to squeeze into. Funny thing, this fear of death. It can play havoc with the laws of science . . ."

"Hilarious," agreed Alan.

They drove out to the Officers' Beach Club at Gold Mohur where Alan had to shake lots more new hands and drink more than he was used to doing. While still a little drunk he went for a swim in the salty, tepid water and then helped a young nurse gather some razor shells from the shoreline for her collection. He told her he was going up country and she was duly impressed, but when he asked her for a date that evening she said she was meeting her boyfriend, who had actually brought her to the club and was sitting right over there . . . Alan looked up to see a tall, blackbearded man with glasses swilling down pints of beer.

"He's in the navy," the nurse explained. "The beard."

"Oh, yes, I wondered about that," Alan lied. In fact her boyfriend held not the slightest bit of interest for him.

"He looks a bit of a bear, doesn't he," she continued, "but in fact he's very nice."

On passing the man, he noticed that he wore a shirt monogrammed with the letters RPH on the pocket. *Obviously forgets his name after a few drinks*, thought Alan, maliciously. *Has to look at his pocket to find out who he is.*

In the early evening, Trevellian took Alan to the rifle range at Steamer Point.

"I can't let you have an SLR to take with you – they're a bit expensive, but this Lee Enfield was used by our chaps until quite recently. It's a good, reliable weapon. Holds ten in the mag."

Alan took the bolt-action rifle, with its old-fashioned wooden stock running the length of the barrel, and weighed it in his hands.

"Christ, it's heavy."

"The SLR's heavier – that's only about nine pounds."

"Haven't you got something smaller? What about a pistol or something?"

Trevellian took out his own revolver and handed it to Alan.

"Have a go with that, at the target over there." He pointed down the range at some squares of cardboard, about twelve by twelve inches.

"That's the safety catch – there – " said Trevellian. "Okay, you're all set. Aim. Squeeze the trigger . . ."

The pistol bucked sharply in Alan's hand and each time he pulled the trigger, the shot went wild. Not one hit the target.

"Still want to take a pistol?" said Trevellian, putting the weapon back into his holster.

"Okay, but there's no guarantee I'll be any better with this thing."

He lay on the ground, adjusted the leaf sight as he was instructed, and managed to put four out of five shots somewhere on the piece of cardboard.

"Accurate job isn't it?" smiled the captain. "We'll make a John Wayne of you yet."

"Not hardly," said Alan, grimly, in a fair imitation of the actor's accent.

He spent an hour pumping .303 rounds into cardboard targets, until he was satisfied he could handle the weapon to a reasonable degree of skill, before Trevellian gave him a display of marksmanship with his pistol, proving, thought Alan, that it was not the song that had been at fault, but the singer.

"It's taken years of practice to arrive at that level of proficiency," Trevellian said. "Don't let it fool you. In any case, you couldn't stop a cockroach with it . . ."

"Speaking of cockroaches . . ." Alan began, but faltered. He lost his courage.

"Yes? What about them?"

"Nothing," said Alan, glumly. "Nothing important."

They drove back to the hotel.

"Tomorrow," Trevellian told him, "the camel."

"Camel?" Alan's stomach felt lead-weighted.

"You've got to learn to ride, haven't you? Do you ride a horse, by the way?"

"No."

"Good, because it's nothing like that. You won't have any bad habits. I'll get one of the Levies to give you some instruction. They're our local force – the Protectorate Levies. Grand chaps."

"Arabs?"

"Naturally, but nothing like Yussuf, the man you met yesterday. These are all clean-shaven military men. Crack fellahs with a camel. See you tomorrow."

"I'll look forward to it," Alan said, not without a trace of sarcasm.

Riding the camel proved to be just as much of an ordeal as Alan had imagined it would be. For a start the beast smelled like an old rug that had been buried under a rubbish heap for a century. It continually tried to turn its head and bite his leg and it would not follow commands unless they were reinforced by its Arab trainer. It was an ugly, slobbering creature that reserved the right to hate whoever it wished, and Alan appeared to be at the top of its list.

"I suppose this is absolutely necessary," said Alan, miserably, from his perch on the hump.

"Absolutely," confirmed Trevellian.

"I thought it might be."

"Give you a couple of weeks and you'll be charging around, shooting one-handed from the saddle. You wait and see. It'll come to you. Just got to get the knack, that's all."

"For one thing, it's bloody high up here. If I fall off, I'll break my neck."

"You won't fall off. Just needs a little confidence. Here, watch."

Trevellian got the camel to kneel and allowed Alan to climb down before getting into the saddle himself.

"Ha!" yelled the captain, and the dromedary set off, first at a loping pace, then a gallop, until the captain's hat came off in the wind he was creating and his hair streamed out from his skull. He went three times around the stockade, weaving in and out of veranda posts, before returning to the spot where Alan stood.

"There you see," said Trevellian, breathlessly, but obviously exhilarated. "Nothing to it. Soon get the hang of it. Now, what about a drink at the mess?"

"Sounds like a good idea," Alan replied, grasping at any excuse.

At ten o'clock that night, Trevellian called at the hotel and found Alan in his room, writing.

"How would you like to see a bit of action tonight? You may have to get used to it. There's more up country."

"Where? When?"

"We've had a tip-off that there's going to be an attack on the cold storage plant in Maala tonight. Do you want to

25

come along? Must be boring for you, spending all your time in this room."

"Not exactly *all* my time," said Alan, wryly. His backside still ached from the afternoon's riding and there were bruises on his shoulder from the Lee Enfield. "Still, it sounds exciting. Just give me a minute will you?"

"Sure." The captain sat on the bed, while Alan tried to concentrate on finishing the paragraph. "What's the tape measure for?" Trevellian pointed to the floor where the instrument in question lay full length, the brass end touching the base of the wall.

"Oh, that?" Alan felt himself flushing. "I borrowed it from that tailor you recommended. Very obliging man."

"Yes, but what's it for?"

"Been measuring some trousers," mumbled Alan, "to get the length right for him."

"Didn't he measure you up in the shop?"

"I'm a bit particular about the length of my trousers. I like them all exactly the same."

"Funny place to leave it – looks like you've been pacing something out." The captain reached down and rolled the measure into a tight roll, placing it carefully on the bedside locker. Alan started another sentence to hide his confusion.

"I'm ready now," he said, after a couple more minutes.

The cold storage plant was situated at the back of Maala, against a honeycomb, perpendicular spur of Crater. The sentry was situated on the roof: normally only one, but three more were placed in the building on this night. Alan and Trevellian were in one of the corridors on the east side, and a barred window provided a viewing point for them both. Along the corridor itself were rows of doors – the kind you see on the huge refrigeration units in butchers' shops.

Though it was a moonlit night outside, the plant was overshadowed by several taller buildings and the visibility was poor. Trevellian had some night glasses which he passed to Alan, who, on looking through them, could define the shapes of the buildings and alleys around them. He passed the binoculars back to the captain.

"Three men enough?" he whispered.

"And one upstairs, don't forget. Oh yes, I think so. It

won't be a full-scale assault or anything like that. Two or three probably. They don't work in larger units."

"Oh."

"And these are good men. Picked them myself. Dunn's already got himself a golly."

For a moment Alan had a mental picture of a soldier being tucked into bed with a golliwog. Then he realised what Trevellian meant. The man had killed an Arab. He was sickened by Trevellian's attitude. A man's life was not a thing to treat with such disrespect – was it?

"I don't think I like that."

"Like what?" Trevellian was peering through the glasses.

"Your – casual language."

Trevellian turned to face him and though he could not see the details of his face Alan imagined an arched eyebrow.

"Bit prim aren't we, old chap?"

"If you like."

They didn't speak to each other after that until Alan saw the coloured lights. They were quite pretty, like a stream of fireflies arcing through the black night, and he was about to mention them to Trevellian, when a thumping sound from the wall below the window outside distracted him.

"Shit!" said Trevellian. "Tracer. Keep your bloody head down, man."

Suddenly the night was full of noise. It seemed incredible that the thunder which almost deafened him came from small-arms fire and Alan clapped his hands over his ears. Trevellian was firing through the window, which he had smashed with the butt of his revolver, and each shot reverberated throughout the catacomb hollowness of the storage plant as if God were clapping his hands.

There was a brief moment of silence.

"Baker!" yelled Trevellian.

"Sir?" a voice boomed back from along the corridor to the right.

"Did you get Group?"

"Should be on their way, sir. Set's a bit garbled tonight but I reckon they got it."

"Good man."

Alan said, "He's got a radio?"

27

"Right. The patrol should be cutting them off from behind . . ." He paused as two more rounds smacked into the wall outside. He yelled again, "Dunn. Can you see them?"

A voice from the roof: "One o'clock, sir. In the old schoolhouse. Top left window. Shall I put a few over there?"

"Wait a minute. Baker, is the patrol closing in?"

Alan could hear a sharp muttering from the other corridor.

"Just going in now. Wait . . . sods. They seen 'em comin'." The sound of gunfire in the distance.

"Didn't want Dunn to fire, because we want them to come this way, not run before the patrol could cut them off," Trevellian explained calmly to Alan. "It's all right now. We've got the bastards pinned." He raised his voice, "Okay, Dunn."

The man on the roof began firing steadily, pouring tracer into the window of the building which housed the terrorists. Alan watched in awe. Surely no one could avoid being hit by such a hail of bullets?

"What I think will happen," shouted Trevellian, "is that, rather than face the patrol they'll either stay there and fight it out, or make a run for it this way. Depends on how much ammo they've got."

"But there's nowhere to go, back here."

"Yes, but they probably think there's only one or two men in here, as is normal. The patrol will be getting reinforcements and they won't have any choice. They'll try to get on our roof and away over the roofs of the buildings to our left. There's only a narrow alley separating them. They'll be sheltered by the taller buildings in front."

"Didn't you think of that – before now, I mean?"

Alan saw the gleam of Trevellian's teeth as searchlights were suddenly trained on the schoolhouse from the far side.

"I've got a man in the alley. He'll shoot their bollocks off as they jump."

Alan suddenly felt ill. "Jesus," he said quietly. He was wondering why he hadn't stayed in his nice safe room at the hotel. It wasn't so much that he was afraid for himself, but he had no desire to witness a carnage, whoever the victims were. This was not how he had imagined it at all. He couldn't see very much, but he could hear it, and somehow that made it worse. He didn't think he would be able to take just lying there listening to men dying, possibly screaming out the last vestiges of their lives in an alley right next to his ears.

Throughout the night there was sporadic firing from both sides but Alan was glad that Trevellian did not use his pistol again. His head was still ringing from those first few shots.

Baker shouted, "They've got a Saladin on the main road," just before dawn came.

"Saladin?" he queried. "Who's got it?"

"He means we have an armoured car on the main Maala stretch – just precautionary, in case some of their pals decide to make a battle of it. It's never happened yet – not in town."

When daylight came they could see a figure in a shirt and *futa* kilt, half-hanging out of a window. It looked like an abandoned rag doll.

"Is that one of them?" said Alan. He was amazed and strangely frightened. He hadn't even heard the man die. How could you die without people around knowing about it? It seemed obscene. People should be aware when a life is draining out, into the unknown. It was a terrible event and not something that should happen secretively. It needed witnesses, in order that the horror should remain imprinted on minds and never be repeated. He swallowed hard.

"Was that you, Dunn?" called Trevellian.

"Can't say, sir. Could 'ave been. That's the window I was firing at. Still alive though. Saw 'im move a minute ago."

Trevellian said, "That means they'll give in shortly. I don't think they'll let him die."

"Why don't they pull him in?"

"Probably can't get near the window – or scared. I wouldn't be surprised if they're shitting their pants in there."

"You think so?"

The captain appraised him coolly.

"Wouldn't you be? They're only men, like you and I. I remember losing my temper and slapping one once. He was so outraged, I think he would have strangled me, if he could have reached me. He kept repeating, over and over again, 'I am man. I am *man*, like you. Why do you do this thing: I am

29

man, *man*, *man*.' I had given him a terrible insult, you see. Didn't intend to, but one of my boys got it in the back the night before and we were sure this fellow knew something. Lost my temper. Never done it since. 'I am *man*, like you.' Never forget that. Don't mistake these fellows for cowards – or callous fiends. They're men, like us."

"Gollies," said Alan, sarcastically.

"God, you're a prig," said Trevellian, and went back to staring out of the window, leaving Alan more confused than before. The man was either a brutish bigot, or he was an understanding, sensitive human being. You couldn't be both. Yet this Trevellian seemed to sway from one to the other. How could you fathom such fickle characteristics?

"Here they come, sir!" Dunn's voice sounded jubilant.

Two Arabs came out of the schoolhouse, like children caught playing truant, and sat in the road with their hands on their heads. Trevellian ran outside yelling, "Baker!" The soldier with the radio followed him.

Alan left the building just as they were putting the wounded Arab on a stretcher. He was screaming now, but it was the cry of pain in life, not pain in death. Alan could listen to that, ugly as it was. There were soldiers everywhere and Trevellian was looking very pleased with himself. On seeing Alan, his face took on a much graver expression.

"Well," he said. "At least we didn't lose anyone to Silent Valley."

"Silent Valley?"

"Our local graveyard. Aptly named, don't you think? Do you want to go back to the hotel now? I'll get one of my men to take you. I've got to make out a report."

"Thanks." Alan felt as if he were in a dream-state. Lack of sleep probably, and the tension. Everything was getting a little fuzzy at the edges. He wiped a hand over his dry mouth. The sun felt hotter than usual.

"All that over a few frozen carcasses and some crates of butter," he said.

Trevellian looked visibly startled.

"What?"

"The attack. On the cold storage plant."

Revelation showed in the captain's features.

30

"You've got it all wrong, old chap. They weren't after dead meat – it was live meat that was their quarry. They just wanted a body to add to their statistics. Instead, we've got three to add to ours. The numbers game."

"Is that what it was all about? Statistics?"

"Can't escape the bloody things. Leaving a desk behind in the office means nothing. The bloody stats follow you out into the field. Not much glory in it, is there?"

"None at all."

"Course, it's different up country. Man against man there. Gunslinger territory. See you later."

He strode off, towards a vehicle. Alan saw him say something to a soldier and the man came up to him and said he would drive him back to the hotel.

Back in his room he went straight to his notebook and tore out the sheet which he had intended to send to the hotel management, about the lack of cupboard space in the room, and began to write his column. He wanted to be able to phone it through before the day shift came in to work at the office in Fleet Street. He liked to think that whoever was there to receive it would be as drugged through lack of sleep as he was himself. It seemed right, somehow.

Halfway through, he sent down for a cup of *mazqul*, the local coffee. He had since learned that it had not been a joke. The coffee really was local. And its ability to keep him awake was nothing short of adequate, since he just made it through the report and then had to have a cold shower in order to feel up to phoning it through. He was not used to spending nights without sleep, though he would become better at it in future.

There was a dance, two nights later, at the Gold Mohur Club. Alan was not fond of dances. He had a well-coordinated action when it came to walking or climbing, but his movements were too disciplined for dancing. He moved like a robot and had no feel for the rhythm. On top of that, it bored him tremendously. He dreaded the time when the band turned to rock-and-roll numbers, which they invariably did after a series of foxtrots and quicksteps. He could jerk through the latter with a semblance of dignity, but the more

31

abandoned dances were completely beyond him. The group consisted of military bandsmen in any case, so the music tended to be a bit stiff and precise.

Luckily, the Beatles had recently turned to slower songs, like 'Strawberry Fields' and 'Penny Lane', so that when the time came, he was able to waltz his way through, to a fashion. As a new male in a stagnant society, it was expected of him to put himself about a bit.

He struggled through three numbers with the matronly wife of a group captain, who to his discomfort squeezed his buttock at the end of the dance. He led her back to her seat. He then felt obliged to ask her pretty companion, a small woman with a pert look and short, dark hair, to stand up with him for the Tom Jones ballad, 'The Green, Green, Grass Of Home'. After a few turns around the floor, during which time it was plain to him that she was preoccupied with something, she suggested they go outside for some fresh air. He agreed.

They walked down to the seashore, where the reflections of the stars were dancing on the water, light on dark. The continual swishing of the wavelets, almost to the time of the background music of the dance, was a peaceful sound and he did not attempt conversation, allowing her to remain absorbed in her thoughts. It was she who broke the silence between them.

"How long have you been in Aden, Mr . . .?"

"Please call me Alan."

"If you like."

"How long? Oh, just arrived, more or less. And you?"

"Sarah. Sarah Mitchell. I've been here two years. They're about to send me home."

He studied her face in the poor light.

"You don't sound too happy about it."

"It's . . . I'm sorry. Bit difficult to explain. I'm splitting up with my husband. I don't want to burden you with my problems." She hesitated, then added, "I recently had a rather strange experience – in the desert. It's partly due to that."

"Oh, I don't mind you unloading on me."

He wondered whether he actually did mind. Normally he

shied clear of domestic dramas, not wishing to get involved in something he found distasteful. But she looked so vulnerable: it brought out the protector in him.

"You've probably heard the story already, from someone else. It's common gossip, when I'm not around. I got lost – in the desert. They didn't find me for three days."

He had heard something, now that she came to mention it. Sarah. Sarah who? The name didn't mean anything, but Trevellian had told him that some woman – one of the wives – had gone wandering off by herself, and . . . Good Lord, yes. Some scandal or other attached to it. He remembered the group captain's wife prattling on about a liaison between her companion and a mysterious man. The only part he recalled with any clarity was the bit about 'not blaming her because Aden was so stiflingly boring with many of the men up country and there being so little to do'. Warning bells had begun to jangle at that point and he had quickly changed the subject.

"Ah, I did hear something," he said, and hated the way the embarrassment he felt came out in his tone.

"It was rather traumatic, so you'll forgive me for seeming a little distant."

"Of course. Of course."

Across the water the lights of Little Aden studded the darkness. He hoped she would soon ask to go back inside. He could not very well suggest it himself, or she would think he was trying to get rid of her. He had to wait it out.

After a while, she said, "Please don't think my husband is trying to get rid of me. Soiled goods and all that. It's me, not him."

"Didn't give it a thought." His collar felt tight. Why did they make the damn things too tight?

"John is a nice man, in his way. But I've been unhappy for some time now. I don't want to go home, you know. I'd give anything to stay here. *Anything*." She looked at him fiercely. There was a moment of uncomfortable silence, before she added, "You don't want someone to help you, do you? I'm pretty good at photography."

He loosened his bow tie.

" 'Gainst the rules, I'm afraid."

33

Her mouth set in a thin line.

"Yes, of course. The *rules*."

"If anything comes up, I'll be sure to let you know. You can count on that."

"I never count on things." She sounded terribly sad. "I don't suppose you've ever had an experience that has altered your life." It was a statement.

He saw a way to divert the subject and grabbed at it eagerly.

"Matter of fact, I have. When I was a boy. A friend and I were involved in the death of a man. A very famous man."

"Oh?"

"Yes. Went through a bad time afterwards. So I know a little of how you feel. Altered my whole perspective on life. Guilt. It evolves into obsession. To a degree that incident is responsible for me being here now. The man that died – his fame came from his exploits in this area.

"Of course, if this whole business – the spread of armed insurrection throughout South West Arabia – if that hadn't blown up, my paper would never have sent me. But I'm glad they did."

She turned her hazel eyes on him.

"The desert has a way of drawing us to it, hasn't it?"

"What do you mean?"

"Well, if there had been no violence out here you would never have been sent, would you? This land creates its own history. People are incidental. It uses them, I think."

He did not like the way the conversation was going.

"That's a very strange concept. You ought to talk to Jim. He says things like that."

"Jim?"

"The friend that was with me at the time of the accident. When we were boys. I'll give you his address before you go. I'm sure he'd love to talk with you about this place. He's more obsessed with it than I am. Collects all sorts of junk about the place – photos, maps – you name it."

"And you don't?"

"Not to the same degree."

"And yet, you're here, and he's still in England."

Alan shrugged.

34

"Luck of the draw. I asked him to come with me, but he's got a wife and mortgage, and a job to hold down. Strong sense of duty, you see."

He looked out over the sea, into an immense darkness that seemed to be moving towards him, ready to engulf him in its oblivion.

Over the next three weeks Alan practised with the rifle and the camel, becoming moderately proficient with both. He went swimming once, with the young nurse, at Conquest Bay. She introduced him to the delights of underwater swimming with a snorkel and mask and he found a new world beneath the waves, of brightly coloured coral and strange fish. Once, he saw a shark – a three-footer, probably a sand shark – which swam by him indifferently. The only thing he really did not like were the moray eels, some of them as thick as a man's thigh. They poked their ugly heads out of holes in the reef and he was told that if they sank their needle teeth into you, nothing on earth would make them let go. Sting rays he didn't mind because they swam close to the bottom, where he never went, and they looked like slow birds leisurely gliding just above the sandy sea bed. The ocean was a fascinating place.

There came the day when he set his face towards the mountains of the Yemen. Trevellian was there to see him off.

"Good luck. I don't know when I'll see you again, but I hope it goes well for you." Trevellian shook his hand.

Alan said, "Thanks. Don't wait up for me."

The sun was just setting. The first part of the journey was to be at night, away from the eyes of any informers.

Four riders and two pack camels went north.

JIM

It was a grizzled November day, with hoar frost covering the trimmed lawns, as Jim made his way down the hill towards Shenfield railway station. Before he reached the paper shop it had begun to rain and he cursed himself for not taking more notice of Maddie when she suggested he take his overcoat. He hated umbrellas and never carried one. By the time he got to work, at the Bank of Saudi Arabia, he was soaked through and spent the rest of the day in damp discomfort.

At three o'clock he received a call from the front desk to say that a woman by the name of Sarah Mitchell was waiting for him in the lobby. Puzzled, he went down to see her. She was a small person, with a haughty tilt to her chin, and she introduced herself in a cultured accent. She explained, after he had shaken her hand, that she had met his friend Alan in Aden, and that Alan had suggested she look Jim up once she was in London.

". . . but you're probably terribly busy now," she said, "so perhaps we could have a drink together, this evening, early?"

"Why not? Do you know the Princess Louise? – you must have passed it to get here."

"I'll find it," she smiled. "Six o'clock?"

"Fine. I'll phone my wife – tell her I'll be late."

"Lovely. See you then."

Jim then went back to his office, wondering why Alan should foist strange women on him.

He almost forgot to go to the pub to meet her, but remembered just before entering Holborn station. He found her sitting in one of the booths, listening to a jazz band in the corner, playing 'Bad Penny Blues'.

"So you met Alan?" Jim said, after they had exchanged civilities.

"Yes, very briefly. At an awful dance. He gave me your

36

address and suggested I look you up. It is all right, isn't it? I didn't want to go to your home because – well, it would look a bit funny to your wife, a strange woman calling. Alan said you worked at the Saudi bank, so I decided to go there instead."

She blew out a stream of smoke.

"I don't know anyone in London, you see, and Alan talked about you for a bit. From what he told me, we seem to have a lot in common."

Jim could not think what he would have in common with a woman newly returned from abroad, but he said nothing of this, instead asking, "Were you in Aden long?"

"Two years. My husband was stationed there. We're recently separated."

"I'm sorry . . ."

She gave a small wave of her hand.

"Please . . ."

He could see that she had been out of the country by her clothes. Although she wore a Mary Quant scarf, she had on a knee-length skirt, while around them mini-skirts barely covered the buttocks of most of the other women. This was quite the weirdest experience he had had in a long time. A woman seeking him out because of a passing remark by a friend. He felt very wary.

"You said we had much in common?"

She smiled, her eyes crinkling at the corners into tiny attractive crow's feet.

"Not *much*. Something. You're interested in South West Arabia, aren't you?"

Interested? Maddie, his wife, would call that an understatement. She said he was obsessed with the area. Had been ever since he and Alan had been involved in that accident as boys. He wouldn't call it an *obsession*, exactly. Sure, he collected maps and books, and the odd piece of trivia, like that *jambia*, and the Moslem prayer beads, but the place did not dominate his mind the *whole* time. That was the meaning of *obsession*, wasn't it? What was he supposed to do now? Launch into an enthusiastic monologue on the Yemen and Hadhramaut? Her eyes were on him, studying his expression.

"I'm sorry. Yes, I do have an interest. It's a place I've

always wanted to visit. Unfortunately, I have my job, which I enjoy very much. Other things. You know, they get in the way."

He found himself staring at her. She was an extremely attractive woman, not just in the sense that she was good-looking, but also that magnetic quality that some people have of drawing one's interest. It wasn't sex appeal either. It was something far less obvious. A vulnerability protected by a thin but hard shell? Not even that. It was an air of carrying some deep secret which only the privileged would learn. And she made you feel that you wanted to be her confidant. That she could reveal some mystery to you, which would alter your whole perspective on life.

"You're staring," she said. "I feel as if I were in a showcase."

"I'm sorry . . ." he blurted.

"And don't keep saying you're sorry," she sounded genuinely irritated. "I'm not fragile. I can take a bit of criticism over my appearance."

"It's nothing like that. You just looked a little sad, that's all. Is it your husband?"

"Not really. Oh, I'm lonely at the moment, but that will pass – and it's not for him. It was my decision to separate, not his. These things happen, sometimes over a long period of time, and in the end they seem quite inevitable and you wonder why you didn't realise it in the first place."

She turned her hazel eyes on him again and he felt lost.

"But you seem reasonably content with life," she continued, "do you have some secret? I want to know what I'm missing."

The jazz band were playing an Acker Bilk number and the music was jarring on his nerves.

"Yes, I'm content. Very satisfied actually. I have a nice home in the suburbs. Been married quite a long time now. No kids, unfortunately. Never got round to them. I like my job at the bank. I'm good with languages and they sent me on a course several years ago – Arabic, naturally. Don't have many qualifications outside banking exams, but then I don't need them because I intend staying where I am. You probably think that's pretty dull, especially now, in the

38

swinging sixties, but that's the way I am." He felt a little heady. "I don't drive, because I hate bloody cars. I don't wear a watch because everyone who works in a bank looks at their wrist a thousand times a day and my wrist isn't very pretty . . ."

She laughed then.

"Thin and hairy," he shrugged, amused in spite of himself. "Spiders shouldn't wear watches."

"It's not thin – it's *slim*. Don't put yourself down all the time. You're a very attractive man."

The words disturbed him, but in a pleasant way.

They spent an hour or two, talking. The conversation began with Alan, moved on to general subjects and ended with them discussing themselves.

They said good night to each other at the tube station. Sarah was taking a train west, while Jim was going east. He took her telephone number and promised to call her some-time, wondering whether he was getting into something which he had always told himself he would avoid.

Sarah Mitchell stared out of the tube train window, seeing only the desert sky, partly obscured by a man's features. The face was burned brown by the sun and wind. Around her, the sands drifted, forming and reforming in sensual shapes. In between the love talk, he whispered names into her ear, but they had no meaning and passed through her conscious, to her subconscious, without imprint. They were merely sounds, tones, that she would recall only in her dreams.

Then the face evaporated and she found herself staring into the sun. It bore into her with bright shafts, as the hot sand burned between her thighs, caressing her skin with its light touch. The warm winds found the secret places on her body, stroking her with its perfumed breath. It repeated the names, in soft moaning sounds, and called her . . .

Blackness rushed in. She jerked away from the train window with a small cry. None of the other passengers looked her way, however. Thank heavens for London indifference, she thought. Then she panicked again, wondering where she was going. With effort, she recalled her destination.

Then she thought about Jim.

He seemed a nice man, but under-confident, insecure. It was funny that he thought himself so safe. Even in just the short time she had been with him, she had sensed he was about to explode. He was holding everything down, frightened possibly that should he let go his whole life would go up in fragments. He was suppressing his inner self, keeping it contained under a tight lid.

She wondered why she wanted to prise that lid open and set light to the fuse underneath. The compulsion to do so came not from her, but from something that had been planted within her. She knew where it came from, but not why it was there. The source was known, but the reasons vague. Strangely, although she did not understand, she did not mind being used. It seemed right. The same thing that was driving her, would drive him some day. Perhaps it was already, but he was keeping it bottled up, like the rest of his feelings. The desert had touched him, long ago. Once you had been in its shadow, even from a great distance, you did not escape it easily.

Not that she herself wanted to escape. She would have given anything to stay there. And she would go back, soon. But she had this task to . . .

What? Oh, South Kensington. Just another station. Lights, people. People. Poor John. He had treated the desert as just another piece of scrubby ground. He had to work there, because that's what the army paid him for, but it meant nothing to him emotionally. When she had described to him how *she* saw the desert, how the dying sunlight of the evening caught the ochre rocks, brought out the dark, dried-blood hues in the landscape, her husband had scowled. Not laughed even, but scowled.

"But what made you go out there?" he had asked. "What on earth induced you to go? Walking out into a place you know you might get lost in. It's a thoroughly irresponsible act. The lives of others have been put at risk because you felt some idiotic poetic mood come over you. What made you do it?"

She had been weary of his arguments.

"I've already explained."

"You've told me nothing. Nothing. Just some vague remarked about being *called*, whatever that means."

"You wouldn't understand. It's not something I can put into words. It's just a feeling . . ."

"Well that's bloody obvious, woman."

He had thrown away the collection of dried desert flowers and told her that he was sending her home. It was out of his hands anyway. The army couldn't have dependants wandering off into the desert when they felt like it. She was obviously ill. Suffering under the strain of living in a hot, violent place. His career had been damaged by her stupidity . . .

Then he had become remorseful, saying he was sorry he was behaving like a boor, but she was not interested in his apologies, or his anger. He was totally outside her sphere of concern any longer. She had other things to do. John was history.

The last day in Aden, she had spent looking out of her window in the house at Khormaksar – out into the nothingness where her true self lay. Would he come? Would he come at the last moment, when the sun withdrew its rays from the desert floor? He was locked inside her soul, and she would not even tarnish his memory by denial. That had hurt John. She had seen the hurt in his face and she pitied him, but what was she to do?

"The goatboy was with you the whole time," John said.

"Even goatboys have to sleep."

"I'll never divorce you, you know that. By God, if I thought this was true . . . but there's no one like that out there."

"Let me have a divorce, John."

"No. I'll fight you all the way. And if I meet this . . . I'll kill him. You understand that. I'll kill him."

Of course, he never came for her.

Lying on the strange bed, in the strange room, with the stranger beside him, Jim could see the tin angels. Sarah had told him about them before they had gone to sleep, some time during the early hours of the morning. To a fourteenth-century monk, the illusion would probably have been associated with some kind of inner revelation, a sudden insight into the deeper meaning and order of the universe. The poet Hopkins had a word for it: *inscape*. In reality they were the floodlights of the adjacent tennis courts which he could see through the low window, but with the sunlight behind them they had the appearance of cherubim with trumpets, heralding the day. In a world which had too many people, and too many machines, Jim was happy to allow his perspective to be tampered with, so long as it was a peaceful, relaxing experience.

"What are you going to do now?" Sarah said, pulling his attention reluctantly back to the real world.

He turned on his side to look at his companion. She was a small woman, with large expressive eyes, and hair cut very short, emphasising the roundness of her features. He noticed that her collar bones protruded higher above her shoulders than most people's, like the beginnings of little angel's wings themselves. She seemed relaxed, her face free of the small tension wrinkles that occasionally formed around the bridge of her nose: they had disappeared when the two of them had begun making love a few hours previously. It had been their first time together and he found it wonderful that her complexion, features and skin became youthful during the physical act of love.

"I don't know – go to work I suppose?" He hoped that was what she meant: his immediate plans. He was not collected enough to propose any long-term plans that might include them both.

Under his gaze she pulled the sheet up over her naked brown body, closer to her chin. It was an involuntary action. He could see by the way she realised, too late, how obvious it looked and pretended to be smoothing the bed. Earlier, she had tried to hide her abdomen with her hands.

"What's the matter?" he had asked her.

"Appendix scar. It's ugly."

"Nothing about you is ugly." He searched for the right words, but could not find them. "These things are just part of you – the whole you – and I find everything about you attractive."

"You're just blind at the moment. Am I the first – since you got married, I mean?"

He immediately thought of Maddie and a hot wave of guilt passed through him. Still, he had done it now. The betrayal. Adultery. That was an ugly word. He didn't want to hurt her . . .

"Yes. The first since then."

She kissed him fervently. "I *wish* I could tell you the same thing, but I don't want to begin by lying to you."

"Of course not." He felt a certain amount of despair enter his heart. Why *couldn't* she lie to him? Or say nothing at all. Why was it essential to lay out the history, for the inspection of the other? Life began now, didn't it?

He turned over in bed and smelt the dryness of her skin. She had an aridness to her body that belied her spirit. They made love again, and again he was startled by the way in which her face became much younger: a serene expression. She nestled into the nape of his neck once they had finished.

He stared out of the window again, at the tin angels, but they refused to be seen in their fantasy role. They were just floodlights.

"What are you thinking of?" she asked, turning to look up at him.

"I was thinking of Alan," he said, a moment later.

She straddled his leg with her own chubby thighs and he could feel the pressure of her mound hard against him: not soft, but warm. It was almost painful.

"Now? *Alan?*" She was teasing him.

"Well not him, especially. But the whole scene out there. The different culture."

"There's a desert in my eyes," she said, and he looked and was worried for a moment when he saw it there.

"Don't look like that," he cried, startled. Then he felt silly. "I'm sorry. I couldn't see myself in there anywhere."

Her mouth tightened a little.

"It's only a single night, Jim. I can't make any commitments to the future on just that."

She rolled away from him and stared at the ceiling.

"I'm sorry," she said, after a while. "I'm making too many

43

assumptions, aren't I? You do what you feel best. I'll be around for a while."

"I know. I know. Give me some time to sort my feelings out. I'm still confused."

She bit her lip as she looked at him.

"If you wait too long, you'll only get more confused. I'm not trying to push you. I'm just giving you a little advice."

"You're the expert."

"That's a nasty thing to say."

"Yes, it was," he said, contritely. "I'm sorry. These things come out without me meaning them to."

She had had one or two lovers. She had told him that. He was the most important for the moment – but how long does a moment last? Did he want for ever? He wasn't sure. He was married. He had no rights whatsoever. He could ask for no promises, nor expect fidelity. Christ, what *did* he want? He knew one thing, which was ignoble of him. He felt a burning jealousy towards those other lovers. He hated them with an intensity that scared him. Those ghosts, damn them. Would they always be in bed with the two of them?

"Let's play a game," she said, "of questions and answers. I'll tell you how it goes . . ." And she did.

He learned something, during that game, about the depths of her feelings for the land which held Alan at the moment – which had held both of them, from a distance, since boys. The knowledge scared him.

"We'd better get up in a moment," she said.

"Why?"

"Because, because . . ." she said, playfully.

"What a shame. I wish we were twenty. On second thoughts, you would have hated me at that age."

"How old *are* you?"

"Forty-seven."

Her head jerked up. "Christ, you're a cradle snatcher. I'm only thirty-three."

For a moment he felt panic – that she would end it there and then. But she snuggled back down and in a small voice added, "You know I don't mind."

She went downstairs to make breakfast while he shaved. He paused halfway through the operation to study the deep lines in his forehead. Surely she must have known? He looked all of forty-seven – if not more. Love wasn't that blind. Not at their age. Hair, greying indiscriminately. Small dark eyes that seemed to sink deeper with every season, like two shy animals retreating into their burrows. *All* of forty-seven. Or was it the different perspective thing again? Did she notice quite different features, placing the emphasis according to her own subconscious list of important physiognomic details? Perhaps she saw someone whom he would not recognise if he met him face to face? *She might be in love with a stranger to me*, he thought. A stranger in personality, character and outward appearance.

Certainly, he didn't feel like Jim – the Jim he knew. He felt like a puppet made up to look like Jim. A mechanical thing which would not allow the human in him to come forward. One reason was, it was difficult to shake off the 'guest in a hotel' feeling, whenever he went to pick something up, or sit somewhere. Nothing belonged to him: was not even a shared possession. Everything was hers and he even had that schoolboy urge to request permission to use the toilet. It was an odd sensation. At home, he would have picked up the phone and dialled without thinking. Here, he asked first. When – *if* – they came to live together, he would have to alter his whole mode of thinking or he would be unable to function.

When he had finished washing and shaving he wrote I LOVE YOU in soap on the mirror. Then immediately he felt foolish. She would probably regard it as childish, in the way that she did his occasional pranks. There was tea and toast on the table when he got down, but he waited until she had washed and dressed before starting.

"I must write to Alan today," he said, more to himself than to Sarah. "Would you like to add a postscript?"

"What for?" Her large eyes stared at him over a mug of coffee, their almond shape distorted by the steam. Were they violet? He had thought they were hazel.

"What for?" she repeated.

"It'd be nice, that's all. He doesn't have anyone else. No female to write to. A little feminine prose might lift his spirits."

45

"How about femin*ist* prose? Do they need lifting? What do you call feminine prose? Flowery?"

"Don't do it if you don't feel like it. It's only a suggestion."

"I want to get to know all your friends," she said, suddenly enthusiastic. "Yes, all right. There can't be any harm in it."

"Is it hearing about the desert that's bothering you?"

She appeared nonplussed for a moment and coloured slightly, before saying, "I've always been interested in the lonely places of the earth. I *like* hearing about the desert. It's you who seems afraid . . . Somehow I get the idea that you think it's something *more* than just sand and rock."

"I'm with the American Indians. They believed that *everything* was alive – trees, rocks, earth, sky – everything has a spirit, a soul if you like. Well, I can go along with that – especially when it comes to places like the desert. Why not? – it was all here before we came, and it will be here after we've gone. Life sprang out of stone and sand."

"Sounds a very primitive philosophy."

"It's not a philosophy – I don't live by it. But don't scorn the primitives. Primitive doesn't mean *simple*. They may have had a greater understanding of the nature of the world than we do, because they were closer to it. Civilisation gets in the way of our thinking – we've lost touch with our roots. Machines and cities have placed a barrier between us and the natural world. I'm not so arrogant as to believe that a primitive knows less about these things than I do, when he is part of it and I'm not. I consider myself the pupil, not the teacher. He has everything to give – I've got nothing of value that I can show him."

"Or her." She smiled.

"Right – or her. Look, why don't we take the rest of the day off. I want to show you something."

"Isn't that a little irresponsible?"

"Yes. Are you coming?"

She laughed. "I love secrets. What do we have to do?"

"Just get in the car. You drive, I'll navigate. I'm the best navigator in the world."

"Modest, aren't we? What's *your* secret?"

"Oh, I can't tell you that, or all the mystery would go out of your life. Let's just say I know the star paths of the Polynesians. I can read the wind and the waves. I have the knack of judging the direction of an ocean swell and can tell from the temperature of the sea water where the nearest landfall lies . . ."

"All that's going to be a great deal of use on the M1."

She opened a drawer and tossed him a road map.

"Just in case your instinct fails you."

He beamed at her.

"I can't use one of these things – I always get lost."

As he sat waiting for her in the car, he thought about the maps he had studied of the South Arabian sands, and the names came to him like words, magic chants, of necromancers and wizards – Al Wāzi'īyah, Ash Shuqayrah in the mountains, Qubaytah, the Attaffa desert region, the Rāsyan watercourse – place names with all the power and mystery of a shaman's secret oath.

They drove down to Manningtree on the Essex coast. They took the journey very slowly, along winding country roads, stopping for lunch at a pub. Since it was February, it was cold and Sarah insisted on spending the afternoon in Chelmsford museum. They arrived at their destination around five o'clock. It was a calm evening and she parked the car behind the mills that threatened to topple into the River Stour.

This was a tidal stretch of the river: broad and flat, and flanked by wharves with names out of the distant past. This was one of the rivers up which the Viking longships, bristling with wicked iron, had slid with sinister intent. To the south was the Blackwater, and more southerly still, the Crouch. The whole coastline was incised by rivers and backwaters, creeks and salt flats, inlets – havens for smugglers of the past – with the marshes between.

He took her to the edge of one of these marshlands, which was said to harbour dengies – taciturn old eremites who lived in the rotting shells of old craft, half-buried in the mud. In the dying light of the day the wide lanes of purple shadow gave the flatlands a brooding, mystical atmosphere that even the most unromantic of people could not ignore. The salt smell was strong, wafting through the reeds, mingling with the pungent aroma of bladder wrack. Beneath that mud was a host of secrets, of wars and warriors, and ships and captains and kings, lying amongst the timbers of bygone settlements that had been sucked down into the shifting alluvium.

"Well?" he said. "Do you feel it?"

She shrugged, the easterly wind tugging at her thick coat and lifting her fine hair.

"I can hear the birds in the reeds, and I can smell – I don't know – something tangy and rotten. But this place – it's nothing like the desert, Jim. You may think it is, but it's just a poor substitute."

"Oh." He was bitterly disappointed and she saw it.

"I'm sorry. I know what you were trying to do for us, but it doesn't work."

What did she want of him? He wanted to share places like this. They were the only ones available to them, within a day's drive. He thought about taking her to the Lake District, or the Pennines, but knew instinctively that they would not satisfy her either.

The wind sent ripples through the reeds. It was as if the land were some giant bird, stirring on its nest, settling deeper into itself.

Sarah gripped his arm tightly.

"I'm sorry, Jim. You wanted me to enjoy today, didn't you? And I have. I've enjoyed being with you. I haven't told you yet, though I've hinted occasionally – one of the reasons I was sent back from Aden, was because I was lost, out in the desert. That kind of thing affects you, deeply. It was one of the reasons why I sought you out. Because I knew, from what Alan had told me, that you would understand just how profoundly such an experience can change a person.

"I agree with your sentiments, about the marshes, but when you've been moved by something a thousand times more powerful in its atmosphere, places like this – they can't touch you any longer. Please, say you understand."

"I understand," he said, flatly.

"Jim. Jim." She put her cheek close to his and he could smell the sweetness of her breath. "We feel the same way.

48

That's what I've been trying to tell you."

He sighed. "I know. I suppose I'm just jealous. I envy you, that's all. I've got to make do with places like this . . ."

"Do you?"

She pulled his mouth down to hers and kissed him. He felt the blood rushing through his head and he had to pull away in the end, to get some breath.

"Come on," she said. "Take your floozie for a walk along the sea wall . . ."

He pulled away sharply.

"Don't call yourself that."

She glared at him and then strode away.

The light was failing rapidly now and the shadows had darkened, were racing across the salt flats and creeks. He turned and ran after her, catching her arm.

"Don't be silly, Sarah."

He put his arm around her shoulders and led her to a pub he knew, which was flanked by two enormous mills with gantries reaching out over the fast-flowing incoming tidal waters.

Once they were inside, with the bar's well-lit alcoves, she brightened considerably, and then enjoyed a fish meal with wine. The colour came back to her cheeks and halfway through the evening she gave him a hug and said, "I'm enjoying this. It's nice isn't it?"

He reached across and touched her face.

"It's nice being with you," he said, and he meant it. He did not envy Alan in the least at that moment. Afterwards, out on the wharf, he looked down into dark waters that wore highlights as a flamenco dancer does, with the appearance of wanton passion. These were lies, he knew. Beneath her scarlet dress, her rose, her flashing eyes, the dancer was weary of all but sleep. Beneath those coloured ripples the river was dangerously cold and tired of all but death.

He kissed Sarah, at the water's edge. Her lips were dry and her eyes inattentive. She was somewhere else, perhaps with someone else. He didn't think it would be long before she asked him to move in with her, and possibly even less time before she asked him to leave. It was all there, spread out before him like the river – his near future. Yet he was

49

powerless to prevent its flow. His small boat, oarless, was caught on the tide and he would be first taken upstream, then, when the turn came, back down to the sea to be adrift on the ocean once again.

Later that week he took another day off. He wanted to get away from the city for a while and travelled north to the peak district and Kinder Scout. It was not a high mountain – hardly more than a large hill, but it was a good day's rambling climb amid interesting scenery. On the train he sat opposite a nun who was on her way to lead a party of climbers up The Peak. They chatted for part of the journey and he was surprised by the worldliness of her. He had always imagined nuns to be timid creatures that saw little except the grey stone walls of convents. This one had seen more of the world than he. She had been in the Congo and had undergone some harrowing experiences. Now she was an avid climber who regularly spent weekends in Wales or Scotland.

"It's a very short life," she said. "One must do as much as one can – and enjoy it."

On reaching his station he said goodbye and hoisted his pack on his back. Among other things it contained his sleeping bag and a small primus stove. It was well to be prepared to stay in one spot: the mist often dropped like a stone over Kinder Scout and the plateau, the peat bog, on top was large enough to get lost on. There were other climbers but contact could soon be lost when you could not see a yard in front of your face.

There was a kind of controlled excitement in his breast as he began to walk up the long winding path that skirted the Neb, to follow Griod's Brook to the summit. At first the going was easy, but soon Jim began to find his climbing boots slipping on the wet stones as the path became steeper. The moor at the top was only 600 feet above sea level, but the path to it was circuitous, following the first part of the Pennine Way to Upper Tor and the Crowden Towers. As he walked, ghosts accompanied him. All mountains are haunted, the spirits of the past inhabiting the gullies and crevices in the rocks. But they were good company, not unwelcome companions.

50

Griod's Brook skittered noisily below him, deep in its gully, like some agitated animal on an urgent journey. He paused, listening to his own heartbeat and the wind soughing through the heather. He was at peace with himself for the first time in many months.

He had problems with his dreams. Nightmares really, except that nothing horrifying happened in them – only strange events which engendered the feeling of terror. He often woke, crying out with fear, not knowing where the fear was coming from. His dreams were terribly lucid and had none of the quirkiness of which childhood dreams were composed.

In one of them he was on mainland Greece – a lonely spot to which he had been driven by a desperate need for seclusion, solitude. But still the isolation left him feeling wanting. He walked and walked. The sun moved down to a sea with an horizon as sharp as a ploughshare and his journey round a headland took him to a tiny bay where the rigid, stony brow of a cliff frowned at the fluid creases in the water below it.

He sat upon the sands and gazed out to sea. Not far from the shore was a small island, mostly rock, but with a few patches of soil bearing shrubs and trees. Immediately he felt an affinity with this small piece of earth jutting from the water and they both looked upon one another in the fading light of the day with a sense of familiarity. There was an intrinsic vitality about this island which he recognised. He had often had similar feelings about other areas of land – inanimate hills or lonely tors – which always seemed just about to reveal their power of movement. He often waited for some gesture. Of course, it never came, unless by a trick of the light.

The scent of wild herbs was in the air and filled him with a kind of exuberance he had not felt as a child. He stared at the island, wondering whether it was near enough to reach with a swim. He was not a strong swimmer and he knew distances over water were deceiving but he could see the fruit on the fig trees, like small, green Montgolfier balloons, ready to ascend, and the broad leaves around them threw out shade which looked cool and inviting.

51

Certainly it *seemed* close enough to swim to.

The water was cool, but not cold. He began a slow breast stroke towards the island which he had studied for places suitable as a landfall. He decided to make for the point where the fig trees grew, there being a short stretch of sand below them. It was a little further than the nearest section, the shape of the island being rather like an oblique wedge, with sheer cliffs towards the shore, sloping down and out at an angle, to the part where the trees grew. Obviously the rain, when it came, flowed down the slope and provided the foliage with the nutrients they needed to survive. Perhaps there were bird droppings, which would help fertilise the big trees?

He fixed his eyes on the bottom of the wedge and made ungainly progress through the calm, blue waters. He found it strange how an object towards which one moved slowly seemed not just to remain at the same distance, but appeared to be moving away.

As he was swimming a light breeze sprang up blowing spray into his face, which made him panic. He trod water and found that it was an offshore wind, which would help him get to the island. It was irritating, whenever there was an eddy which flicked the tails of wavelets into his face, but it would make his swim less difficult.

Yet still the island seemed to get no closer. His limbs began to tire and he thought about turning back, but the breeze had become a strong wind and not only hampered him in that enterprise, but was gently insistent that he went on. He continued heading for the island.

The sea became remarkably cold and great shadows moved across it, either of clouds or currents – he could not tell which. He felt incredibly alone.

When he reached the island, it moved out to sea with him, holding him prisoner with the love that a child has for an injured bird it has found, jealous of any other who shows an interest in it. It had caught him and it was going to keep him – for ever.

He screamed at the island to take him back, to his own kind – back, back, back, before his bones were like white shells on its small beach. The island ignored him.

He would wake up shouting, unintelligibly, into the

emptiness of his bedroom, with his partner trying to calm him. These were the kind of dreams he had – vivid, startling in their clarity – almost like another life with sharper edges to it and a preternatural order.

After leaving the rill, he reached the scree of the Fox Holes, near the summit, and heard noises above him. There were sheep, with their feet clacking on the loose shale. He could smell their faeces and the under-odour of their damp wool.

At the summit, he removed the heavy pack and stared out over the bleak moor. The peat bog opened before him like a dark, frozen ocean. Among the array of humps and mounds lay deep valleys of soft peat which could suck a man to his death.

He picked up his pack and moved on. The wind had become an insistent force against his frame, a huge cold hand pushing him in the chest. The going was hard. His boots sank in the peat, gathered layers of it on his soles. He trudged onward with slow, laboured steps. The moor dipped and rolled on all sides, its lugubrious scenery moving with an uneven rhythm as he walked.

A tor loomed like a giant, suddenly dwarfing him, as he came out of a gully. His heart jumped. Just a rock. Nothing but compressed silt. Nothing but a mixture of common elements.

His fingers froze against the straps of his pack. He flexed them and pushed on, treading carefully in the rivulets of weak sunlight, away from the shadows, that lit the clumps of hard ground with pale luminosity.

At Blackden Rind he took a short rest and ate some chocolate, his eyes roving over the shadowy rock forms that seemed to close in around him like slow beasts shuffling towards a herding area. Nearby was Madman's Stones: tall, perpendicular tongues of rock with leprous features.

"What?" he said aloud to them, half hoping that the fungoid lips that grew on their surfaces would give him answer.

Finally, what he had been hoping for happened.

The mist came down in wet veils, too fast to allow him to reach a point of descent. He would probably have to spend the night where he was and it was doubtful whether he would make it back to the city before midday the following morning.

With something approaching happiness, he took out his sleeping bag with its waterproof cover and prepared to settle for a long, cold, damp night in the open.

ALAN

Like the delicate transluscent bone of a small bird, a white scorpion lay unnoticed just beneath the edge of the sleeping bag. In the firelight the side of its body glistened. It was doing nothing, prepared for nothing. It did not know that humans regarded it with a fear disproportionate to its potential to cause harm. It did not know that it was looked upon, loathsomely, as an instrument of evil: one of those creatures like the spider and the snake, that comprise the demonic set of the natural world. It knew only hunger, fear, discomfort and love – in man's view, a very brief, fleeting love – but nevertheless, love of a kind. Its own form was not loathsome to itself, nor was it beautiful, nor strange. Occasionally it was instinctively attractive. Survival. That was its prime purpose. The immediate survival of itself, which was taken care of by hunger and fear and discomfort, and the long-term survival of its species, which was provided for by scorpion love.

Not far away, perhaps two scorpion miles, sat four men eating unleavened bread and swilling it down with coffee. One of them, the whitest-skinned of the four, was having great difficulty digesting his food and his expression showed how bitter the coffee was to his tongue whenever he took a sip. This creature – this man – in three short days, had slipped down to a lower level than that of the delicate scorpion, in that he possessed only three of the four survival instincts of that creature, if thirst can be included as part of hunger. Love, even the narrow, limited love of the kind known to scorpions, was no longer any part of him. Except for his hunger, fear and discomfort, he was dead.

"You'll get used to it. It takes time."

The words, uttered in a slightly Australian accent, came from a slender man who formed one of the party. He called himself Yussuf and said he was the son of an important sheik, a prince if you like, educated in Australia. He was Alan's

55

interpreter and companion, though at the time Alan was no companion for him.

"I'm determined to."

Alan swallowed another chunk of the biscuit-brittle bread. Around him the rock desert moved with small, living creatures. The air was chill, unlike on the coast, as the temperature fell with the sun. He hunched his shoulders under his thick coat and dreamed of a warm, soft bed somewhere in another life, another world, as distant as a childhood memory. He was tired and irritable and afraid, like a new boy on the first day at public school. Yes, that was exactly how he felt, he thought, like the first day at that damn school, stripped of the protectiveness of his parents and the comforts of home: stripped of all familiar sights and sounds, and feeling utterly abandoned, lost, bewildered, thoroughly insecure. He was vulnerable to everything and everyone, because he didn't know the rules and there were those around who exploited that fact. Everything you did, every move you made, was wrong in some way. There was always someone waiting, like a bad angel hovering just out of sight, ready to descend, for that wrong move. They didn't want to warn you, when they saw it coming, because that would spoil the fun. They wanted you to make that wrong move, so that they could descend on you in triumph and carry out or witness the punishment.

The two Bedu, accompanying Alan and Yussuf, were murmuring amongst themselves in Arabic. *Secret languages. Keep the outsider outside. Don't let him into the private circle, the inner sanctum.* The tone was a strange mixture of contrasts, carrying the softest of sounds alongside guttural harshness. To Alan it was like listening to a Brahms concerto in the presence of an old man insistent on hawking. Occasionally the level rose and certain words sounded aggressive, violent, but this did not register on the impassive faces of the Bedu.

Yussuf took something from his saddlebag.

"You have a book?" said Alan, eagerly. "I meant to bring several, but in the excitement . . ."

Yussuf nodded and began reading by the firelight, while Alan looked on, enviously. The bread was a hard lump in his stomach and he knew he was going to have an uncomfortable night. A little read before turning in would have made all the difference: given him something to think about. He would ask to borrow the book later.

Laying back, he thought about home and went into a short wakeful dream about walking into 'the Caribbean Club', behind the Aldwych, and ordering oysters followed by Montserrat mountain chicken. God, what he wouldn't do for a bottle – no, *two* bottles, dreams can afford extravagance – of sweet white wine.

The days had been excruciatingly boring, as well as unbearably hot. During the day he would have sold his grandmother into white slavery for a cool shower, but the coldness of the night drove such thoughts out of his head. The grey sand got everywhere. His hair seemed to be made of it. The slightest wind made his life a torment, blowing the sharp grains into his face, until he felt he had been pared to the bone.

Ridge after ridge after ridge. They were never-ending. Each ridge, maddeningly, was subtly different from all others, but not enough to dispel the boredom, only enough to attract the edge of his attention. If they had all been exactly alike, he could have forgotten about them and disappeared into a world of nullity, but there was just enough difference to keep him this side of oblivion.

The sun. God, that *sun*. Had he really paid money to go to the South of France just to lie underneath it? What he would not do now for endless grey autumn days, with skies the colour of Cumbrian slate! The sun came down, out of the heavens, and rested on his shoulders, bearing down on him with its full weight, pressing his sweat-sore buttocks and testicles harder into the lumpy saddle, until he was raw. The sun was insistent, glaring into his eyes whichever way he turned, filling his head with unwelcome light. He was constantly giddy and sick, but afraid to mention it to the nomads because he knew that already they considered him an inadequate human being. He desperately wanted to prove himself worthy.

Yussuf had fallen off to sleep. The book lay by his side. Tired as he was Alan stirred the fire, to give him some extra light, and reached across to scoop up the volume. He settled

57

down by the flames with a sense of pleasant anticipation awakening his numb senses. The sensation was almost painful, like feeling returning to frozen limbs.

He opened the book and squinted at the words. Then he moved closer to the flames, until he was almost on top of the fire, holding the pages out to the light.

Ugly, bitter disappointment.

"Oh, for God's sakes!"

He flung the book from him in anger. Yussuf's good English had lulled him into a belief in fellowship. The book was in Arabic. He couldn't read a word. Spiders had written on those pages, dipping their legs in ink and running amok.

One of the Bedu woke up and saw the book lying in the sand, its pages creased where it had landed, open and face down. The man leapt to his feet instantly and Alan was horrified by the rage he saw in his features.

"What's the matter?" he said. He searched his mind for his meagre Arabic. *Mahlish*? No, that meant "never mind".

The Bedu reached across and was about to deliver what would have been a nasty blow to his face, when Yussuf, now awake, intervened. A hot argument ensued between all three Arabs, while Alan sat miserably awaiting the outcome.

Finally, grumbling, and darting fiery glances at Alan, the two Bedu settled down again. In his nervousness, Alan broke wind and one of them gave him a look of pure hatred, pinched his own chin and said, "*Spa*," or something similar. Alan had learned the gesture, if not the word. It meant *shame*.

Yussuf picked up his book and brushed the pages free of sand. The smooth-faced man came and squatted on his haunches in front of Alan.

"That was a foolish thing to do."

Did he mean the incident with the book, or the fart?

"I still don't understand," he said, unhappily.

Yussuf held up the leatherbound volume.

"This is my bible – the Koran. They thought you were being irreverent to our religion. We are particularly sensitive when it comes to Christians. He saw you throw away the Koran, in disgust. You're lucky he didn't kill you."

"I didn't – I had no idea it was the Koran. I thought it was just an ordinary book. I'm sorry. I'm not thinking straight. It

58

was obvious really – I suppose you were learning it?"

"Yes. It is unfortunate. I'll explain to them tomorrow."
He paused. "You're not very happy, my friend."

It was not a question.

"Yes, yes. I'm fine. Just overtired and out of tune.
Someone's tightened my strings, that's all. I'll get over it. I'll
get used to this place, if it kills me."

"It might very well do that."

Alan set his jaw. "Like hell it will. I won't be beaten by a
few shoddy miles of desert."

Yussuf smiled. "When I was in England, I used to have tea
with my landlady every Sunday. Her cakes – they were like
sugared clouds, and I hated them. But I was determined to
enjoy everything about England, because my visit was short
and I might never get there again. I ate those cakes with an
attempt at relish."

"Did you ever get used to them? Enjoy them?"

"Never. My stomach turns even now at the thought of
them. Every night, after one of those teas, I would go to the
pink bathroom and vomit."

Yussuf again retired, taking his precious Koran with him
and Alan went to his own sleeping bag. As he reached for it,
something scuttled beneath. He felt the rhythmic pounding
of his heart increase in pace. There was something nasty
underneath that bag and he didn't really wish to look at it. He
snatched up the bed, but the scorpion had found a crease in
the earth's crust into which it had squeezed itself, out of sight
of the human.

Alan stared at the spot where his bed had been, unable to
see anything moving. Still, he did not think he would sleep in
that particular place. There were too many small stones. He
would find a softer spot. He found an area at the bottom of a
dune, where the sand at least moved around the contours of
his body. Nothing would disturb him now – maybe a skink
might tunnel below his bed, if it was in its way, but he wasn't
worried about lizards. They were okay. It was things with
brittle legs that bothered him.

There were dreams, of water seeping into his bedroom as a
child, until it gradually filled, like a tank to the ceiling, while
he, contrary to the laws of such things, remained compressed

59

by its weight. He found himself struggling for breath, fighting against the black pain in his lungs. He could not move.

He could *not* move.

His arms were pinned hard to his sides and his legs were pressed together so tightly that the bones from one dug into the flesh of the other. It was dark – the impenetrable blackness of the grave. Round about his head, the sleeping bag formed a pocket where the air was trapped. Suddenly, he realized he was awake, and let out a stifled scream.

The air was rapidly becoming stale and his head began hammering with pain. He moaned, again and again, in the knowledge that he was going to die. Then he could hear voices – garbled, gabbling voices that spoke with the tongues of demons. He was in Hell. He had already died and he was in Hell! "Oh, God!" he screamed, and the sound remained with him, in its small enclosure.

Then the weight on his body began to lift and gradually he found he could use his arms, his legs. He thrashed around, when the freedom came, fighting to stand up and run.

Light and air. He blinked against the blinding brightness and gulped down the air in grateful draughts. Light and air. How sweet they were.

When he could see, there were three of them, standing above him.

"What happened?" he croaked. His throat felt like sandpaper and agonising shafts of pain penetrated his temples. He needed a drink very badly.

"You were buried," said Yussuf, "under the sand. The dune collapsed, like a landslip. You should never sleep under a dune. The wind . . ."

Alan took a proffered drink gratefully, slaking his terrible thirst.

"Was there a storm?" he asked of the guide. "A strong wind?"

"No, the dune must have collapsed gradually. It buried you completely. We heard your voice and dug."

The other two men had lost interest in him now and were busy breaking camp, which they did in a practised way, with economy of energy. The chill of the night was gone and the sun was hot on the horizon. It seemed to roll up from below the world and out into the desert, ready to melt all within its range. Raw areas of sunburn on Alan's skin – his nose and brow – began to become inflamed as the rays of the molten ball burned into them again, raising the temperature. The cold night airs had brought his temperature down, but now it began to soar again. He could feel the bands of skin tightening, stretching, where the burns were worst. Covering the tender places, he turned to Yussuf.

"How do things like that happen?"

"What?"

"A landslip like that. Is it common?"

"It happens." The man was silent for a moment. Then he said, "How much did Major Trevellian tell you?"

Alan was puzzled.

"I don't understand. What do you mean, about the geophysical aspects?"

Yussuf shook his head, his deep brown eyes gauging something in Alan.

"About me."

"He said you were the son of some sheik or other – I'm sorry, I didn't mean to insult you or anything – it's just that I can't remember the name of your father."

Yussuf waved that away.

"What I'm trying to say is, the desert is not as familiar to me as you might think. I've only been here for two years."

"Oh, yes. You were in Australia – then you mentioned England."

"A short time in England."

"So?"

"So I haven't the association with this land that gives me the authority to say that I *know* it. I don't know it, yet. I intend to. I'm learning all the time, but as to knowing what's commonplace – you're asking the wrong man. I can survive out here, but I'm no expert on all the desert's moods."

"You talk as if the desert's a live thing."

"So it is – in a way. It's unpredictable – does things you don't expect. You have to be on your guard all the time. Watching. Know what I mean?"

Alan studied the landscape, the wild rock formations,

61

thrown up as tongues of lava – the earth trying to lick the base of the sky – and the cliffs with their basalt colonnades, nature in its more symmetrical guise. There were stretches of rock and scrublands between, and the occasional dune or drift that had found an object to pile up against. Although the scenery looked harsh and resisting, there was nothing overtly threatening about it to Alan's eyes.

He thought: the desert can be anything you want it to be. Just a stretch of nothingness, or a menacing entity that resented your presence. At that moment, it was Phlegethon, the river of fire in Hades, into which those who have shed blood are thrown. A river of fire and boiling blood. Perhaps he was here to atone for that earlier incident in his life? Jim would have thought like that. No, he was here because he had been sent by his newspaper to report on activity in a natural region of rock and dust. There was nothing preter-natural about the landscape. It was just a wasteland.

His sandals were by the fire ashes, where he had left them, and he began to follow Yussuf, dragging his sleeping bag behind him. Just as he was about to pull on his footwear they had visitors.

The first he knew of their presence was when Yussuf touched his arm, and he looked up to see two figures on dromedaries, moving slowly down the escarpment of a rugged hill to the west.

"Careful," said Yussuf, softly.

His two Bedu were already carrying their rifles and Alan saw one of them slip the safety catch. His heart began thumping, but whether it was with excitement or fear he wasn't sure.

"Who are they?" he asked, but received no answer for a moment. The figures came closer – lean, hungry-looking men.

"Qotaibi," muttered Yussuf.

"Are they Royalist, or Republican?"

"Neither. They're a tribe that recognise no masters or loyalties, except to their own kind – the Wolves of the Radfan they call them."

"I've read about them," said Alan, and his veins ran hot. He remembered a story about two British airmen who had crashed in their territory. Something about decapitation and heads being displayed on wooden stakes. Was it true? He couldn't remember where he read it. Some of these accounts were exaggerated, some even invented. Right at this moment he was happy to believe it was an invented tale. A story dreamed up by a flier to impress his girlfriend, to enhance his own image in her eyes. Definitely.

"Don't speak. Cover your face."

Alan pulled his headcloth over his nose and mouth with shaking fingers. Was this the moment? He had told the woman on the train he was prepared to die, but now that it had become a probability, he realised just how unprepared he really was.

The sharp faces came closer. They were aptly named – the Wolves of the Radfan: their wolfish features looked cruel and unyielding as they paused, some twenty yards away, and called out the Moslem greeting.

Alan stepped back a pace, involuntarily, and his naked foot found bare rock. The sun had been up two hours now and the rock was as hot as a flat iron set for pressing cotton. The pain was excruciating and he knew the tender skin would be badly burned, but he did not dare change position again.

The air was taut with tension. The greeting had been reciprocated, but apart from that, no one had moved or spoken for what appeared to be at least five minutes.

One of his Bedu spoke again and a rider dismounted, walking directly up to Alan. The man's rifle was held loosely, but it was aiming in the general area of Alan's privates. He stared into the tribesman's eyes and found no sign of compassion there: nothing but inanimate stone and sand, and the simmering heat of hatred for the stranger in his land. Though the face was heavily grooved with creases and lacking in the outward signs of nobility, there was an arrogant pride etched deep into the features which Alan had seen before, on the faces of the senior boys at public school. It went deeper than the creases in the skin. It went through to the heart. An expression went through Alan's mind. "*Every tribesman believes himself a sultan.*"

"*Salaam ali cum,*" said the tribesman.

Alan made the formal reply, with difficulty.

63

The Arab flicked his rifle.

"*Taal.*"

Alan's mind went into its encyclopaedic mode. *Taal? Taal?* What was that? Christ, he knew the word. He *had* to know the word. Meanings flitted through his mind as he discarded one after another.

"*Taal!*" The word was rapped out, louder, with a trace of anger behind it. He was going to be shot. God, he was going to die! What was Yussuf just standing there for? Why didn't someone say something? – come to his rescue with guns or words? Anything.

He was about to shout, "Press. Correspondent. Newspaper man!" when the word came to him. *Taal. Come.* The man wanted him to step forward. Why? Did he have any choice?

He placed a foot in front of him and immediately the rock burned into his already scorched sole. He shouted, unable to help himself. It was too much. Pain on top of pain, and the tension, the overwhelming fear of death. It was all too much. He hopped around, from foot to foot, the tears of frustration and pain welling up in his eyes: tears of anger too.

The tribesman suddenly erupted into loud, raucous laughter, and his companion began laughing too. Yussuf and the two Bedu followed suit – all five of them screeching with mirth at the humour of this thing – a European jumping from foot to foot and wailing with every step.

"You bastards," seethed Alan.

He found his sandals and put them on gingerly, still aware of the laughter at his foolish antics.

The Qotaibi then went into an animated discussion with his two Bedu, during which there were many gestures in his direction. Yussuf stood apart, his keen eyes flickering from face to face.

"What's happening?" asked Alan, limping to the only man who spoke his language.

"They're explaining our presence. We're lucky. They're not looking for trouble. They've been told you're a Swedish journalist, working for Amnesty International. It doesn't mean very much, but it's better than being English."

"Would they have killed us?"

64

Yussuf gave him a smile and patted his gun.

"Don't underestimate me. I can use this thing as well as they can. Someone might have been killed, but not necessarily us. It's best to avoid a fight if at all possible though, especially with neutrals. There's nothing to gain by it."

"They've heard of Amnesty International?"

"Sure. The AI have been to Aden. These snippets of information find their way up country. You seem to think they're ignorant. They're not – and they have radios. They make it a point to keep up with local politics."

The tribesmen then walked to their camels, grazing on some scrub nearby, one of them doing a little dance on the sand, saying, "Hoo! HOO!" in imitation of Alan's earlier actions, before mounting his beast. He was laughing. Alan's feet were still very painful and he swore under his breath at the clowning.

"Steady," said Yussuf. "They're not gone yet."

'Once they were out of sight, the three Arabs said their prayers, which had been delayed, first by Alan's earlier predicament and then by their visitors. Alan stood by, awkward in his isolation from this personal but public show of worship. They were locked into a world which excluded him completely. He watched them fumble with their prayer beads and do their *salaams* with a feeling of envy awakening within him. He hated secrets – secrets kept from him – and would like to have been let in on this one. Not because he needed a faith, he told himself, but because he was curious about the way in which it seemed to change a man's perspective on the world. Islam permeated every pore of their existence and it surely altered the way in which they viewed life and even the material world. He wanted to see it through their eyes. Did it look rosier? Or more magical? Or – what? – just *different*?

When they had finished, and rolled up their prayer mats, he said confidentially to Yussuf, "I'm a Mason you know."

"A what?" The man raised an eyebrow.

"A Freemason. Haven't you heard of them?"

"Yes, I've heard of them, but I thought you weren't supposed to tell people."

Alan was uncomfortable under his gaze.

"Well, we're not actually, but I thought, out here in the desert . . ."

"To tell you the truth, mate," the Australian accent suddenly became very pronounced, "I can't stand these secret societies you British seem to love. Bit too schoolboyish, if you know what I mean."

Alan got a little hot.

"No, I don't know what you mean. It's the same as all this, isn't it? The Islam bit?"

"You're comparing a religion with a few overgrown schoolboys playing at Druids? Get lost, chum."

Yussuf's camel came to its knees and he mounted it.

"And before we go any further, I'm fed up with this farce. There's too many layers – I'm beginning to wonder who I really am. My Moslem name is Yussuf, though for the purposes of the army, it's Sabalala, the name I was born with. Corporal Sabalala. I haven't been a Moslem long, but I took it up because I wanted to – not because I was told to. So don't say any more about Islam, or you'll get my boot up your arse, officer status or not."

Alan was aghast at the news. He looked up at the man sitting high in the saddle.

"Well – what are you? If you're not an Arab?"

"I come from Suva – never heard of it eh? Well, it's in Fiji. You've heard of *that*?"

"Fiji – and you're a corporal?" said Alan, faintly.

"A corporal and proud of it. Took me a long time to earn those stripes – the army's not free of prejudice you know. I may look twenty, but I'm nearer to thirty. Now, are you coming?"

Alan mounted his own camel in a kind of daze. He had been sent out into the desert with some madcap Fijian corporal in the British army – he assumed it was the British army, and not some international force from the South Pacific or something – he'd never heard of one, if there was. A *corporal*. Not even an officer. And one crazy enough to be seduced by the local religion. He was going to write a nasty letter to Trevellian about this one. Palming him off with a *corporal*. A sheik's son – now that was something worthy of his attention.

Alan's wounded pride smarted worse than his desert-inflicted wounds. He took out his salt tablets as he rode and downed them with a draught of water, remembering his intake of liquid was expected to be about two gallons a day. It sounded a great deal. It *was* a great deal.

Later, he was sick, when the sugar coating of the tablets wore off and his empty stomach was exposed to pure salt. He wondered whether Polynesians needed as much salt as Europeans. Or whether they had some sort of chemical difference which compensated. He took out his pocket mirror and inspected his nose. It was raw. He polished the mirror with a finger of spit and put it back into his pocket. Inside and out, he was a wreck.

"Don't flash that thing," shouted Sabalala. "It can be seen miles away."

Bloody corporals, telling him what to do!

"I was told," he said stiffly, "that a mirror is an important part of our equipment. If one gets lost, one can use it as a signalling device."

"Just don't flash the thing, that's all."

Up yours, corporal!

When they halted at midday, in the shade of a rock overhang, he took out the last letter he had received from Jim. It was creased and grubby now, and he tried to smooth out the wrinkles before reading.

Dear Alan,

How are you? I hope you're holding your own in that place that has occupied our thoughts for so long. I try to imagine what you must be feeling – and experiencing – but it's difficult for me, surrounded as I am by the hustle and bustle of London traffic.

I have some news for you, sad in its way. Maddie and I are thinking of splitting up. Things haven't been going too well lately and we've decided it would be best to separate. For a while, at least. The thing is, Alan, I've met someone else – Sarah Mitchell, the woman you met in Aden and gave my address to. We share the same interests and while I could never slight Maddie in any way – we've been through a great deal together, after all – I've found something with Sarah that

67

is special. I don't need to tell you how I feel about her. I'm sure you understand.

Maddie took it very well, with dignity, but I've had to watch her go through a bad time. Sarah says it's all a question of needs. She and I need each other. I'm sure you'll consider me a prime bastard after this, and I deserve it, but somehow I couldn't help myself. I'm not offering that as an excuse – there is no excuse for betraying loyalty and trust – I'm just trying to explain how I feel.

I myself find adultery both understandable and unforgivable. Understandable because we only have one life and no one should be responsible to another for the way in which they live it. Unforgivable because, besides wounding somebody of whom one is fond, without cause, it destroys trust and reduces promises to the level of lies. It sours the past. This is a paradox that gives me sleepless nights and has me so confused sometimes I feel physically ill. I'm not playing for sympathy. I'm just trying to explain that it was not an easy decision to make. Even now I'm not sure. I don't suppose I ever shall be.

Well, there you are. I've bared my soul. I find life with Sarah exciting at the moment, but I don't kid myself that such a state is permanent. We're still caught up in the newness of it all. That will fade and I hope something more substantial will remain. I find her a good companion, with much to offer. We feel the same way about many things, especially about the desert. She's been there – you *are* there. I guess I'm the odd one out.

Warmly,
Jim

P.S. From Sarah. Alan. I just want to thank you for giving me Jim's address. As it's worked out, I found more than I could have hoped for and I'll always remember that it was you who brought us together. I haven't read this letter. That's private, between you and Jim – but I imagine he's told you about us. Wish us luck. You never know. You might be seeing us sooner than you think. Sarah.

So, Jim was about to leave Maddie? No, mate, he thought.

You're not a prime bastard. You're just a bloody fool. The worst thing about these triangles was that all the people involved were basically nice. He didn't know too much about Sarah, but she seemed to have integrity and wasn't one to inflict pain needlessly, or destroy for the sake of it. Alan and Maddie had never got on, but of one thing he was sure: she was one of the most level-headed and caring women he had ever met. Jim must have had a touch of winter madness to give her up. These things were incomprehensible to him.

He put the pages away and carefully folded the envelope, pushing it back into his pocket. As he did so, he noticed how sweat-stained and filthy his clothes were, even beneath the heavy coat. They looked as though they had come from some gypsy's rag-bag. They had looked so smart when he first left Aden too! He was deteriorating. Already some of the stitching was beginning to rot beneath the armpits.

When the time came to mount again, his camel refused to kneel and even attempted to bite him as it circled round on the end of its rein, with him pleading and cursing, alternately. Eventually, Sabalala had to rap out a command and the beast dropped (reluctantly, it seemed) to its knees. Alan was beginning to detest his mount. There was absolutely no rapport. It had been one constant battle between them, since they had left Aden, with the dromedary pulling away from the other camels and Alan having to force it back into line again, leaving him aching and exhausted at the end of each day. Everything seemed designed to make Alan's life as difficult as possible.

In the afternoon, they came to a pass in the mountains where the sides rose vertically and great pillars of rock looked over them in threatening gestures. The menacing landscape with its dour aspect depressed Alan considerably. By nightfall, he was beginning to hate his managing editor, the newspaper and this land to which he had been sent, with equal fervency.

On dismounting from his camel Alan felt not only wet, but sticky around the thighs. On checking he found that he had two huge sores and that the blood from these was seeping through his shorts. Miserably, he approached Sabalala.

"Corporal . . ." he began with dignity.

Sabalala rapped, "Don't call me that."

"Sorry. Look, I've got a problem. Have we any first aid stuff with us?"

"What's the problem?"

"Sores."

"Let me see."

Alan drew himself up, stiffly. He wasn't having some smooth-skinned Fijian who couldn't even show his age decently, looking at *his* thighs. He'd heard stories about Polynesians. They considered homosexuality a normality, didn't they?

"Oh, well," said the Fijian. "If you're going to be funny about it, you can suffer, mate."

"What about the first aid kit?"

"A few bandages. Not much more. Come on, whip your shorts down. No one's going to laugh at your hairy legs."

Alan took off his coat slowly and then pulled up the long legs of his shorts to reveal the bloody mess of the inside of his thighs. Sabalala inspected the sores briefly, then spoke rapidly to one of the Bedu. The man he had talked with went off, into the scrub, muttering away to himself, and eventually returned to toss a plant into Sabalala's lap.

The Fijian took out two bandages from his saddlebags and told Alan to get his shorts off. This time he did as he was asked.

He suffered the indignity of the Fijian's hands about his thighs as the man placed some leaves on the sores and bound them in place with the bandages.

"What is it?" he asked.

"*Rumran*. It'll draw out the sores. You've got a whole first aid kit around you all the time. *Sarh* for eye trouble. Or *harmal*, if that doesn't cure the soreness. *Ben* tree for snake-bites. The bark of the *tolak* for fever. *Sene* . . ." He grinned. "That's a purgative."

"That's one thing I *don't* bloody need at the moment. Where did you learn all this stuff?"

"The army taught me some of it. The rest I've learned from these fellahs. You pick it up, bit by bit. Give you a few months out here and you'll know as much as the natives."

70

"I doubt it. Thanks, anyway."

"That's okay. Don't choke on it." Alan bit his lip.

"Look, I'm sorry about earlier. I'm – I'm a bit out of my depth in this place. Everything here seems designed to irritate me. I'll – get used to it."

"That's okay. You'll have to. My orders are to get you to the north, then you're virtually on your own. You can stick around with me if you like, but it might get a bit rough and don't forget, I'm a spy in this place. If I get caught, you'll most certainly get roped in too – they'll laugh at that newspaper stuff."

"I'll give it some thought."

They prepared the beds for the night and made coffee and flour cakes. One of the Bedu caught a small *wabar* which they cooked and ate under the peaceful canopy of the night sky. Sabalala cleaned his weapon with some light oil and a pullthrough. The taller Bedu began humming a tune and the other fell in with him. The scene began to become almost idyllic.

"What made you join the army?" Alan asked of the Fijian.

"Good question. I often ask that myself. I guess I didn't have a lot of choice. When I was ten my father died and I bummed a lift to Australia to work in the market at Sydney, sending money home to my mother and two sisters. Later on I got caught up in the racetrack scene – gambling. Made a lot of money . . ."

"You're good at that?"

"At gambling? No, mate. What used to happen was, I'd give one of the jockeys a few quid to spread around his mates, leaving out the guy that was riding the outsider. He'd be so incensed, this guy, he'd ride flat out to win and the others would hold in to let him. 'Course, all my bets would be on the outsider. Used to rake it in."

Alan felt the indignation rising within him.

"But that's cheating."

The Fijian gave him a look of mild contempt.

"You could say that. You could say that paying me two dollars a week to hump boxes in the market was cheating. I worked sixteen hours a day at the age of ten. What were you doing?"

71

Alan refrained from answering.

The Fijian continued. "Anyway, I'm not looking for your approval. They caught us in the end and we got the choice – join the army or go to jail. Some of us chose the army." He paused to toss a twig into the fire. "It's not such a bad life. They sent me to school, to learn Arabic and a few other things. I get paid. And at least I'm not stuck on some farm on the outback, watching sheep all day long."

Alan couldn't see a great deal of difference between that and the kind of life Sabalala was leading at the moment, but he didn't say so.

A few days later they had reached Jabal Isbil, which they skirted to the west, heading for Al Watadah in the north. The peak of Jabal Isbil stood at around 3,000 metres and they were having to travel across a plateau only 500 metres lower. It was cooler up here, during the daytime, but the nights were bitterly cold and the water froze in the goatskins. Alan's hands became chapped and he found it difficult to write in his notebook. Occasionally they found shelter in uninhabited forts that seemed to grow out of the solid rock.

The Bedu seemed constantly amused by Alan's obsession with the time and called to each other whenever they caught him looking at his watch. He never understood what passed between them but he hated being a source of amusement.

When they were sure of being isolated from villages Sabalala taught Alan how to use his rifle on live game, but he told him he would never become a good shot.

Alan was a little put out by this.

"Why not?"

"Because you don't have any flair with the weapon. It's all 'by numbers' with you. Don't worry, there are worse things in the world than being a mediocre shot with a rifle. After all, you can only kill things with it."

He was determined to prove the Fijian wrong, and practised whenever he got the chance. He did improve slightly, but not as well or as quickly as he had hoped. One night he managed to shoot a kite hawk which had alighted on a rock not far from the camp, but for some reason this did not impress his companions in the least. He kept one of the tail feathers as a trophy.

As the days passed, he kept hoping for his spirit to blend in with the atmosphere of his surroundings. He wanted to feel part of the scenery around him: become a Bedu in all but nationality. Always, though, he felt like an outsider. The desert seemed determined to end his life as quickly as it could: to get rid of this irritating foreign body on its back. There was the incident when his camel bolted, near to the edge of a ravine, and only the quick thinking of Abdulla, the short, clean-shaven Bedu, prevented a fatal accident. There was the time he followed a pi-dog into a ruined fort and almost fell down the shaft of a disused well in the darkness of its interior.

Gradually, he came to look on the desert not as an enemy – that would have ennobled it – but as a recalcitrant dog: something which had to be brought to heel. He learned to look ahead, watch for the signs; to anticipate and thwart its attempts before they reached crisis point. If he could not become part of it, he would master it.

Abdulla and Ali became another challenge for him. He wanted desperately to impress these rugged tribesmen with their haughty airs. Eventually, he realised he was never going to do it by playing them at their own game and introduced a new one: dominoes. They were fascinated by the little oblong blocks of wood covered in white spots and he spent his time teaching them to play, until they were so obsessed by the game they would plague Sabalala with requests to stop long before it was necessary to make evening camp. At first, to their disgust, Alan won every game, but as the time passed their brains tuned themselves to the nuances of the game and eventually it was either Ali or Abdulla that came away winning. Alan did not mind this as much as he thought he might, because in return they taught him the skills of surviving in the desert and they no longer looked down their hawk-beaked noses at this pallid Englishman and his inability to fit into their environment.

"If I had thought to bring some cards with me," said Alan to Sabalala, "I could have taught them bridge. You too."

Sabalala, who found the task of interpreting very demanding after a day's ride, expressed his relief in no uncertain terms that the cards in question were back in civilisation.

One day Ali came to Alan with a request that he or Abdulla should be the man to carry the box of dominoes, not the Englishman.

"You're welcome," said Alan, thinking that any small weight out of his saddlebag could only be an advantage to him. He handed them over.

"What's the idea?" he asked the Fijian.

Sabalala spoke with Ali and then grinning, turned to Alan. "They don't trust you to stay alive. He says if you're going to fall over the edge of a mountain it's best they have the dominoes with *them* – that way they won't be lost."

"Bloody cheek," said Alan, regretting he had handed them over. They might feel less inclined to look after him now that they had the things in their possession. No wonder they had been assiduous in their efforts to protect him from the desert's pitfalls. He thought he had won them over with the strength of his personality and that they had begun to admire this Englishman's tenacity and had developed such a respect for him that they would follow him into hell and back, his loyal, devoted Bedu. Instead, all they had been worried about was the loss of the dominoes! It was a hard thing to come to terms with, when one thought one was doing so well. Where were all these natives of *Boy's Own* comics? Presumably dead.

One afternoon, as they were riding through a *wadi*, they were attacked without warning. A bullet raised a puff of dust in front of the lead camel and Alan found himself crouched in amongst some rocks, trembling with excitement, without knowing how he had got there.

"You all right?" whispered Sabalala, next to him.

"Yes. Who is it?"

"God knows – at least they don't want to kill us or one of us would be dead now. It's probably a warning not to proceed further up the *wadi*."

"What do we do then?"

"Stay here till nightfall – then go back the way we came until we can branch off and continue west."

74

They never did find out who the aggressors were. Some dissidents from a local village, Sabalala thought, protecting their hideout. Alan wrote in his notebook the following day: "Encounter with hostiles in a *wadi*. Shots exchanged but ambushers escaped. Terrain becoming more difficult and going arduous. The added danger of violent encounters keeps us constantly on our toes . . ."

He wrote this as the two Bedu were playing dominoes by the firelight, growling softly at one another when they had to 'knock' and pass. Sabalala was constantly called upon to arbitrate, which he did with grave enthusiasm.

A lizard ran through the arch formed by Alan's legs as he wrote, resting his notebook on his knees for support.

". . . The uncertainty of life in this area makes one marvel at the ability of the nomad to survive in such a harsh environment. Poisonous creatures abound, water is scarce and the privation . . ." The phrases flowed from his pencil with the barest glance at the truth. He was here to give the readers what they wanted, not the unembroidered facts. The facts were that the life was hard but they could survive very well. However, it was his duty to embellish the facts, which were ninety-eight per cent boring if looked at in the raw.

The game by the fire became heated and Alan put down his notebook to join in. The two Arabs did not seem to mind losing so much to each other if he was playing, presumably because he was supposed to be the expert and he always came last now, thus allowing both Bedu a measure of success.

Two days later there was a bit of a crisis. After they had successfully passed through a line of Egyptian soldiers who had been guarding the exit to a long, snaking valley, Abdulla discovered that one of the dominoes was missing. His anguish was so great, he swore he would go back, retrace his steps, to find it, even if it meant fighting the whole of the Egyptian army. Sabalala pleaded with the man but his distress overwhelmed any appeal to his reason or caution.

Just as he was about to set off, Ali shamefacedly produced the double six from somewhere on his person and a great argument ensued as to whether he had deliberately withheld it in order to be able to start first on the next game.

Alan sided with Abdulla, whom he thought was right to

75

accuse the other of cheating, while Sabalala pointed out that it was easy to misplace one of the dominoes, since the two Arabs were so intent on keeping their opponent's eyes away from their numbers they frequently memorised them and tucked them up their sleeves, out of sight.

Alan said that this could hardly happen with the double six since it was the first domino laid, but Ali was adamant that he had not known it was in his possession until he felt about his person. In any case, he told Sabalala, keeping a domino on him would ensure that he had an extra one to start with and that would have put him at a disadvantage. Abdulla seemed mollified by this statement, which seemed to make sense, but Ali had to agree to allow the other Bedu an extra turn at carrying the box, as punishment for his negligence and carelessness. This compromise was reached reluctantly, by both parties. All four men were secretly relieved that it had not come to a fight. Arabs don't fist fight: they come right to the point, and that point is either a knife or a gun. Alan wondered how his editor would take the news that he had been shot in an argument over a game of dominoes, some- where in the hills of Yemen. It would raise a snigger, if nothing else, amongst his enemies in the office.

Sabalala's job was to gather information, not fight, and Alan became vexed with the corporal when they did not make a stand sometimes, instead of skirting patrols of Republican forces or guerrilla groups of the NLF.

"I'm here to observe not participate," he told Alan. Sabalala had a small transceiver in his equipment which he used to pass back information on military activity in the hills, to the base, at Aden. Occasionally, they stopped at some village, leaving Alan kicking his heels outside, while they went in to talk to the locals.

After spending some time about fifty kilometres east of Sana'a they followed a line of villages out of the hills, to the Hadhramaut where Sabalala was to receive an airdrop of fresh supplies, including batteries for his transceiver.

One day, when the sky was a watery blue and they had crossed a seemingly endless plain of gravel – about as interesting as an empty car park with its horizons pushed back to the edges of the world – Alan first saw the great *Wadi* Duan, which drops a thousand feet, suddenly, from the level of the desert. Along the natural walls of this chasm were built castles, fashioned from the same materials as the rock face into which they were set, so that they possessed a natural camouflage. He was profoundly impressed by this sight and began to realise that there was more to the peoples of that region than he had previously suspected. The *wadi* itself was breathtaking enough. He mentioned this to Sabalala who told him that the *Wadi* Hadhramaut was even more dramatic and he realised he had yet seen little of the country on which he was reporting.

That evening he wrote to Jim, urging him to find a way of getting out there. He would drop the letter at the next 'safe' village, along with his more lengthy reports for his paper: those that could not be passed over the air via Sabalala's transceiver.

"You must experience this place," he wrote. "Its chaotic nature would appeal to you enormously."

It was about this time that he began to fall prey to that curiously undocumented malady known as *simoom* madness. The *simoom*, a hot, dry, dust-laden wind, was infamous for its suffocating effects, both on the body and the brain. Alan was an easy victim.

JIM

The party was at the Malaysian Centre for Cultural Exchange and the apprehension Jim had felt on accepting the invitation reached its climax as he was introduced to several of the guests. It was full of people who moved in a sphere of society above that with which he was comfortable.

Although Jim was now a senior executive at the bank, he felt his humble origins were all too evident. Jim could get by with tradesmen and shopkeepers, amuse colleagues at his own level in business and impress clients with his knowledge of banking, but his social graces were limited and without the training necessary to oil the mechanism needed at such a gathering.

"Enjoying it, darling?" Sarah. She was dressed in a black, off-the-shoulder evening dress and he hardly knew her.

"Yes. Great time. Don't worry about me. You enjoy the party. I can take care of myself."

"Of course you can. I didn't think otherwise." She gave his arm a squeeze. "I like showing off my new man."

She drifted off, but not without a backward, secretive smile, towards a couple decorating the fireplace with their young, graceful bodies.

Leaving Maddie had been a traumatic experience – not for her, since she took the news stoically and was anything but demonstrative – but certainly for him. He was turning his back on someone who had given him nothing but love and affection for as many years as he could remember. Why? Because he was bored? That seemed a terrible reason to leave. No, that wasn't it. It was simply that he had fallen in love again, and a new love is one of life's most exciting experiences. It paints the world in fresh colours and even the most mundane things are suddenly quite wonderful. Since he was not one of those men who fell in love in three-year cycles, he had gone down hard.

It had not been an easy decision to leave. He did not trust

78

this new love as he had done the old. He saw himself ending up in a seedy flat in some derelict part of London, bitter, solitary and afraid. However, the magic of Sarah – and it was magic – seemed worth the risk.

She was not fond of television and he had rediscovered the delights of reading. For the first time he had obtained a copy of the Desert Hero's autobiography and it was a fascinating document. How thoroughly the man had immersed himself in the Arab culture! One passage had been particularly awesome in its implications.

. . . the well by the twin rocks, which rose like two elephant tusks embedded in the sand to form an arch-like entrance to the valley, was the property of the al-Kaffa tribe. I had been sworn into the tribe as an honorary member and they were closer to me than brothers. The penalty for stealing water from the well, without permission from the al-Kaffa, was death – instant death – without trial or question. I was riding through this section of the empty quarter, journeying east, when I came across a group using the well. They were three in number. It was my duty, as a member of the al-Kaffa, to execute the thieves and I would not have hesitated, had the robbers not made away during the night hours. It was evening as I approached the place and I decided to wait until dawn before riding in, but in the morning they were gone. Water is a precious commodity in the desert and while this form of justice may seem harsh to an Englishman with a dozen taps in his house and virtually unlimited supplies of the liquid, it was a code by which I had chosen to live . . .

Surprisingly, for Sarah was non-violent to the point of deploring the trend towards blood-and-thunder in modern films, his new partner in life had agreed with this philosophy, since she said that if you choose to live in another world you must abide by its rules.

Sarah was back at his side again.

"Come on, darling. I want to introduce you to some

79

people. Our host's over there. He'a a very nice man called Jaman Kota . . ."

He found himself being led across the room, between a trio of bored-looking youngsters, towards a small dark man in native dress who was having his ear bent by someone in a business suit. The second party was leaning forward, over his own drink, with a face full of seriousness.

"Well, of course we can give your new poet – I'm afraid his name slips my memory for the moment – we can give him a launching at the exhibition. I know it's basically an import-export show, but surely cultural exchange . . ." The business suit stopped in mid-sentence when he was aware of eavesdroppers.

"Sorry," said Sarah. "I was just going to introduce my friend to Jaman. Do go on . . ."

"No, no. It can wait. Business. This is a party after all." The business suit gave them a grey smile and drifted away with a mumbled apology to his listener.

"Jaman, this is James. You remember I told you about him?"

Jaman grasped his hand with pudgy fingers.

"Ah, yes. Sarah's new friend. How do you do? So nice to meet you."

Jaman's face was round and pleasant, with a slight hardness to the eyes. When he spoke his lower lip did not seem to move at all, which Jim found disconcerting, since it immediately became a magnetic feature and he found himself unable to look elsewhere.

"Sarah tells me you are a banker."

"I work for a bank."

"So? Perhaps I can put some business your way, James? There are various concerns with which I am connected – not necessarily in Malaysia, but all over the world . . ."

"Sounds interesting."

". . . for example, I have connections with the *qāt* business in the Yemen, which I understand you know something about."

"I know absolutely nothing about *qāt*." This was not quite true. He knew it was a leaf crop that could be made into a form of tea, or chewed as a drug.

"No, you misunderstand. I mean you know about the country – the Yemen. Such an unfortunate business going on there at the moment, but not likely to affect people like you and me – men of commerce. I have a large transaction in progress there at the moment." He touched Jim's shoulder and looked conspiratorially to the left and the right. Leaning closer, so that his breath made Jim gag, he added, "The deal is very lucrative. We . . . ah, food," he reached out and took something from a tray which a waiter was thrusting between them. Sarah and Jim followed suit. It was some kind of meat, spicy, which left a slight burning sensation at the back of the tongue.

"You like exotic foods, James?" said Jaman.

"Yes," he lied.

"I'm afraid I adore food. It's my one great vice."

He showed them a row of perfectly even white teeth.

"My passion – I'm not married you see."

What the hell had that got to do with it?

"Have another? Better still, come over to the buffet table. We can choose from the various plates."

As he led them across the room, Jaman said, "I have all my food – well, much of it – flown out from the Far East. Extravagant, terribly extravagant. Still, it's my one great passion . . ."

Jim made some kind of noncommittal noise in the back of his throat, which was still suffering from the burning sensation of the meat.

The buffet table was spread with a variety of dishes, none of which Jim recognised. Jaman began pointing out several different kinds of fruit and meat, inviting Jim and Sarah to try each one, telling them the Malay for each titbit and occasionally explaining what it was in English.

"Snake?" said Jim, pulling his hand up short when it was an inch from the proffered plate. "I'm sorry, I don't think . . ."

"Oh, James. You have no idea how delicious it can taste." Jaman took a ball of the pale-looking flesh himself, smacking his lips ostentatiously as he ate it.

"My Chinese chef knows exactly how to prepare this dish. It is – delectable."

81

"I'm sure it is," replied Jim, not moving a muscle.

Sarah pointedly took a piece herself, glaring a little at him as she chewed it.

"Hmmm. Super. You really ought to try some, Jim."

"Not on an empty stomach," he joked, but received no smile from either of them.

"Finicky," said Sarah to Jaman, as if Jim were a fussy child who would not eat his cabbage.

"In that case, James, I shall cease telling you what they are and let you choose in ignorance. What you don't know won't upset you, yes?"

"I think that's probably best," he replied. Out of politeness he reached for something that had no name and swallowed it quickly without tasting it.

"Yes, absolutely. Quite delicious, Jaman."

"Good. Good." A hand descended on his shoulder.

"Now, about this Yemen business. You would need to go there in person of course – I shall have a word with your managing director tomorrow morning. I'm sure when he knows the financial details, he'll be more than willing to loan you to me for a while. What about your personal plans? Nothing in the way there, I trust?"

Sarah replied, "No, he's quite free at the moment, aren't you, Jim?"

Jim went hot and cold alternately. What the hell was happening here? He had the sensation of being thrust into the neck of a bottle head first and he wasn't enjoying it.

"Now, wait a minute . . ." he began, but Jaman was talking again.

"It's essential I have someone I trust, you understand? There are too few people around one can trust these days, isn't that so? You come highly recommended, my dear friend, by this lady here. She shall be permitted to go with you of course. A female companion is essential out there, in order to show them you are not interested in *their* women."

Jim saw this was a great opportunity to realise his ambition. But something still held him back. For one thing, he felt he was being used. Sarah had set this whole offer up, without consultation, and it mortified him to think that she might be regarding him as an instrument to get herself back to South-West Arabia.

The other thing was, he was afraid. There was no specific fear – just a general foreboding that was strong enough to make him hesitate.

"I'm not sure," he said. "It's not as easy as all . . ."

There was distress in Sarah's face.

She cried, "Oh, Jim. Of course it's easy. All you have to do is say yes."

"No!" He meant, "No, it isn't as simple as that" but Kota's face stiffened at the abruptness of the word and he shrugged his shoulders at Sarah and strode off to another part of the room.

"You've insulted him," said Sarah.

"You should have warned me. I wasn't prepared. I don't like having things like this sprung on me without knowing about it first."

She said, "Well, that's it then, isn't it? Don't say I never try to help you." She swallowed the last of her drink fiercely and then walked away.

Jim worked himself into a corner and stayed there, miserably throwing down gins whenever a tray came within reach. He felt humiliated and angry, without knowing why. I'm being unreasonable, he thought. People are trying to be kind to me and I'm reading all sorts of motives into their actions. I should stop being so childish.

A young woman was sitting on the floor a few feet away, staring miserably at the rest of the guests. Jim squatted down beside her, sensing a soul mate. She was a blue-eyed blonde with porcelain features and her legs were stretched out in front of her, the dress forming a basin between her knees.

"Hello. You on your own?" he asked.

The blue eyes focused for an instant on his face.

"Who are you?" she asked, rudely.

"The name's Jim. I came in with Sarah Mitchell, that lady over there." He pointed to Sarah, who was engaged in conversation with the group of youngsters he had noticed earlier.

"Sarah *who*? Oh, you mean Sarah Ashcrofte."

"Ashcrofte? No, Mitchell. Her name's Mitchell."

Suddenly the girl laughed. "Oh, *I* get it. She's reverted to her maiden name. She's married to John Ashcrofte – a major or something in the army."

Jim felt stupid. Why hadn't Sarah mentioned that? It was just like her. She was full of silly secrets, that need not be secrets at all.

"Actually, they're separated," he found himself explaining. "We live together now."

"And she never told you? Oh, well. Not my business." She took a sip of her drink. "Hell, I'm sorry. I don't mean to be aggressive, but I've had a bad day."

"That's okay. I'm having a bad evening."

She suddenly regarded him with interest.

"You don't like parties?"

"I don't like this one. I'm out of my depth. I don't know any of these people and I don't think I really want to."

"Thanks," she said, wryly.

"Oh, I didn't mean you," he amended, hastily.

"No, I know you didn't, but you do. God, this stuff is disgusting. What is it?"

"I don't know. What are you drinking?"

She stared down into a glass of magenta-coloured liquid, screwing up her doll-like features.

"The punch I think. Tastes like syrup."

"Do you want something else? I'll get it if you like."

"Would you? A white rum if they've got it. With a dash of Coke?"

"Be glad to."

In the taxi on the way home, he tried to apologise, but though she didn't seem angry she was distant and he imagined a simmering fury inside her, which she was holding back.

"Why didn't you tell me you'd changed your name?" he said.

She glanced sideways at him.

"I haven't. What do you mean?"

He stared out of the window, watching the lights whip by in the night. They formed a blurred pattern in his brain, as it struggled to function.

"A woman at the party called you Ashcrofte."

Sarah laughed. "Oh, *that*? My married name. I'm entitled to use my maiden name if I want to, aren't I? I just hadn't thought of mentioning it before. It hadn't cropped up in conversation. I'm sorry, I can't just pull out my history on a broad sheet of paper, and hand it to you. It'll all have to come out naturally, in little bits. I'm sure you have your dark side too."

"I suppose so." He stared moodily at the lights again. There were some things he wanted to forget. Some things he would never tell her.

"Here we are," said Sarah. "Home."

Later that night, he woke as she moved away from him in bed.

"What's the matter?"

"Nothing. You're hot, that's all. I can't sleep with your arm around me when you're so hot."

He sighed, moving further away from her. After that, he couldn't get to sleep again and stirred, restlessly, trying to find a comfortable position. He felt reptilian, repulsive.

"Jim?"

"What?"

"Could you use the sofa? You're fidgeting too much. I can't sleep."

"I'm sorry. Shall I go back to Madelaine? Maybe I won't disturb you from there."

"Oh, God, you're so childish."

He left it a few moments and then, grabbing his pillows, went down the stairs to the sofa. It seemed cold and unwelcome at first. The sofa was hard and lumpy. However, he imagined himself back on the moors, sleeping beneath the stars, and he soon dropped off into a deep slumber.

Some time, in the middle of the night, Sarah came downstairs, presumably to get a drink.

He woke, and said as she passed, "Welcome to the leper colony." She failed to answer him, merely going to the fridge and taking something with her, back up the stairs.

Sarah lay awake staring at the ceiling in the near darkness.

She felt depressed and unhappy. Things were not going as she intended. Jim did not seem to understand that it was important for him to go to Arabia. She would like to go too, of course, but that was a separate issue, and not so imperative. If she could explain to him *why*, it would have been easy, but she didn't know why. She just felt compelled to direct him on his course to his own destiny. Surely if she could explain her feelings, they wouldn't be feelings any longer, only facts. It was like trying to explain *why God*.

He had told her that evening that he felt he was being used. So what? They were all being used, weren't they? Did that matter? Good heavens, her own mother had used her. She had liked John Ashcrofte, when they were introduced, but she never intended marrying him. It was her mother who had put her up to that, knowing that an army officer is likely to be posted abroad and that she could persuade the young couple to take her with them. Her mother had spent much of her life in India, and liked the colonial life. It was pleasant, she told her daughter, not to have to worry about the mundane things in life. Abroad one had cheap servants to do all the housework and cooking – servants that one could not afford at home in England. And the climate was so amiable in places like India and Africa, so long as one did not have to venture out into the sun too often. Her mother had gone with them to Singapore and had died there within three months, of a stomach disease. That had left her with John. They had got on well enough, but he was not the one she would have chosen, left to her.

In Malaya she came into her first contact with a completely foreign culture and it excited her enormously. Her weekend bungalow was on the mainland, near Kuala Lumpur. Although it was too far for just a two-day weekend, she would spend several weeks up there on her own, while John was away on duty somewhere in Malaysia. The jungle was only thirty yards from her back door.

She would stare out of her window at the immense wall of foliage, impenetrable, even to light, and would be filled with a sense of its brooding aggression towards her. She was an outsider. The apes would come out of the trees for sugar lumps wrapped in silver paper: they belonged to that darkness – but not she. Yet she did not mind this feeling, because she knew she was insignificant. It was not her, personally, that the jungle disliked, but everything and everyone that threatened its existence.

She even went on short expeditions, arranged by local Malays, into its hot damp interior. There, amidst the bamboo in all its hundreds of varieties, and the palms and vines and undergrowth, all locked together in one mighty embrace, she felt its force, the pressure of its being. It had silver, noisy mouths, in the hanging-jawed waterfalls, which roared at her suddenly, on breaking through into a clearing. And out of the dark-green hills came long, brown rivers, each with a life of their own. There, she saw what the jungle could do with religion – the religion of men. It crushed their temples to powder with its invincible strength and swallowed them whole. There was no force equal to it.

At night, she would watch the moon rise over its back and would allow herself the pleasure of awe as tier on tier of its broad reaches were revealed to her in the yellow light. She would listen to its many voices and succumb to the weight of its mood.

It was not difficult for her to accept the desert in the same way, once she and John were sent to Aden. In fact, the desert was not as hostile as the jungle, because the threat of mankind meant nothing to it. It was already a wasteland. Also, the desert was not a contained spirit: it was free, open and full of light. She had feared the jungle, but she loved the desert.

It was because of her experience with these two live entities that she had become so angry with Jim, for trying to compare the puny Essex marshes with such places. The latter were nothing, nothing compared with the desert and jungle. You could not lose your soul to such insignificant regions when you had known the giants.

She heard Jim stir downstairs.

What was she to do? How was she to fulfil her promise, if he would not go? She had removed obstacles: Madelaine, the need for work. And still he was afraid to follow the path that must be followed. A certain sense of duty was keeping him here: she must use his sense of duty to get him away. Alan's letters to her had become a little amorous of late. She would encourage that and begin to reject Jim. It would be hard, because she was very fond of him. But it was necessary to break the last tie with England. And if Alan were in trouble – he would feel it his duty to help his friend . . .

BOYS

The two boys put down their fishing rods and began skimming stones across the surface of the river. Where the stones touched, the water threw itself up in uneven loops of molten silver, for it was one of those bright English summer days that old people stretch, until it covers all the summers of their youthful years. They forget the days of rain and wind and remember only the sunshine, the frogs plopping in the pond, the smell of dusty wheatfields and the white, weather-board church glinting above a hill of mustard crops.

"You remember how we used to fish in the river? God, it was always sunny in those days, wasn't it? I can't remember a time when the sun wasn't out and we hadn't got a rod in our hands . . ."

A single day, that would become many days: multiples of itself.

One of the boys idling on the bank was called Al – a lean sandy-haired youth with the premature shadow of perpetual sadness already forming in his face. You knew, if you were aware of the signs, that his mind had been formed by order and ritual, was fashioned only for the reception of such, and since the world tends towards chaos, he was bound towards a life of disappointment.

The name of the other youth was Jim, a short, stocky, black-headed boy with a constant dreamy look that appeared to be a smile, except that he was unaware of any universal joke and the expression was merely a setting of the facial muscles in their most comfortable position. Both boys were capable of humour, but of the two only Jim gained spiritual benefit from it. The bolts of joy embedded themselves deep inside him, whereas they merely skimmed the surface of the sandy youth like stones skipped across water.

Jim, in contrast to Al, lived in a misty world where time was unimportant and events occurred spontaneously, with-out reference to scheme or plan. He was always in trouble, as

89

such boys are, with authority, who drew up rules to frame life as they thought it should be, and expected the Jims of the world to fit inside them.

Al stopped whipping his arm over his shoulders.

"You know that Sheila Johnson? You reckon she would?"

They had begun to enter an era of their lives when fishing was of secondary importance: when certain physical and mental changes were taking place which were delightfully disturbing.

"Dunno. Phil Staker says he's had a handful – in the back of the coach when we went to Whipsnade."

Al's face darkened with seriousness.

"He's a lying pig's orphan. According to him every girl in the school's wearing his handprint on her . . ." He came to a halt. The word *breasts* seemed a bit prissy and he knew he would redden with the use of slang. They were both totally inexperienced with regard to the bodies of young ladies, but, like most boys of their age, believed themselves to be islands of reluctant virtue in a sea of promiscuity. Often they lied to each other, believing themselves truly alone in their purity. Sexual encounters were desperately attractive, mentally, but frightening, both in the idea of venturing into the unknown, and the possible consequences of that journey. They exhibited all the signs of tension, their bodies pulling them one way and their fears and morals the other.

The chaotic charges of sexual electricity coursing through his body was especially alarming to Al, who wanted logical answers as to the source and meaning. He had sneaked books from the library, with titles like *The Psychology of Human Encounters*, but the answers were hidden beneath layers of evasive medical jargon, more difficult to unearth than an archaeological artefact. Even if he found an answer he was unable to decipher it, not yet possessing the Rosetta stone of sexual experience.

Jim, who wanted to become a doctor, knew more about the workings of the human body than Al, but it was a mechanic's knowledge, which he found difficult to apply to himself and his discoveries.

A few years previously, they would have stripped off their clothes and gone bathing in the nude, but with sexual tension comes inhibition, so they merely lay on their backs on the grassy bank and soaked up the sunshine. Consequently, instead of becoming refreshed, envigorated, by a swim in the cool water, they became drowsy and sluggish, forbidden thoughts dulling their normally alert brains.

When the trees filled with starlings, setting up a clamour prior to settling for the evening, Jim knew it was time to go home. Al had already consulted his watch. They tied the rods to the crossbars of their bicycles and rode across the meadow to the road, each lost in his own thoughts.

There was a hole in the hedge, barely wide enough for both bikes abreast, but they enjoyed the minor danger of going through together, timing it so that their machines clashed at the point of entry, and bounced away from each other on exit. On the other side was the road.

They raced for the opening, the dying sun glinting on their handlebars, losing for a moment their preoccupation with sex in the chivalric excitement of bikemanship. Timing it precisely, the riders hit the dip in the shallow ditch simultaneously. The handlebars clipped each other and Al's foot caught the pedal of Jim's bike. His trouser turnup was hooked and held. Normally, he would have extracted himself without too much difficulty, but the late afternoon's lethargy had blunted his reactions and as he fought to free himself, the pair of them ran out of control.

"Christ!" shouted Jim, more in exultation than concern, as they both flew out of the hedge, locked together, leaves whipping their faces, into the middle of the road.

The motorcycle was about twenty yards from them, its roar lost amongst high banks and thick hedgerows. They saw the rider braking hard, his machine slewing away from him and spurting fountains of sparks. Then he was catapulted high and hard against a tree, while the vehicle did a series of somersaults, passing the two boys by inches and finally slashing a long groove in the sun-softened tarmac. When it came to rest its lights suddenly went on, then died. For a while one of the wheels continued to spin, the light flickering on the polished spokes.

A car came along shortly afterwards and they flagged it down. The driver helped them lay the motorcyclist on the grass verge, before driving to the police station on the outskirts of the village. Neither he, nor the boys, had ever seen a dead person before, let alone handled a corpse, and all were considerably shaken. The boys were taken to their respective homes to be quizzed by confused and horrified parents, prior to a night during which, for the first time in two months, neither of them thought about Sheila Johnson's breasts.

Two weeks later the boys met in the barn they had used as a den since they were six-year-olds. For once, even Jim's face wore the furrows of care. They sat on a bale of straw, pulling at loose stalks desultorily.

Jim said, "You know who he was, don't you?"

"Can't help it. Mum never stops talking. Anyway, I read it in the papers."

"Christ! He discovered South Arabia."

"Not discovered." Al was more of a scholar than Jim. "He was an adventurer. He crossed the desert there – helped the Arabs fight. He was – a hero."

"We weren't to know. Hardly anyone's on that road – usually."

"I couldn't get my foot off. I couldn't get it off."

"He did things no one's ever done – crossed deserts that even the Arabs couldn't. Wrote a book about it . . ."

"My trousers were caught. You should've –"

"I couldn't do anything. I didn't even see him till –"

They sat there, staring into the gloom at the back of the barn, where they had once hunted rats with an air rifle. The rodents had always been too clever for them. When they had carried the gun, the rats were nowhere to be seen. Without it, the creatures ran across the beams in full view, with their pointed faces twitching, and scuttled over the straw with impunity. The one time Jim had one in his sights, Al screamed at him to pull the trigger and he froze, his heart thumping fast. Suddenly, the rat was no longer a rat, but a creature – a nameless animal – with a heart beating like his own. He lost all his distaste for the creature and in his imagination he saw the lead pellet ripping savagely through the soft flesh – saw the animal twitching and jerking in death

92

– and he could not squeeze the trigger. Al would have done, but then Al did not own Jim's imagination.

"We should do somethin'," said Jim.

"What?"

"I dunno. *Something*."

An owl shuffled on its perch high in the roof. Their attention was momentarily distracted.

The barn was on a knoll above the flat countryside of the Essex coastland. All around them, for as far as the eye could see, were yellow cornfields, with the occasional rise and fall of a barrow, like a golden dune, hiding the secrets of fallen warrior chiefs.

"It was our fault," said Jim. He wanted to say more, but the words would not come to him. He had felt a change within himself, since the death of the Arabian hero, but he was unsure of Alan. To have voiced what he felt, without knowing, would have left him feeling foolish.

"It wasn't," said Alan, fiercely. "It was an accident. We couldn't help it – it just . . . happened."

Jim suddenly blurted out, "Are you having dreams?"

A cloud-shadow swept like a dark wave over the cornfields below, drowning the gold beneath its rapid flow. They both watched it, through the open-sided barn, until it had gone.

"What kind of dreams?"

"I dunno. Nightmares. I keep dreaming that rocks and things keep comin' alive and chasing me. If I'm in a town, all the people lock their doors, just as I reach them, so I can't get in – can't escape the things that are chasing me. If it's in the country, I get tangled in the trees or I keep trying to jump a gate in a field and hit the top bar every time. All the time these creatures are after me – like in a science fiction comic. You have dreams like that?"

"No," replied Al, in such a way that Jim knew he was not telling the truth.

They lapsed into silence again, before Alan said, "My parents are sending me away to a school – in Buckinghamshire. They said you're a bad influence on me." Jim was shocked and Alan, on seeing his face, added quickly, "It's not me. I don't think that. It's them. You know what parents are. They think they know everything."

"What kind of school is it?"

"Just an ordinary school – boarding. They said it's best for me – for my education. They said they should've done it a long time ago." In comparison to Jim's parents, Alan's were quite wealthy. They owned a large farm and ran a riding stables. They could afford to give their son what they felt was best for him.

Jim said, "Does that mean I won't be able to come riding any more?"

"In the holidays you can. When I'm home."

Jim bit his lip, not because of what Alan had said, but because he had tried to hurt him by pretending that the only thing he would miss would be riding the horses in Alan's parents' stables. He wanted to retract the words but it was too late. If any damage had been done it was irreparable. To attempt any explanation now would have left Jim too vulnerable to Alan's sarcasm. While they were friends, they were also enemies, their feelings for each other balanced delicately on an ambivalent relationship. Much of their time was spent arguing hotly about trivial matters and occasionally they came to minor blows.

"You can have Sheila Johnson to yourself now."

"Yeah. Thanks a lot. She told me she'd rather go out with someone like you."

"She did?"

"Yeah. Then she added that she threw up every time she thought about going out with you."

Alan punched a bale of straw. "She would, the cow. I can't stand the sight of her."

"Me neither."

"Can't think what I ever saw in her."

"Me neither."

"That's the trouble with some of these women. They think they're God's gift. Maybe I'll ask her to go out with me, just so's I can watch her throw up."

"Maybe if we both ask her at once she'll stiffen up and die."

They were quiet after that. The subject having turned to death once again, the distraction Miss Johnson had caused no longer took their minds away from the accident and once more it dominated their individual thoughts. It was to do so, on and off, for the rest of their lives.

When they left school, Alan went on to university while Jim tried various jobs before settling down in a bank. It was not that he liked the money market, but it paid well and one did not necessarily need qualifications in order to get the job. One could not advance very far without taking exams, within the system, but they were willing to take you on so long as you were prepared to immerse yourself in a world of paper and figures.

Alan left university to become a political journalist. There was little contact between the two men during these years and it came as something of a surprise to Alan that Jim did not fulfil his ambition to become a doctor, not realising that Jim had given up that idea as soon as he decided he was not capable of entering the medical profession.

Alan remained single but Jim married Madelaine Shirley Bell, a colleague from the bank, at Hawkswell Church on a rainy day in October. Once all the excitement was over they found they were comfortable with each other, though Jim left his present bank to join the Bank of Saudi Arabia, since they saw a little too much of each other when working side by side all day long. Even the best marriages can cloy on double cream.

Alan often thought back to that time when Jim, in the barn, had asked him if he had bad dreams. Though he hadn't admitted it at the time, the dreams were terrible, and they had never gone away. He was almost used to them by the time he was forty: would have missed them if they stopped. Fortunately, as a bachelor, his screams in the middle of the night woke nothing but the cat, and even his pet got used to his middle-hour ravings. All regularities become routine.

Sometimes, at night, he would walk along the Thames embankment, when his sleep had been disturbed, and watch the lights on the dark water. On these occasions he would often come across vagrants, tramps, for whom he had a particular distaste, which he could not have explained, even to himself.

There's no need for it, in these times, he would tell

himself. Not in a welfare state. The squalor and the dirt
offended him and their way of life, the winos and dropouts,
seemed such a waste of human energy. He liked walking
himself, but to make it an occupation struck him as pathetic.
If they had been gypsies, why that was a different matter.
Gypsies were nomadic by nature. They had a certain nobility, as a wandering race, such as the Arabs possessed.

One evening, after he had been to a formal party at Queen
Mary's College in Mile End Road, East London, he was
feeling particularly satisfied with life. He studied the train
timetable with a sense of enjoyment. He liked the neat rows,
with their appearance of precision. Clean columns of figures,
representative of structure and order. As he folded the
pamphlet and put it in his inside pocket, he noticed a group
of gypsies sitting beneath a buddleia, near the railway
embankment. It was the shrub itself that caught his eye, for
beneath the grime and dirt that had crept from the railway
sheds on to the plant, he could see the mauve blooms
struggling to add some colour to the dismal appearance of the
neighbourhood. Then he saw the figures beneath.

"Good evening," he said, as he realised he had been staring
directly at them. They were five in number: a burly youth
of about twenty, two children like miniature scarecrows
with coalpit faces, a sharp-featured woman of indetermin-
ate age and an old man, shrivelled, like a dried mandrake
root.

They stared at him in silence and he suddenly wondered
whether or not they spoke English.

"Watcha want?" the woman said, suddenly. Her voice was
as deep and harsh as if she had been swallowing kitchen
bleach.

"Nothing. Nothing at all." He felt extremely uncomfortable. "I was just curious – admiring the bush. I hadn't seen
you – squatting – beneath."

The three adults looked at the buddleia as if they were
seeing it for the first time. The two children began squab-
bling over something and the old man, his face almost hidden
by a greasy cloth cap much too large for his narrow skull,
reached out and flicked the nearest ear, extracting a screech.

On impulse, Alan moved closer to the group.

"You – what do you do here? Collect scrap metal?"

The woman: "You the police?"

"What? No – nothing of the kind. I'm just out for a walk. I've always been interested in the nomadic life . . ."

"You wot?" snapped the youth.

"The nomad – the wandering kind of life. The way you people live."

They stared at him suddenly. The youth asked, "You got some scrap?"

The old man sniffed. " 'Orses. We're 'orse dealers, not pikeys."

Horses? Where on earth would they breed horses in London? On the waste grounds, or perhaps they kept their caravan in the city and went out to the country, Essex or Middlesex, in order to carry out their business? A sort of reverse commuter role?

"If 'e's got scrap, we can get rid of it," argued the youth. "I ain't fussy where me money comes from."

" 'E's got no scrap. Look at 'im."

Alan was aware that he was in evening dress, but it gave him a feeling of security, rather than embarrassment. Put a barrier between him and these people. Barriers were useful when you were out of your depth.

The young man produced a box of matches.

"I could do with a fag."

Alan said quickly, "I don't smoke."

The two children were tugging with grubby hands at his trouser legs now. What on earth were they doing? He didn't want to brush them away and he couldn't walk off with them clinging there. None of the adults made a move to assist him. He stood, helpless, amongst the glares.

"I've got some brandy," he said. It was true. He carried a hip flask as a precaution against the cold. Fumbling in his overcoat pocket, he produced a leather-covered bottle, a present from a former girlfriend. He offered it to the old man, who took it instantly.

"Don't mind." The cap was unscrewed.

"Leave the gentleman's legs alone, you little . . ." said the woman. The children took no notice. Grimy fingers pawed at the cloth.

The old man took a guzzle of the brandy, then the woman and finally the youth.

"Good stuff," he said. He handed it up to Alan, without the top. Alan held it stupidly in front of him. They stared at him expectantly and his confusion mounted. They wanted him to drink. Could he wipe the top with them all staring at him like that? They might have some sort of ritual which made it bad manners to do such a thing. Like American Indians passing the pipe.

"Another?" he suggested hopefully, holding out the bottle again.

"You first," said the youth.

With extreme distaste which he hoped did not show in his face, Alan raised the flask to his lips, tasting, he was sure, spittle. He wanted to vomit, but fought it down, hard. Without actually drinking he tipped the bottle up. Then handed it back to them.

"Finish it off."

They did as asked, passing him the empty flask.

"Why do you live the travelling life? Is it the freedom?" He was determined to get something out of this situation. It had been expensive in terms of dignity.

"Why?" They looked at him with genuinely puzzled expressions.

"Yes, why?"

"I'll tell you why," answered the youth. " 'Cos it's bloody fun in the winter, freezin' yer arse off in a van, when the cops keep movin' you on every time you light a fire, and you can't get water, 'cos all the taps is froze and the 'ouses won't open their doors to you, and the wimmin don't want no clothes pegs or bits of 'eather, so you can't get no food – and the gamekeepers fill your arse with buckshot when you try to, and warm it up a bit, and one of the kids is sick, but you can't get no doctor to see 'em, and the local gentry come down, claimin' you've stole this and that . . ." He kept up this tirade for several minutes, until the woman said, "Oh shuddup. 'E gave us a swig, didn't 'e?"

Alan at last managed to wrench himself away from the infants and hurried off down the road. After a quarter of a mile, he slowed his pace and found that he was still carrying his empty flask. The silver top was missing and the kid leather had dirty fingerprints all over it. He threw it on a waste heap and wiped his mouth with his handkerchief in disgust. He remembered the woman's rotten teeth and the hard scab of mucus on the old man's upper lip. How did he manage to get himself into these situations? They were not *bad* people. They just weren't his kind. He couldn't stand dirt and they seemed inseparable from it.

As he waited for his train he noticed a woman on the same platform who had been at the party. She was dressed in a white silk evening dress and looked as if she had just stepped out of a beauty salon. This was his kind of person.

He managed to sit opposite her on the tube and made some opening remark about it having been a nice party and hadn't he seen her there?

"Yes, you did," she said, a little stiffly, which he put down to shyness. "I heard you talking about the situation in Aden – the violence out there."

"Oh, did you? I'm a political correspondent – that's my interest. Do you have an opinion?"

She leaned forward and said, "Yes, I have an opinion. I believe all war is wrong."

He smiled indulgently. "It's not a war, you know. It's merely a bunch of scruffy Arab terrorists."

"Don't play with words. People are killing each other. We shouldn't be there in the first place."

Suddenly he was on the defensive again.

"Some of us think it's worth fighting for."

"It isn't you that's doing the fighting." Her blue eyes blazed into his. "You're sitting here comfortably safe on a London train."

"The men who are out there are all volunteers. They joined up to fight." He ignored the attack on his manhood and honour, believing she did not understand what she was saying.

"This may come as a bit of a shock to you, but all young men do not join the armed forces because they want to fight. They sometimes join because they have had no education and they need a job – any job. They sometimes join to get away from a home background that's intolerable and it's the only

99

way to escape. They sometimes join because they have fathers who hold the same perverse opinions as you do, and being impressionable, wanting to prove themselves to men who are not worth proving anything to, they set out to show them that they are not the useless, gutless individuals their fathers keep telling them they are. They sometimes join because they want to fly aeroplanes or see foreign countries and are horrified to find themselves in a war situation . . ."

"Bit stupid then, aren't they?"

"Naive, not stupid. They're young – sometimes only schoolchildren who haven't had time to sort out their values."

He grunted in discomfort. This woman clearly needed setting straight.

"I am prepared to die for what I believe in," he said. "I suppose you find that crass."

"No, I admire it. I too am prepared to die for what I believe in."

"Well then!" he cried triumphantly.

"I'm afraid you misunderstood my argument," she said, rising to go as the train stopped at a station and the doors hissed open. "I'm prepared to die for what I believe in – I'm just not prepared to kill for it."

She left the carriage and he slumped back into his seat. Goddamnit, he thought. This just isn't my night. This just isn't my night.

He was so vexed with the woman, and himself, that he missed his stop and had to take a taxi the rest of the way home.

Jim's wife, Maddie, was one of those very busy people who fill their lives with work beyond work. She held down a full-time job, was on several committees, always had an educational course on the go and believed that attendance at the squash court was essential to life after death. Small, pretty and energetic, with above average intelligence, she filled Jim's life with a vibrancy that remained with him even during her absence.

Since her fidelity was beyond question, though she frequently spent many nights away from home, Jim was very contented during the early years of their marriage. Whenever her work for the merchant bank took her away, he would go climbing in Snowdonia, or the Pennines, or take himself off and backpack into the wilds of Scotland, knowing that her light and colour would soon return to the house, to throw its patterns across his life. She was good for him that way.

Although Jim himself was not particularly ambitious, she encouraged him expertly, injecting strength into his weaknesses and praising his small triumphs, until he held quite a responsible position at the bank. Always at the back of his mind, though, was the feeling that it was temporary. That something would occur to place them on different spheres of understanding which would be irreconcilable. It was nothing to do with love: it was to do with forces less comprehensible and since love itself – the understanding of its nature and source – has puzzled poets and philosophers since mankind's first fall, it was unlikely that Jim would be able to comprehend what those sundering forces might be.

He had tried to tell her once that they might find themselves parting one day, and that it had to do with an accident he had been involved in as a youth, but she misunderstood and thought he was trying to leave the door open for himself. The accident still played a great deal on his mind and he followed the news from the Middle East with more than mild interest.

In September 1962, Imam Mohammed al Badr, the priest-king ruler of the Yemen, a country in South West Arabia, was overthrown by a *coup d'état* inspired by the United Arab Republic. Egypt had invited the Imam to send some of his young men to Cairo to become educated and rightly suspecting the motives for the offer he had dispatched, as a token, the son of a lowly blacksmith, wrongly believing that such a youth would be incapable of organising a revolt on his return, should he indeed have aspirations to power.

Egypt trained the Yemeni youth in terrorism and he returned to his own country to organise a successful revolt against the Royalists, who were driven out of the cities and into the northern mountains to begin a long campaign of guerrilla warfare. The Imam escaped with his family, from the shelled palace in the capital, Sana'a, to lead the loyal tribesmen against Egyptian troops supporting the left-wing Yemeni Republicans.

By 1966, there were some 60,000 Egyptian troops in the Yemen, attempting the formidable task of winkling out ferocious Bedu from the hills. The Egyptian soldiers, many of them conscripts, were no match for the sharpshooting Bedu who hunted in family groups and could keep whole regiments of the enemy pinned down in unfamiliar territory for weeks, until the radio messages for bread and water became almost pitiful and the constant sniper fire whittled down their numbers to the point where a desperate rush at the Bedu was the last resort. The terrain was unsuitable for armoured vehicles, which meant the Egyptians were having to fight on the terms of their adversaries, and such incidents were common.

Around that time republicanism began to move south-east, into the various sheikdoms of the Hadhramaut, a plateau region inhabited by Hadhramis – farmers and Bedu – and down towards Aden. Hadhramaut sheiks were supported by the British presence in the Protectorate, but this land, once the source of great wealth – myrrh and incense – found itself torn by war. The incense tree, with its ash-coloured trunk and precious green transparent gum, became a shelter for Arab snipers and its days of former glory, when its resin was burned on the altars of Memphis and Jerusalem, were forgotten. Around the tomb of the Prophet Hud, great-great-grandson of Noah, who was transformed by God into a huge stone, still standing, the bullets whined. It was still regarded as a sanctuary in the mountains, since those who violated it would be beaten to death by leaping and screaming sticks and stones that lay about its entrance, but whoever went in had to come out, eventually, and this oasis of security was but a temporary respite for the man weary of violence.

The influence of the Republicans was already fomenting unrest amongst the Adenis, eager to be rid of the British, and several violent incidents had taken place in the port. Unlike the Yemen, with its rivers that never reached the sea, Aden was arid sand and rock. It was hot and humid both by day and night and tempers were on a short fuse. There were two main British bases – the port of Steamer Point and Khormaksar, the air force camp – both fairly close to the hotbed of the volatile population of Crater, the extinct hollow volcano which housed a town. Here rose the Front for the Liberation of South Yemen, a revolutionary organisation that was eventually to come into conflict with the dissidents in the Hadhramaut, the National Liberation Front.

Late in 1966, Jim received a phone call from Alan saying that he had been posted to South-West Arabia to cover events there for his newspaper. He suggested that Jim might join him.

"What the hell would I do there?" asked Jim.

"Oh, I could wangle you on to the payroll. Don't worry about that. You could take leave of absence or something – from the bank I mean."

"Yes, but what would I do?" The whole thing sounded totally impractical, irrational.

"You could ride shotgun," suggested Alan, lightheartedly. "You know – protect my flank."

Jim was incredulous. "You're not going there to fight, surely? I thought you were going to . . ."

"Oh, I know," interrupted Alan, "but who knows what'll happen once I get there. People get involved once they get into these places. I shall offer my services as a source of information, obviously."

Obviously? Obviously Alan was out of his mind. He had some warped vision of himself as a romantic spy for the British and while Jim did not approve of terrorist methods, he was anti-imperialism and a socialist. There was no way he was going to aid either side.

"You must be joking, Al. I've got my wife to consider. How would she feel if I went traipsing off to Aden to act as your lackey? Besides, we're not fighters – *I'm* not."

"*He* was."

"He?" For a few moments Jim hadn't the faintest idea who Alan was talking about, until the man said, "The accident – you remember. That's where he made his name. Out there in the desert. We could make amends . . ."

"What are you talking about?"

"Well, make up for what we did by – by – by being there.

103

Seeing what he saw. Doing what he did."

"This is 1966, Alan. You're talking about history – something that happened a long time ago. Who do you think you are – Thesiger? Lawrence? Philby? –that age has gone. You can't recreate an era that died a natural death."

Alan seemed to be getting impatient with him.

"Oh, for Christ's sakes, Jim. Stop making feeble excuses. We shall be *there*. We're both forty-seven years of age – the age at which he died. You realise that?"

"Yes."

"Well then. It's now or never. Can't you *feel* it? It's like I'm on the end of a fishing line. I'm hooked. I'm being reeled in. I can't help myself."

Jim admitted to himself that there was a lure, which somehow involved the dreams which were constantly with him: a magnetism drawing him towards the land he had thought so much about since he was a youth. He could feel the attraction, strongly, but it was more a case of making a decision, rather than feeling helplessly drawn towards an irresistible force that would not let him go until it had him in its clutches. There were subtle differences, obviously, be-tween his feelings and Alan's. His natural inclination was to go, but he told himself that duty was stronger. His childhood friend seemed caught up in an uncontrollable passion with an *idea* and Jim had always suspected ideas as motives. It was like being in love with love, rather than a person. Jim knew he would be at home in the desert, because he had been there, in his own homeland. He had camped on the moors of the West Country and in the bleak mountains of Scotland. Open spaces were his concubines.

"This isn't some silly exercise," insisted Alan. "There are real benefits to be had. Fame . . ."

"I don't want fame."

"Well, come because you *want* to."

"I can't and that's that. I'm entrenched in suburbia and here I'm going to stay. Good luck, Alan. Keep in touch. I'll write . . ."

"Jim!"

"What?"

There was hesitancy at the other end of the line. Finally,

when there was no answer he carefully replaced the receiver. Maddie came into the room just as he was doing so.

"Who was that?" she asked.

"Alan. He's going to the Middle East – his paper's sending him there."

"And? There's something more or you wouldn't be looking so pensive."

Sometimes she could read his mind. When he lay awake at night, thinking of things that he had no wish to divulge – to his wife or anyone – she would ask him what the matter was. He once asked her how she knew he hadn't been asleep and she replied that it was nothing supernatural, that his breathing had a certain rhythm while he slept and when he was awake she could sense the tenseness in him. Not read his mind exactly, but too damn close for comfort. A man had to have some secrets or his whole soul would lie bare and there would be nothing left of him.

"He asked me to go with him."

He expected her to say something like 'how preposterous' or 'the man's mad – what does he expect you to do? just throw up your job', but true to her nature she never did anything predictable when it came to the really important things. Oh, she was predictable enough when it came to the commonplace, but she seemed to have some hidden insight which told her when to spring the unusual on him.

"And are you going?"

"Of course I'm not going. What, leave everything here? That *would* be irresponsible, wouldn't it? If he wants to go off on some – well, he's being *sent*. It's quite different. There's no way I can just throw up everything and follow him."

"You could – or rather, you would, if you felt strongly enough. Nothing would stop you."

"I can't – there's – there's something I haven't told you."

"What?"

"I'm – pregnant."

When he found himself in a corner he always tried to joke his way out of it. Sometimes she got annoyed and at others she simply ignored it.

"Look, Jim, I don't *want* you to go, but if you feel you have to, don't make me the excuse to stay behind. I don't want you, in later years, blaming me – either consciously or otherwise – for holding you back. Do you understand?"

"I'm going to get a drink. Do you want one?"

"Yes please. A scotch with water."

He went into the dining room of their bungalow and took the scotch out of the tantalus, taking a deep swig from the bottle. Then he poured them both two generous measures, adding water to hers. When he carried them back into the living room, she was engrossed in a book and took the glass absently.

Why didn't he go? Because he was *afraid*. He admitted it to himself. He was scared rotten yellow. Not of losing his job or even of ruining his marriage, though he was comfortable enough in both, but of something within himself. He was afraid of a revelation: that the desert would reveal something to him of which he would rather remain ignorant. He knew, instinctively, that to go there would be to touch the edges of, or even enter, a spiritual zone where the natural laws of science – the hard logical rules of order – would disintegrate into something indefinable. He would come out – if he came out at all – markedly changed. He remembered a terrible line from Conrad's *Heart of Darkness* when the narrator, Marlow, spoke of Kurtz's mental state. ". . . I wasn't arguing with a lunatic . . . *But his soul was mad*. Being alone in the wilderness, it had looked within itself, and . . . it had gone mad."

There were things at work out there in the 'wilderness', which took little note of time, space and the laws which men had decided were immutable. Scribblings on paper, sudden insights resulting in discoveries, theories which showed how the universe ran like clockwork, mathematics with indisputable balances and equations, patterns which proved order existed in the seeming chaos – these were cast into spiral winds in the wilderness and scattered like dust. These were suits of armour for the Don Quixotes of civilisation. They felt protected by them. Used them as security blankets in order that they could go about their daily lives in the knowledge that nothing terrible could happen to the world which did not have its cause in reason. Nothing terrible could happen to them that was not of their own making. Anything apparently preternatural had a good sound reason behind it

106

and could be argued away with logic.

Out there, in the desert, Jim knew he would be facing a kind of destiny – not the only one, for a man might have several depending upon the decisions he makes himself. Free will was an element, but only an element, in the alloy that was forged into his life. He had not the courage, at that moment, to face what lay in wait for him in the deserts of South-West Arabia. Perhaps he never would have and might end his days, a grey retired bank employee who chuntered about exchange rates and bonds, and thought nothing of what lay beyond the world of concrete and machines?

Yes, certainly he was not ready for those empty nights and unending stretches of nothing, where a man might come face to face with himself and be terrified by what he saw. Where he might come upon himself, in darkness or in light, and find the deserts within his soul.

Alan had not really expected Jim to join him, but he felt it was worth a try. It would have helped him to overcome some of the anxiousness he felt about going out to a trouble spot. He was not a war correspondent and really didn't know why they were sending him.

"We need a fresh look at things," the editor told him. "Someone who can report on the human aspect – who's not already clogged up with preconceived notions."

That did not hold much water with Alan. It was too thin – too shallow. He tried to think of why they would want him out of the way for a while. Was there to be a merger, a sale? Or maybe someone was going to be promoted over the top of him and they didn't want a fuss until the new person was established in the job? None of these seemed terribly likely. Besides, he was relatively small fish and would not have influenced any sale or merger. He had recently been promoted, so he wasn't expecting any new advancement. The next slot would be a desk job and he didn't want that anyway.

Well, whatever the real reasons, he was going, and despite what he had told the woman on the train that time, he wasn't quite ready to die for his country, or his newspaper. There were other, more heroic types around, who were quite prepared to run the risks for a column of exciting narrative. Let them lie on the floor with the bullets whizzing round them – he was going to be careful. You weren't much good to your paper dead – that is, they could sell a few more copies on the day they showed your mangled body in an exclusive photograph, but the rewards hardly covered the cost. Anyway, making a few live 'situations' out of hearsay was not beyond his powers of imagination or his integrity. The daily news was transient, evanescent, and would be forgotten by the time the next edition was off the press, so what was there to be noble about? A smear that lasted a day would not hurt him or his unwitting readers and would enhance the reputation of the paper.

Was there anything else to fear? The ghost of the man who had died on the motorcycle? Absolute rot. Rubbish woven out of his nightmares. Oh, he didn't deny he felt uneasy about going there, which, if any place on earth was haunted, that certainly was. But what was the desert after all? A wasteground a little bigger than those that abutted the railway sidings in the East End. A stretch of dirt, that was all. A few bits of rock, perhaps, not yet eroded, but on their way to joining the rest of the dust piles. Nothing more. Maybe even a ragged sand-torn tree or two? Nothing to get excited about. He would miss his sports car and the appliances he had gathered over the years at his flat, of course. There was a party at June's place in two weeks' time. He would miss that. And the new Pinter play was due out. Still, that would wait. He had no doubt of its ability to run until he returned. The thing to do would be to get a nice first-class cabin on an ocean liner, so that the layers could peel away slowly before he was thrown into the – what did they call it? the armpit of the East? something more obscene probably. Yes, go out by boat. Do all the jolly roger stuff. Quoits on the deck, rubbers of bridge at midnight, perhaps even an illicit romance? He could get up early one morning and watch the flying fish leaping the boat, or lose himself in himself, contemplating the waves, he could . . .

Christ! Why wasn't Jim going with him!

JIM

Morning above the city was crooked with tall, corner buildings and appeared to have the viscosity of yellow glue, smeared across the sky by a weary sun that had lost its enthusiasm for its job. Along the railway sidings and canal banks, the junkies of the plant world sucked what goodness they could find from its light, along with the oil and grease on which they had been hooked since birth. From grimy holes, feral cats stared out, glad that their world was that of the night and the glutinous morning did not belong to them.

Jim woke with a raging headache, by a dirty canal. Nearby, three city tramps were brewing something evil in a tin can over a fire of old oil rags. He viewed the sky with distaste, then climbed to his feet to join the winos.

"Got any tea going, lads?" he said, thickly.

"Whut? See, get a can, boy. Ye get nobut a mouthful, mind."

The speaker was no older than Jim, but from outward appearances might have been his grandfather.

"A mouthful's all I need," he said. "Went on a bender last night." He stared around him at the wasteland covered in rubbish. "Christ, where are we anyway?" A train rumbled by, close to their heads, drowning any reply in the exchange between steel and steel on the bridge above.

"Where?"

"Stepney."

He squatted down with the trio and began to go through his pockets, looking for a cigarette. This caused a considerable amount of interest amongst his companions, until all he drew out was a very crumpled letter. He studied the envelope again.

'*Mrs S. Mitchell*' it read. That was wrong for a start.

He had found the letter yesterday – the day after his detective work – tucked behind the breadbin. She had wanted him to find it, otherwise she would have destroyed it.

109

The letter began: *My Dearest Sarah*, and ended, *All My Love, Alan*. The words between these two phrases were cleverly interwoven and effectively excluded all others from the world except the addressed and the addressee. It was, quite simply, a love letter.

"Bloody perverts, that's what they are," he muttered. "Who the hell makes love by post to someone they've hardly met? It's got to be perverted."

"They're all soddin' perverts. Every fuckin' man-jack o' them bastards. Bloody bastards. Fuck them bastard perverts . . ." The tramp's face was about half an inch away from Jim's, and he was shouting every word, his face twisted with impotent rage. His teeth were the colour of discarded cigarette butts in a urinal and the breath was polluted with the matter they had gathered to themselves. Jim could see parts of his internal anatomy that should always remain hidden.

". . . you're a bloody bastard," the tramp roared, becoming personal and flailing a bony fist in the air about Jim's head. "I'll smash your . . ."

"Settle down," said Jim in a testy voice. "Where's the tea you promised me? Come on, I can't hang about here all day."

The man stopped yelling immediately and his face, after going through a moment of dumb transformation, would not have been out of place on an apostle. He reached for the tea can with shabby-gloved hands and passed it to Jim very carefully. The other two were deep in some unintelligible argument that had nothing to do with anything but a distortion of the language and filling the empty morning with sound.

"Hell, that's hot," said Jim. "But it tastes like nectar after stale beer."

"That's right, lad. Sammidges?"

"What's that? Oh, sandwiches. No, you eat 'em, mate. I'll have some more of this tea though." He reached into his pocket for some money and placed it on the ground beside the tramp.

"Bloody money. Who needs'a bastard," snarled the man, picking it up and savagely thrusting it into an inside pocket of his greasy overcoat.

110

"Quite," said Jim. "Mucky stuff. That's why I've got rid of it." He sipped the tea placidly and nodded towards the other two, who were still at loggerheads over something.

"You know what I'd like to do now?" Jim said. "I'd like to get a pack on my back and just go – anywhere. Scotland preferably."

"Scotland."

"You've got it." He took another sip of the dark brew which was floating with tealeaves the size of woodchips. He handed the battered bean can back to the tramp.

"Sounds good, doesn't it? But it can get pretty cold up there, this time of year."

He pulled his soiled, crumpled jacket around him and scratched the stubble on his chin.

"You look bloody awful," he said to the tramp. "I hope my eyes aren't as bloodshot as those you're carrying."

The canal had a thin layer of ice at the edges which had trapped rubbish in artificial poses. Jim suddenly felt very cold and wondered why it had only just got through to him. He remembered stirring several times in the night, during his fitful sleep, and feeling the cold trapped in his bones. The sight of the fire on waking must have provided some pyschological warmth. He found he was shaking now and he stretched out his hands towards the flames. Alcohol lowered the blood temperature, but the tea had done him some good.

In the distance were some playing fields and a game of football was about to begin between some early-rising youngsters. He could hear them bellowing at one another.

"Never been a team man, myself. Always preferred sports where the individual relies only on himself. You know what she said to me?" The other two tramps were quiet now, staring into the dying fire. "She said she couldn't help what she was doing. No explanations. Just, 'I can't help it, Jim.' Can't help doing things that need a cold and calculated plan? Something's very wrong here, but I can't get anything else out of her. Maybe she's telling the truth? Maybe she really doesn't know why she's doing all these things? But there must be a reason. There *must* be. There's something missing – some vital link that hasn't come to light – yet. But I don't know where to look for it." An aircraft was flying overhead, silver hanging in the murk.

"Pity it's a machine. God should've made eagles that big and then we wouldn't be such cocky bastards."

"How's that?"

"Us – the human race. It would do us good to have a few giant predators around to keep our arrogance in check. Hell, she was desperate enough to get me away from Maddie. The trouble is, she's not such a bad sort, underneath, but she makes me angry. All this manipulating. What's it all about? Wrecking lives. Setting friend against friend. I really don't understand it – it's out of character. Underneath, she's a good person. I've always trusted my feelings about people . . ."

The eyes remained fixed on his.

"Well, it's no good staring. What are we going to do about it?"

"Dunno."

"No, neither do I. Nothing to be done, is there? Just got to – go on."

"Bloody bastards, the lot o' them."

Later that day, when he had cleaned himself up a little, and the despair was at its height, he went to the house he had left just a few weeks previously. It took a lot of courage to knock on his own door and he prepared himself to hide his shame under a cloak of humility.

Maddie answered the door.

"Can you – let me come in?"

She regarded him steadily, her face set. He couldn't blame her. He had walked out with hardly an explanation, one morning after breakfast. He had tried to generate a row, to give himself some sort of excuse, and she had not risen to the bait. Even as he was doing it, he had realised the ignobleness of his actions. Now he was paying the price.

She was thinner, he could see that.

"What for?"

"I – haven't got anywhere else to go."

"You can't come back." She tilted her chin. Her cheeks were shiny and warm-looking. "I'm having a good time."

"I know. I know I can't just walk in and out as I please. I just need a bed – or a couch," he added hastily. Then a terrible thought struck him. "You haven't got anyone else here?"

There was no answer and an unreasonable flash of jealousy went through him like a knife. He couldn't imagine her with anyone else – then, when he thought about it, he could, and it cut into his soul with a serrated edge.

"I'm glad you're having a good time," he said, miserably.

"You stupid bugger," she said, angrily.

He nodded. That he couldn't argue with.

"What time is it?" he asked, morosely.

"What difference does it make? God – you – you never know the bloody time, do you?" She grabbed his wrist, then flung it from her. "Why don't you buy yourself a watch? You're useless. I saw Peter Brookes yesterday. You know you've been given the sack, don't you? He said you've hardly been in to work the past six weeks and they're fed up with you. God, you hadn't even told them you'd left home! You can't hold down a job, you can't keep a wife, you can't even bloody drive . . ." That had always bothered her.

The news about the job, although not unexpected, was an additional blow to his failing spirit.

"I could learn."

"What?"

"To keep a wife."

"No, Jimmy. It's over. I've been through the mill and surprisingly I came out all right on the other side. It's over – and it's your own fault." She tossed her short hair.

"There's no one here. Not at the moment. Come on in then. It's too cold, even for creeps like you to be walking the streets."

He stepped inside gratefully.

"You never used to swear so much," he said, shaking nonexistent snow from his jacket.

"I've taken it up recently. It's good for me. I can do what I bloody well like now, can't I? Look, I'm smoking again." She snatched a packet of cigarettes from the kitchen table, as he followed her in, lighting one furiously.

"Ah, that tastes good."

She blew the smoke through her nose in a gesture of defiance and contempt.

He giggled. He couldn't help himself and she glowered at him.

"Smart arse. Well I'm not the one who's come crawling back . . ."

"For heaven's sakes, Maddie. I just want a place to lay my head. The kitchen table will do fine."

He climbed on top and lay out, full length. The kitchen was warm and though he had meant it as a joke, weariness suddenly overtook him and he found himself in danger of falling off to sleep.

"Maddie?" He fought to keep his eyes open.

"What?"

"I'm sorry."

He did not hear the answer.

"Tea."

He sat up quickly. She was in a different dress. The yellow one she had bought in Cornwall while they were on holiday.

"Tea?"

"You've been asleep – for about an hour. I thought I'd leave you there. Brother, you and that woman must have been energetic. I could never get you into that state. Not if I tried all night."

He was bemused, muzzy.

"It wasn't her. It was when I was with the tramps."

Her eyes opened wide.

"My God, you really have been having yourself a time."

"No. Not that – I just slept with – *stayed* with some tramps last night. They had a fire and I was cold. I think that's why I stayed. I can't remember exactly. I was pissed."

"You look it. You'd better go upstairs and get cleaned up. You're making my kitchen smell. I'm going out soon . . ."

"Why aren't you at work?" he asked, the thought suddenly striking him.

"It's Saturday."

"Is it?" He rubbed his face.

"You can use the couch tonight."

"Thanks, Maddie."

"Don't thank me – it's your furniture too."

"Where are you going?"

"Out."

"You – you won't bring anyone back? Not while I'm here. I couldn't bear . . ."

114

Her eyes blazed. "You're insufferable. You think I want any of my friends to see *you*? Just don't wait up for me, that's all."

She was back at eleven o'clock. He heard the front door open and she crept up the stairs softly. There were some ashes, still glowing, in the log-fire grate. He fumbled in his jacket pocket and drew out the letter again, lighting it from a red-hot cinder. It seemed to burn like ordinary paper, as if it were not responsible for his present state of dejection. The words inside, erotic as they were, did not flare into brilliant, exciting colours, nor exude some captured fragrance of forbidden desires. The log he had put on earlier had sent out spurts of blue and green flame, and had wafted scent into the room – the perfume of some summer breeze that had been trapped beneath the bark. He had expected the letter to do something similar. After all, it had come from an exotic land – a land of nomads and carpeted tents; silk cushions; sherbet and high-breasted maidens. It had been sent to a secret lover who had no doubt covered it with kisses and slept with it tucked inside the panties that went with her pale blue nightie.

It should have done more than just *burn*.

Jim stayed with Maddie for several weeks and she showed no inclination to get back together again, as man and wife. Finally, he realised they weren't ever going to do it. She had found an independence she enjoyed. He was not greatly distressed, though he told himself he should be. One night they were sitting by the fire, surrounded by memories of their former life in the shape of ornaments and pictures, when he said, "Seems funny, doesn't it, sitting here, and yet being apart, so to speak." He reached forward and picked up a statuette they had bought in Wales. It was entitled 'Hocus-pocus' and was of two witches entwined like thick vines.

"What's so funny about it?" She looked up from her book.

"Nothing, except that if anyone walked in they would think we were perfectly happy."

She took off her reading glasses and regarded him thought-fully.

"Aren't you happy, Jimmy?"

"No, but then I don't think I ever have been – completely happy. Oh, for brief periods, perhaps, like the first couple of years of our marriage, and parts of childhood. But for most of the time I feel a kind of – emptiness."

"I'm sure everyone has an empty space inside them, Jim. No one – no thing – can fill that for you. People try of course. They think falling in love will do it, but it only works for a while."

"Is that true? It seems to make sense."

"I think it is. At least it's true for me. I've seen people trying to fill that space – romance, travel, work, enthusiasms. They go from one thing to another thinking that each time they've found the answer. They change houses every two or three years – or partners – or buy things: furniture, artworks, yachts if they can afford them. None of this works. Not for long, anyway."

He stared into the fire. Ever since the incident as a youth he had thought the emptiness was something to do with the accident. That he had brought retribution on himself in the form of a hollowness to his life. Now she was saying that she felt it too! That it was normal – common to most people.

"I could never talk to you like this before. What's happened? Did we have to move away from each other to find conversation like this?"

"We couldn't have spoken in the same way. It would have seemed a betrayal, wouldn't it? To say you weren't happy?"

She leaned back in her chair, pulling her cardigan over her shoulders and drawing her legs up underneath her. He had seen her do the same movements perhaps a thousand times during their married life, but somehow there was a new intimacy to them now that she was no longer his bedfellow.

He said, "I suppose so. Isn't there any way of dealing with the emptiness then?"

"I don't know. I don't think so."

Jim relaxed, back into his armchair. Why did she have to be so much wiser than he was? She probably wasn't saying anything new or profound, but it was something he should have worked out for himself.

Suddenly, he valued her very highly. She was forty-four years old, still bearing strong traces of the prettiness which had attracted him in youth. Her hair was a little frizzier now, and a different colour, but the blue eyes, high cheekbones, wide mouth, were all as they had been when she was nineteen. Her bearing was much more confident and her social graces surpassed his own by many degrees. She was the same person – yet different, and the difference was all addition – positive improvements. The mature woman of forty-four was streets ahead of the girl of nineteen. In losing her, he had lost much more than he had ever gained when he first found her. Using a crude metaphor, which did not take into account her fine mind and spirit, the painting which had attracted him with its colours and form when it was freshly done had become a masterpiece without him realising it. And he had thrown it all away.

"*Come and grow old with me. The best is yet to be.*"

"Pardon?" She looked up, in surprise.

"Nothing. Just a couple of lines from Byron. We'll always be friends, won't we, Maddie? I need you as a friend at the very least."

"I don't see why not. So long as we don't make too many demands upon one another. You can't stay here for ever, you know."

"Oh, I know that. And I don't want you to sell the house either."

"You know I'll pay you half."

"I know. I'm not worried. I have plenty of money saved, you know that. We're both fairly comfortable, financially."

The log in the fire sloughed its bark, slowly, as he wondered what on earth he was going to do with himself.

"And you got it wrong," murmured Maddie. "It's '*Grow old along with me.*' And that isn't an invitation – I just think Browning deserved to be quoted correctly."

Precision. He had never been able to match her – or anyone for that matter – in preciseness. It was something he could quite well do without. Browning, Byron? Yes, it did matter, he supposed, if it was important to you. He had been trying to use it, though, for a purpose, rather than hold it up for inspection. Not, 'Look at this beautiful book, with its ornate cover etched in gold-leaf centripetals and fashioned from the finest cow hide' but 'Look at this philosophy it expounds –

117

we could live our lives according to these ideas, and perhaps be happy . . .'

A month later, after he had been on a walking trip through the Yorkshire Dales, climbing along the ridges of Swale and down into the valley of Wensley, he received a frantic phone call from Sarah.

"He's in trouble. I know he is. I haven't had a letter in *weeks*." She was talking about Alan and her distress seemed genuine. "You know what it's like over there? There's a war going on."

"It's hardly a *war*, Sarah."

"People are being killed."

He stared at the back of Maddie's head through the kitchen hatchway. She was making supper for herself and a man friend and he had to be out of the house by eight o'clock.

"Tell you what. I'll meet you in the Princess Louise, in Holborn. What's the time now?"

"Seven-fifteen."

"I'll be there by eight. Can you make it? It's difficult to talk on the phone."

She agreed.

She was sitting in a corner booth when he arrived, anxiously glancing at her watch. He gave her a wave and ordered himself a drink from the barmaid. Sarah already had one.

Sitting down beside her, he felt her draw away from him and the action annoyed him. He took the seat opposite.

"You sure you wouldn't like to meet in separate pubs?" he said.

"I'm sorry. I can't help it. It's not a conscious action – it's involuntary."

"Somehow that makes it worse. However, what's the problem?"

Her face twisted into a mask of the tragedy queen.

"It's Alan. I haven't had a letter in weeks now, and the last one from him was very strange. Here." She took out an envelope and extracted some pages, pushing them across the table towards him.

He nodded and began reading.

118

He winced at the opening endearment, then quickly scanned the irrelevant passages until he came to the part which he
realised was causing her concern.

". . . I must make the desert buckle to my will. It doesn't
like me. At first I felt it was just rejecting me and I reacted by
treating it with scorn. But now I think it's seriously trying to
kill me. There have been several incidents – yes, several. I
must tell you – you must understand what's happening to
me. The night it tried to bury me. That night. BURY ME!
Then there was the sandstorm. I was lost for two days.
Corporal Sabalala – he's the one, the sheik's son who turned
out to be an undercover agent for the British. Fijian, not
Arab. I was on my last legs when he found me. He said I'd
wandered so close to a well, how could I have missed seeing
it? The sun of course. It blinded me. I *know*. It's in collusion
with the damned desert. Both of them against me. But I'll
win.

"The desert sees me as an enemy. It's infinite – no, eternal
– this spread of sand and rock. It can swallow a man as easily
and thoughtlessly as a – watch a frog swallow an insect. Like
that. It has unfair advantages.

"I'm not mad. I know what I'm saying. Think about
stubbing your toe on a chair. Sometimes it seeems as if the
chair does it deliberately, doesn't it? I want you to promise
me something. If I die out here, get me home. I don't want to
be buried in the heart of something that hates me. Sabalala
wants nothing to do with it. He calls me a fool.

"The fighting here is fierce but sporadic. I don't mind that
so much. I'd rather be shot than buried alive, though I must
admit, I rarely put my weapon down for fear of being caught
unawares. The Bedu call me *Abu-al-Bundug* – the father of the
rifle – because I carry it always, cradled in my arms like a
baby. I think it's meant to be a compliment, but one can
never be sure that such titles are free of irony. They're an
enigmatic people.

"Corporal Sabalala is a fascinating man. I really believed he
was an Arab. But then his disguise is perfect. He speaks
fluent Arabic of course, and he doesn't have to fool the
Royalists with his disguise – they know who he is – but there
are many neutral tribes here, who take no side with Royalist

119

or Republican. They're a xenophobic people ('I am against my cousin, but my cousin and I are against the stranger') and one has to blend with a local group in order to stay alive.

"I've acquired a very Arabic-looking exterior, with a dark skin and an aspect that even Sabalala says passes as authentic at a distance. Of course, I have to keep my head covered. Not many Arabs have fair hair. I can't compete with Sabalala though. He's in a different class altogether. There are several Fijians in the British undercover service. They call their operations 'Keeni-Meeni jobs' – it's a Swahili word apparently, which describes the unseen, sinuous movement of a snake in long grass. Quite a romantic life in a way, if the desert's not against you.

"The other day – when? – anyway, we were going through an *aqabat*, a mountain pass. Then that sun. That's the way it happened. Like this – the sun was low on the horizon, behind the mountains, and captured my attention by shining on a *hisn*, built high up on a place called *Jabal Ashqab*. It was the sun – the sun was inside the fort and filled its interior with brilliant light. A trick of course – I *know*. Glassless windows and gunslits bright and holy-looking – vertical slabs of gold, you see? It made me catch my breath and I wasn't ready. Then Sabalala pushed me from my saddle – sent me sprawling in the dust. A rock struck my camel, where I'd been sitting – broke the poor creature's back. Actually, I never liked that camel. Well, it didn't like me and you can't – do you see what I mean? The point is, we couldn't see where the rock had fallen from. High up on the *hayt* was a piece like a broken tooth. The desert again.

"Tomorrow we go to see Sherif Hussein, ruler of Beihan, on the Yemeni border. He provides safe houses for guerrilla operations. We all need a rest badly. I shall give this letter to one of Sabalala's contacts there, to post to you from Aden.

"I've decided not to send any more reports back to the newspaper I work for – they won't print my stories about the desert. I feel it would be better to publish them after it's all over, in book form. I don't need the money and it's becoming increasingly difficult to write good copy in this desolate mountainous area, where I can't let my attention wander for a moment without finding a camel spider or

120

snake crawling over my foot. Or some enemy Arab firing from a *sangar* at our dromedaries. (My camel – my poor beast – I never did get on with it. It was so strong-willed and had a bad temper. I still have a scar from a bite mark on my shoulder. The other day it actually urinated over my legs as I was tethering it. Still it's gone to some camel heaven now. I did not *enjoy* shooting it.)

"I'll close now. The evening star . . ."

Jim stopped reading at this point, feeling the hairs on the back of his neck prickle. He reached for the envelope to replace the pages, and as he opened it some grains of sand fell out, on to the table. Sarah leaned over and blew them away, abstractly.

The pub was beginning to fill with people from the cinemas and theatres now, and there was a great deal of background noise – clinking glasses and chatter – and Jim wanted to be out of it.

Sarah said, "You notice how the syntax and grammar break down when he comes to talk about the desert?"

"I'm not an analyst, Sarah."

"I know, but you can see that there's something very wrong. He becomes – I don't know – over-emotional. Most of the other stuff seems quite normal."

"Well, what do you want me to do about it?"

Jim was concerned, too, about Alan's preoccupation with death, but he was also worried about the fact that his friend was becoming involved in the fighting. He wasn't out there to fight, for Christ's sakes, he was there to write for his newspaper. Now he had abandoned that.

Sarah looked a little crestfallen and he suddenly felt quite sorry for her. She had obviously built her hopes for the future around this man she had never met – or had she? Was this just another of her devious tricks to get herself out to the Yemen? He wished he could see into her mind – illuminate the truth. She seemed so sincere, but then there was the history of her scheming to take into account. God, he was so confused.

"Is he crazy?" she asked.

"How do I know? He sounds unbalanced but maybe it's the environment? Take him away from that and he might be

121

okay. It can't be easy, adjusting to that kind of life. I don't think for one moment that he's right, but it may seem that way to him. His personality doesn't fit the circumstances. It sounds to me as if he's merely accident prone in that kind of situation."

Sarah's mouth set in a hard, firm line.

"Why didn't you go with him, when he asked you to? You could have looked after him. You speak Arabic. You glory in the outdoor life. You're much more suited to that kind of thing than he is."

Jim's anger came through. "Dammit, woman, I don't know what your game is, but these are our lives you're playing with."

She returned fire with fire.

"You're the strong one. You could have made him listen. You could have stopped him from going."

He was exasperated. How could he argue against such convoluted logic? There was no sense in her words. One thing was true – he *had* prepared himself for Arabia. Perhaps not consciously, but she was right about the fact that he was much more suited to that kind of adventuring than Alan. Alan was a scholar, not an adventurer. A man *could* be both. That much had been proved, but the man has to be exceptional, gifted, and neither he nor Alan could lay claim to such wide-ranging talents. *Together*, they made that man.

Arabia had been an obsession with him, ever since the accident, but it was an ill-defined obsession with an ill-clarified purpose. The desert had been calling him, through his dreams, but he was never sure whether that came from within him – spurred by the guilt he felt – or whether there was a deeper, darker force at work. It was so difficult to tell, since he could not go back to the moment of truth and identify the direction from which it had come. The event had marked the time, but not the source or the direction. He could not tell whether it was a call from an external point, or an internal spur. Whether he was being driven or dragged.

Alan had had this solved for him by Sarah. It was not in Alan's make-up to respond to an emotional call. It had to have logical shape and form. His practical mind would not allow his actions to be dictated to by some mystical motivation. Alan was governed, *had* been governed, by his intellect, not his emotions, and though the essential ore of life in both men had been smelted by traumatic experience, a sensation, Alan needed a reason he could recognise to turn the mystical nature of the *primum mobile* into something solid.

Destiny had caught up with Jim at last.

"I'll find him," he said to Sarah. "I'll find him and bring him home, though whether you'll want him once I get him here – well, I'll be very interested to see. It would answer a few questions for me."

"You don't believe I want him, do you?"

"Frankly, no. Maybe you think you do at this moment – I don't know, I've lost all my faith in assurances – maybe you're being manipulated by something outside your control?"

"Anyway, I'm grateful, Jim."

He placed his hand on hers without thinking, but there was no instinctive withdrawal this time. For a moment he felt tender towards her, then the feeling disappeared and was replaced by indifference. He supposed, when he met Alan again, he should punch him on the nose for stealing his lover, but even the thought was fatuous. There was something far more significant at work than a man stealing his best friend's girl. The events all seemed part of some elaborate plan, conceived by the lords of darkness, whoever they were.

When he got back to the house, Maddie was alone and he told her. At one point there was a little triumphant smile on her face which irritated him intensely.

"What's that for? That silly grin?"

"I've just been thinking about your analysis of Alan – you said he needed a good reason for going."

"Yes."

"Well, you've got one too now, haven't you?"

He was stunned and uncomfortable.

"I think I might have gone there one day – just to see it."

"Would you? You'll never know now. Oh, Jimmy. I'm not making fun of you – in fact I'm very concerned about you. You *are* a romantic, and no one could say otherwise – it

123

doesn't mean that you don't need a substantial reason for going. You will take care, won't you?"

"How come," he said, "you always make me feel about ten years old?"

"You're lucky. I wish someone would do that for me. I feel about a hundred."

A week later he took a flight to Aden. He was met at the airport by an army major.

"Sorry, old chap," said the bronzed serviceman, "we're not allowing civilians into the country now. They should have told you before you left. Politics are getting too dicey."

"They did tell me. How did you know I was coming?"

"I didn't. Immigration rang me when they got the passenger list through. I'm afraid I'll have to take your passport away from you until you catch the flight back tomorrow morning."

Three men in tropical suits, almost identical, passed by the immigration desk.

"What about them?"

"They're all here on official business. Yours was the only name on the list that we hadn't passed, apart from the locals, who are free to come and go as they choose. Do you mind telling me why you're here? What are you, freelance or something?"

"Freelance what?"

"Reporter – or something like that? Or what? Amnesty International's already paid us a visit you know, and we don't recognise any fringe groups."

So that was it. They thought he was here to spy on them for some organisation or other. Since he had not got a good reason for being in Aden, there was not a great deal to be gained by arguing. He could see a number of military guards posted about the airport, weapons cradled in toasted arms. The British troops were on *active service* now. The first time that had happened since the war.

"Why so sensitive?" he asked. "What have you got to hide?"

"Look. Let's not have any trouble. I've told you what the situation is and I'm afraid I'm just carrying out orders. If you've got an uncle in high places that you're going to flick out like a trump card, forget it. You'll have to take that up with the people in Britain." He was clearly nervous and trying to fill any holes that might appear. Jim was obviously a mystery and the military do not like mysteries.

"What if I don't want to go?"

"No choice. I've told you . . ."

"I know. You've got your orders. Well, relax, major. I'm only here to see my sister. She works at the hospital – a nurse."

"What's her name?"

"I don't want to get her into trouble. I'll catch the flight out tomorrow, as you suggested. Sorry to put you to so much trouble yourself. I hadn't realised what the situation was here – that it was quite so bad."

The major relaxed, visibly.

"I've found you a room in the officers' quarters at Khormaksar. The Red Sea Hotel's been attacked twice this week. Place is becoming a bloodbath." He picked up Jim's case. "What did you say you did?"

Jim smiled. "I didn't – but I'm a banker. I work for the Saudi Bank in London. Your intelligence service isn't very hot is it?"

The major stiffened. "Actually it's quite good, but you didn't give us a lot of time. This way."

Outside the air-conditioned building the heat swamped Jim immediately. He was tired after the flight and wanted time to think. The major carried Jim's suitcase to a waiting landrover. Jim kept hold of his briefcase. It was full of Maria Theresa dollars – silver coins that the Arabs called *riyals* and currency even in the desert.

There was a hot breeze blowing and the landrover's wheels threw up dust where it had blown into small drifts on the tarmac. Jim was struck by how brown and dry everything looked after the greenness of the English countryside. There was the occasional palm, but very little else. White kerbstones, a testament to the military mind, wherever it takes itself in the world, dazzled beneath the sun's glare. Who would think of painting kerbstones in the heat, blood and dust of a fading colony? Tradition! Discipline! Keywords of

the Empire maintenance crew. An Arab boy in a *futa* was sweeping the gutter with a handleless witch's broom. Appearances!

The officers' mess was fronted by an area of coarse grass, watered by a sprinkler. A pomegranate with blooms like wounds grew in the centre of this lawn. Exactly in the centre. On either side of the side steps that led up to the reception hall were potted plants taller than a man.

"I'll leave you here," said the major, putting Jim's case down in the hall. There was a strong smell of cedar about the place and Jim noticed that much of the wood had been heavily oiled. A ceiling fan squeaked out a regular message above their heads. "The corporal will look after you." There was a man standing close by, wearing stiff khaki. He looked as though he bathed in starch.

"Thanks very much, Major . . .?"

"Trevellian. Charles Trevellian. I'll probably see you later, at supper. Sorry about all this."

"Can't be helped – but I don't want my sister persecuted because of a whim on my part."

"Good God, no. Won't go any further, I assure you. Well, until later then."

The major strode off, through the twin sets of doors.

"No air conditioning, corporal?" said Jim, as he was shown to his room by his guard.

"Not here, sir. This is the old mess. The new one's got air conditioning."

"How long's that been built?"

"A few years, sir, but we had to open this one up again when accommodation got scarce. When they started posting people in for the withdrawal."

"I see."

When darkness fell, Jim slipped out of the back window and made his way down to Khormaksar beach. He had studied the maps he had brought with him and knew the location of the harbour. He followed the shoreline, passing through several sentries, his European features passport enough, to the waterfront at Steamer Point. Several dhows were anchored there and he approached three before finding one willing to take a passenger up through the gulf and into the Red Sea. *Riyals* changed hands and Jim returned to his room, intending to ship out with the tide at two o'clock in the morning.

He packed his essential goods, including a revolver and the remainder of the *riyals*, into a rucksack, hiding it in his locker.

At nine o'clock, Trevellian came to his room.

"I've checked with the hospital staff. There's no nurse with the same name . . ."

"Married," said Jim, quickly. "She married some man named Baker. Did you ask for Nurse Baker? You promised me you wouldn't, you know."

A loud but distant 'whumpff' made the windows rattle. Trevellian dropped a half-smoked cigarette on the tiled floor and crushed it with his foot.

"There's an ashtray here," said Jim.

Trevellian ignored the remark and stared out of the window at a flare of light, presumably the result of the explosion. Somewhere in the room a mosquito whined.

"You'd better be right about this. I don't want to have to put a guard on you. I was serious this afternoon."

"I thought you'd already taken care of that."

Trevellian moved across the room and opened a drawer to the chest which stood by the locker. There were socks and underwear inside, deposited by Jim earlier. He closed it carefully.

"By the way, you haven't signed the visitors' book," said Trevellian. "Perhaps you'd care to do that and I'll meet you in the bar for a drink afterwards?"

"Right. Where's the book?"

"It's on a table in the main entrance hall. I'll show you."

Trevellian led the way and pointed out the book as he passed through, going into an open doorway which led off the hall. Jim opened the leatherbound volume and picked up the pen which lay beside it. He signed his name in the column headed 'Guests'. Out of idle curiosity he flicked through the pages, looking for Alan's name. It was not there, but as he searched he noticed another name he knew.

'Major J. L. Ashcrofte.'

127

He closed the book thoughtfully.

Trevellian was sitting at the bar. A Somali hovered amongst the bottles, obviously waiting for his order.

"Could I have a cold beer, please? Any kind will do."

"One beer, Chico."

"Yes, sir." The beer was produced. *Crossed Keys*. Jim had never heard of it.

The Somali remained in front of the two men, his shiny black hands resting on the bar.

Trevellian said, "*Imshi*, Chico. We want to talk."

"Yes, sir." The Somali looked disappointed. Perhaps he normally joined in any conversation at the bar? He moved down to the other end of the room, his white jacket crackling, looking peeved.

"I sometimes give him a drink," explained Trevellian. "He's a Moslem but he likes the occasional beer. I didn't see you at supper tonight."

"I wasn't hungry."

"Fair enough." The major lit another cigarette and ran a hand through his blond hair. "You people are a bit of a pain, you know. Not you especially, but it's my job to meet any civilians and some of them won't take no for an answer. We had a freelance photographer arrive last week – had to carry him kicking and screaming to the Happy Bird – the aircraft. He couldn't have been more than eighteen."

"Really?" Jim was going through his mind for a subtle way of broaching the Ashcrofte subject, but in the end decided to come right out with it.

"I noticed a name in the visitors' book – a Major Ashcrofte. Do you know him?"

"John Ashcrofte? Of course. He's gone to Bahrain now. Used to do a bit of work up country, in the Radfan, until that business with his wife . . ." He stopped, suddenly. "Where do you know John from?"

"I don't. Never met him. I met his wife once. She helped negotiate a loan through my bank – for a theatre agency. Quite an attractive woman."

"Sarah Ashcrofte," Trevellian said, reflectively. "Yes. Was quite a looker."

"You knew her too?"

"Of course – that was in the days when the families were still here. Before they sent them home. Everybody knows everybody on a post like this. Incestuous kind of place."

"Was that the trouble you mentioned?"

"What?"

"Well, the fact that she was attractive. I just thought – with her husband away, up country, while the cat's . . ."

Trevellian went bright scarlet.

"Good Lord, no. Nothing like that." He paused and stared hard at the fan above the bar, grinding away slowly. "Least, there was nothing so far as I recall. Some of the wives, perhaps, but not Sarah Ashcrofte. No, hers is a strange story. She wandered out one day, north, into the desert. Had some idea about looking for her husband, one imagines. No one really knows. We found her two days later, or was it three? Anyway, she was suffering from heatstroke. Never the same after that. Affected her mind." He stubbed out his cigarette. "Strange business."

"How did she survive out there?"

"Some half-witted goatherd who didn't know what to do with her kept her alive."

"He didn't . . . touch her?"

Trevellian nearly choked on his beer.

"Why do you keep saying things like that? He was only a boy of twelve. And anyway, she was in a high fever."

"I – she said that she met someone out there."

"Oh, *that*. All in here, old son," he tapped his head. "The boy said he'd been with her the whole time and no one had been near her. I don't doubt she dreamt of being carried away on the back of some sheik's white charger – don't all women have such fancies? Always was a bit of a romantic, so I understand from her husband. Used to go wandering off into the Malayan jungle too. Eccentric little lady."

"What was she doing? When she was found?"

"Nothing. Just walking. She was dehydrated and we only just pulled her through." He looked up. "Was she all right, when you last saw her?"

"So far as I could tell. Yes, she looked fine. It was only a brief meeting, you understand."

"Yes, of course." He seemed to brighten. "Just shows you

129

what this place can do to you. You'll be well out of it. Wish I could jump on the Happy Bird and zoom off back to Blighty. Got to wrap things up here first though."

Jim said, "What about showing me a bit of night life?"

"Night life? Here? There's a fictitious brothel called 'Jasmine's' which some inventive soul dreamed up, many moons ago, either to satisfy an erotic fantasy or as some kind of joke – a rather perverse joke, since we've lost two young airmen who stupidly braved the backstreets in search of this El Dorado of sex. Both shot through the head. That's the closest you'll get to any night life, I promise you."

"Surely there's somewhere better than this? What about the Beach Club? Are you supposed to be on duty tonight? Perhaps I'm talking out of turn."

"No. No I'm free." He looked at his watch. "Why not? I can keep an eye on you just as easily at the Beach Club, can't I?"

Jim smiled. "What a dirty trick. Come on then. What are we waiting for?" He went to his locker and took out his rucksack.

"What's that for?" asked Trevellian.

"Some presents for my sister. I thought perhaps we might call in at the hospital, on the way back here."

"Good idea. I'd like to meet this sister of yours. What's her name?"

"Sally. Sally Baker. But she doesn't like zobits." Jim cruelly used the slang term that rankers use for officers in the air force.

Trevellian went a bit starchy.

"I didn't mean that."

He led the way out to the driveway. A driver saluted them both as they climbed into a landrover.

"We can have supper at the Beach Club if we hurry," said Trevellian. "The stuff at the mess is pretty awful. I'm not surprised you gave it a miss." He glanced sideways at Jim.

"Hadn't even thought about food," said Jim. "Still, sounds like a good idea."

"And if your sister isn't on duty, we can soon get someone to get her out of bed."

"Quite," said Jim.

They drove along the coast road, passing military vehicles every now and then, around the craggy wall of Crater, hiding its terrible secrets within its volcanic interior. Jim thought of one of Alan's earlier letters, when he was still receiving them instead of Sarah. ". . . who would have thought of such a crazy idea? A town inside a prehistoric cone of igneous rock? – the white, cubed houses like sugar lumps at the bottom of a dark, clay bowl . . ." In another letter, "It is the burnt eye of Polyphemus – if one imagines the earth as a Cyclopean giant – useless, except to mankind, who will exhaust the usefulness of even useless things, in order to protect their interest. It is a natural but almost impregnable fortification." Jim liked the first simile better than the second, for its simplicity and lack of academic pompousness. The car passed along Murder Mile and towards the Beach Club, just before Conquest Bay.

As Jim had suspected, there were no closing hours at the Beach Club, and after a lot of introductions to an all-male group, the serious drinking started. At about half past one Jim made the excuse to go to the toilet and left Trevellian in the middle of an anecdote which was raising hilarious laughter amongst his colleagues.

Jim went past the toilets and out of the back of the club. A guard was strolling the perimeter of the barbed-wire fence and Jim quickly picked up a crate of empty Coke bottles and carried it around to the main entrance, depositing it by the side of the building. He then entered the main doors, retrieved his rucksack from the hook in the hall, where he had left it earlier on, and went straight outside again. Hitching his pack on his back, Jim strolled casually towards the beach entrance, guarded by another soldier.

"Nice night," he said to the sentry, pretending to observe the stars.

"Yes, sir." A pause as he passed. "You're not thinking of walking, are you, sir?"

He laughed. "Good Lord, no. Just going to look at the sea. Major Trevellian will be following in a moment – tell him where I am, will you?"

"Certainly, sir. Down by the waves."

"Right."

He walked as slowly as his agitated nerves would allow him to, towards the water, then along the shoreline. The further away he got, the faster he walked, until he was running, full pelt, adjacent to the gentle ripples that lapped at the sands. Some time later he lay flat between two rocks as a vehicle whined along the road, twenty-five yards away.

Jim reached the dhows just before two o'clock. On finding his craft, he boarded it, made his presence known to the Somali captain, and asked the man to ship out as soon as he was able. Then he went below decks, into a hold full of rotting potatoes. He waited.

A few minutes later he heard the flapping of the lateen sail, felt a lurch, and the boat was under way. After about ten minutes he went up on to the leeward-sloping deck and gripped the worn, wooden rail. Lights were slipping away behind them.

There was a fresh, briny smell to the air which was invigorating and Jim gave a little whoop of triumph. Trevellian was probably running around like a mad-arse, cursing soldiers right, left and centre. The hiss of the waves against the bow gave the impression of great speed, but Jim realised they could be caught easily by a launch, if anyone suspected where he was. He wanted to be round the *ra's* as quickly as possible.

The Somali was at the wheel, and the seamen, some Arab, some African, were still busy at the rigging: black, shiny-skinned shapes that worked with efficiency at tasks they knew well. He felt in competent hands. They had been sailing dhows like this for thousands of years, using inherent, inherited skills longer than a lifetime takes to learn.

He reflected on the information he had gained from Trevellian. It had merely served to deepen the mystery of his former lover. Something had happened to her in the desert and he was quite sure now that whatever it was it would remain a secret for all time.

If it was revenge the desert wanted, then it had waited a long time. But what was a *long time*, to an entity that was ageless, timeless? The years between the accident and that moment were just a fleeting second in the life of a desert. It was a chilling thought.

132

Spray hit his face, cool, salty. It took his mind away from the possible menace he was to face at a later time. He felt like a boy scout again. He licked the salt from his lips as the master signalled that they were going to jibe, steadying himself for the change of tack, watching the huge sail melt into shivering folds – then crack out into a full sheet again. The dark sea stretched out before them and on the starboard side the darker land hid low banks of stars. Not far away was the coast of Africa. The archaic craft ploughed forward, big-bellied but graceful, treading the ancient road of slave traders, ivory ships and vessels carrying magic in the shape of rhinoceros' horns. All being well he expected the voyage to take about three days. They were to follow the Arabian coastline, up towards Mecca, though they would find a landfall long before the holy city was due on their starboard bow.

He stayed on deck to watch the dawn rise up over the coastland hills. Never before had he witnessed such a beautiful sight. Not beautiful for its hues, but for its primal harshness, though the red ochre rock did indeed colour the world a hellish, firebrick hue. Prehistory passed to starboard – still and innocent of life – neither welcoming nor hostile. Its shadows a million years old – more – crept slowly down to the shore like dark, nebulous beasts, to drink of the sea. Jim felt a sense of isolation, a contentment only to be found in solitude. He was glad no one was with him to share the sight. His feelings of integration with time and place would some-how have been diminished with company. It was as if he himself stretched back, like those hills, to a time before men walked the earth. A time before the hands of science had begun to shape the environment with their ruthless and wanton efficiency into a machine that would carry them into oblivion.

The only incident which marred the voyage was a fight between two sailors, during which one rammed a raw potato down the other's throat. As the man writhed, blue-faced on the deck, Jim attempted a tracheotomy and the crew almost mutinied. They thought he was trying to cut the man's throat. It was one of those times when communication is of paramount importance, and it disintegrates because of panic.

Luckily the knife, which did not pierce the windpipe correctly, touched a nerve which caused the sailor to disgorge the blockage involuntarily. When the master had time to explain to his crew exactly what Jim had been attempting, they crowded round him, slapping his shoulders in appreciation. Perversely, it was the sailor's attacker who praised him the most and the man became a positive nuisance in his efforts to please Jim for the rest of the journey. It was only later that Jim realised the men had been lovers.

JIM

Single-masted dhows such as the one Jim was on had been sailing the Arabian seas for centuries, virtually unchanged in appearance. Some actually were over a hundred years old. It was not difficult to put aside the world of the 1960s when one was on the deck of an ancient vessel, following an ancient sea road. Far to the north was Mecca, the holy city, lying in a barren hollow in the hills. Within that city was the Ka'aba, a square temple said to have been built by Adam, but later supposed to have been reconstructed by Abraham and Ishmael, putting in one of its corners the Black Stone given them by the Archangel Gabriel. Nearby, was the well of Zamzam, from which Hagar drew water to save her son Ishmael's life after Abraham had cast them both out to die in the wilderness. As a European Jim felt, rightly or wrongly, that these Old Testament connections with the land that had occupied his thoughts for so long provided him with a sense of familiarity and belonging. They were the stories of his Sunday school years, ingrained in his spirit.

The dhow hove in to the port of Mocha at night and, now dressed in traditional Arab clothes, he slipped ashore under cover of darkness. Although his skin was still white, he managed to cover most of his body with the loose-fitting garments.

He wandered the streets of the town for a while, soaking up the atmosphere, but careful to keep to the shadows. The town itself was a maze of narrow, winding streets of sand-coloured houses, some with heavy black doors covered with floral designs and sentences from the Koran.

Finally he grew thirsty and, covering his face, he stopped a coffee seller and bought a cup. The old man peered at him on hearing the request, but though Jim's accent was faulty, there were many visitors to Mocha from Africa and India, and it only aroused mild curiosity.

That night he went to the edge of the town and fell asleep

135

on a rubbish tip. During the early hours he awoke to hear a commotion amongst the pi-dogs that frequented such places and saw a fully-grown leopard nosing around amongst the garbage. He took out his pistol very carefully from his pack and waited, with his heart beating a little more rapidly than normal. He had forgotten that leopards were native to the Yemen. There were many smells on the tip, to cover that of a man's odour, and the leopard passed quite close by, seemingly without noticing him. Finally, it left, loping out into the fields beyond the town.

The climate of the Yemen is by no means as severe as either Aden or the Hadhramaut, having mild summers and cool winters. He was thus able to become acclimatised gradually. He decided to walk between Mocha and Taiz, the first inland city, for this purpose. The distance was over a hundred kilometres, but he had plenty of time before meeting Alan. While he was here, he was determined to exploit his experience to the full. Despite what he had told Sarah, it was not Alan's crazy letter that had brought him to Arabia, but a sense of having to bow to the inevitable. He had had to master his fear and leave. Now that he was here, that fear had abated somewhat, but he would be foolish to let it dissipate completely. He would need it to keep his wits sharp. Alan did seem to be in a certain amount of trouble, but nothing could be done quickly and it would not help his friend any if he too were to become a problem. Alan already had people to watch over him, though he knew that his boyhood friend was strong-willed when it came to going his own way. Now that he was here, it seemed strange to him that he had avoided the place for so long. It felt like coming home.

The business of the exchange of love letters between Sarah and Alan puzzled him. What made them do that? He could only think that on Sarah's part, she had despaired at Jim's refusal to bring her here and hoped that Alan might send for her. If she really believed that, she did not know Alan. It was Jim, his partner in guilt, that he needed with him, not some outsider. He suspected that Alan had fostered the relationship between himself and Sarah in order to prove his superiority over Jim. There had always been a certain amount of rivalry between them and Alan was a power-seeker. He liked to be

136

in control. In taking Sarah away from Jim he would add, in his own eyes if no one else's, to his image and prestige. It was an old story. Steal your best friend's girl and you settled all accounts. Why did people have to be so insecure?

The uncomfortable thought for Jim was that there was a third entity involved, which almost seemed to be working hand in hand with Sarah. The entity that was responsible for Alan's state of mind: the desert. Its influence was far-reaching. Alan was here because of its machinations. Sarah had clearly been bewitched by its atmosphere – and she had been the one responsible for removing any obstacles, real or imagined, in Jim's way. Jim felt he should laugh these ideas away, however, because there was one point where the whole thing broke down. What possible reason could the desert have for wanting to bring them here? Even supposing he *was* prepared to accept the American Indian idea that places have spirits. It was one thing to talk about the numen of *place* in the kitchen of a terraced house in the middle of London, but quite another to accept that it is manipulating your life. On the one hand he knew he was a human being with free will, but on the other, the left hand, there seemed to be forces at work against which his so-called free will was powerless.

The end result was, he *was* here.

He could say it was choice and by his own volition, but the fact was, he *had* come.

Just supposing, he thought, the desert has brought us both here for a purpose, whatever it might be? It would surely begin by punishing them for robbing them of its hero. Even given that it had brought them here for the ultimate revenge – to kill them – there would surely be some sort of punishment? He laughed to himself. The idea *was* ludicrous.

Or at least, it was until he remembered that Alan had already undergone a form of punishment.

The plains beyond Mocha, through which the road to Taiz ran, were not the desert proper, but the mind only encompasses as far as the eye can see. From where Jim stood, sandy gravel wastes reached out to a sharp horizon. There was nothing spectacular to interrupt the view – no weird rock formations or smooth dunes – but Jim still felt a sense of beauty about its starkness. He could fill that space with whatever he wished. Xanadu might rise from the dust, shimmering in the heat waves.

On the road itself, the scorpions and lizards basked, ignoring the tread of their enemy in their blissful state of heat. Eddies of dust whirled along the highway as if they too required a smooth passage across the plains. A faultless blue sky, as fragile as thin china, formed a perfect dome around him.

Jim rejected any offers of lifts from travellers with a wave of his hand and a gruff '*La*'. He did not wish to expose himself to questions at this early stage. Gradually, his skin was darkening and he felt it fortunate that, unlike Alan, he had brown eyes and dark hair. There were sandy-haired, blue-eyed Arabs, but so few as to be quite unusual. Jim did not want to arouse the slightest suspicion. He wore the green headband of the *Hadji*, the Moslem pilgrim who had made the journey to Mecca, in the hope that those who saw him would believe he was on the return journey from the holy land and wished to walk. He slept by the roadside and ate what fare he could find to supplement his provisions.

At the village of Mafraq the foothills began, which led to the climb to Taiz. He was managing twenty kilometres a day and gaining in confidence all the time. He saw many armed men, some of them Egyptian soldiers, and became very wary. The small groups of soldiers looked pathetic. They were boys, far from home, taken from their work as shop assistants or university students, and cast into a foreign land. They looked lost and dejected, and not a little silly in their ill-fitting uniforms. To Jim, all military forces, with their strutting and posturing, were ridiculous. It was only the number and strength of large armies that saved them from being entirely idiotic.

The hills produced the splendour he had been anticipating and their lack of uniformity was pleasant. At certain times he was alone in the world and the burnt sienna, landscape, especially at sunrise and sunset, transported him back to its birth. It was raw and uncompromising in its silent, ragged aspect. This was the land of Saba, or Sheba, where savage

138

beauty had been dissolved in molten violence and had solidified to rock. Sarah had been right. The marshlands were infants compared with this place, where history had hardened to gneiss and hidden itself in the shadows of red valleys, inseparable from natural stone. Often he came across a *sangar*, which appeared to have been formed by nature, rather than man, like an old scab on the body of the rock. These, and the larger fortifications, had grown back into the stone out of which they were built, their fierce beauty pockmarked by violence and stained with blood.

But the most imposing aspect was the sense of timelessness, which swept down from the hills and flowed through the valleys ready to engulf and obliterate any foreigner who might threaten its ancient lore. They became one – the cirrate rocks, the spurting stone, the grooved valleys and slabbed overhangs, the forts licked by tongue-like walls, the goat tracks scarring the hills – they became one with the neatly fitting cinnabar sunsets. Then the long, cool nights before the ejaculation of the new dawns.

He entered Taiz at night and found his way to the *suk*. There among the lighted stalls he began to enquire about the purchase of a rifle, goatskin waterbags and a dromedary. Unfortunately, he immediately aroused suspicion. The city dwellers were not quite so used to foreigners with strange accents as those at the port. He was arrested before he had time to complete his business.

They took him to a fortified house and locked him in a small room for a very long time. He did not know how long, because they took his new watch and the room had no windows. The single dim bulb was permanently lit. A bucket served for a toilet. There was no furniture and he had to lie on the stone floor to find any rest. Food, of a kind, was thrust into his hands along with a jug of water, at irregular intervals. Eventually, a smoothly shaven Indian in a dark suit entered the room.

"Good morning, sir. I am a lawyer and I have come to be of help to you."

Jim rose from his squatting position in the corner of the room, with a feeling of relief. His bones ached from sleeping on the cold stone, his circulation was poor and his head felt muzzy and thick. The air in the room was stale and his ears were ringing constantly for some reason. He was having trouble with his bowels which had left his anus sore and painful.

He took the lawyer's hand and shook it.

"Thank God for that," he said, running his fingers through his matted beard. His time in the cell, however long it had been, had taught him the real meaning of despair. Never in his life before had he experienced that terrible paradoxical state of boredom and depression mixed with quiet terror. At first he had wept, prayed and raved. Later, he had slipped down, into himself, to find a person he did not know. Someone without hope.

"I thought I was going to be here for ever," he added, and it was all he could do to keep the tears out of his eyes.

The lawyer busied himself with some papers, saying his name was Patel and that he would soon clear up any misunderstanding.

"That's all it is," said Jim, eagerly. "A complete misunderstanding."

"Of course," Patel smiled. "These things happen. You must not blame the authorities for being suspicious – these are dangerous times. The Yemen is going through some teething troubles. Insurrection, you know."

"I understand. Will I be allowed to leave soon?"

At that point a table and two chairs were brought in and the lawyer spread his papers across the top of the former. Then he took out a clean white sheet of paper and sat down. Jim took the other chair, shifting uncomfortably as the fiery pains from his anus invaded his pelvic region.

Patel carefully unscrewed the top of a gold-nibbed Parker fountain pen and wrote Jim's name at the head of the sheet in a neat copper-plate hand. Jim could not help noticing how clean the lawyer's skin was. His whole appearance was dapper and spruce, and he smelt faintly of coconut oil. Heavy, horn-rimmed glasses gave him a kind of froggish look.

"Now, sir, shall we begin? What are you doing in the Yemen? Please explain in your own words."

Jim scratched at his beard and some pieces of dried food fell

140

on to the table. He brushed them away, aware that he must stink. He apologised for that, before saying, "I'm here to meet a friend. He's a correspondent for a British newspaper and is reporting on the civil war."

Patel wrote carefully in his own language, just under Jim's name. Jim explained that he believed his friend was ill and he had flown out from England to try to persuade him to come home. That was all there was to it. Nothing more sinister than the call of friendship between two men. Surely Mr Patel understood such things? The lawyer nodded, writing steadily.

"My dear sir," said the lawyer, when Jim had finished. "This is a terrible thing, to be locked up in here simply because you came here to help your friend. We must do all we can to secure your release without delay. I understand you had a considerable sum of money on you when you were arrested?"

"Yes. I can pay your fees, if they're not too exorbitant."

The Indian waved a hand in front of his face.

"Please, please. My fees are the least important of matters at this time. Is there anything you require in the meantime? A bed perhaps? Some furniture?"

"If I have to stay a little longer, yes, please. And could I have some ointment – for my sores?"

Patel smiled. "Why of course. You could have requested these things earlier. These people are not monsters, you know. I'll attend to it immediately."

He called the guard, shook hands with Jim and left the cell.

Jim shouted, "Mr Patel. Your paper."

The sheet still lay on the table.

The door was locked.

Some time later they came and took away the table and chairs. The sheet of paper was ignored and it fluttered to the floor and remained there. Nothing else arrived. A hard lump formed in Jim's throat and he reached a point when he could stand it no longer and beat the door with his bucket.

No one came.

Nothing happened for a whole lifetime.

Nothing.

Jim became familiar with the bleakness within him. It was

his constant companion. Most of the time he lay curled up on his side in the corner of the room, his mind either whirling with thoughts of the outside world, or blank. Sometimes he thought he saw things in the room: shapes that caught the corner of his eye. Sometimes he dreamed he was awake and then became confused when he actually did wake up, because there was no change in his situation.

He had another visitor. An Englishman.

"A friend of mine left a piece of paper in here," said the man. He spoke with a north-country accent.

"I used it," muttered Jim, nodding towards the bucket.

"Ah." The man looked around the walls of the cell. "Aren't you marking off the days? I thought prisoners always did that. And scribbled things – graffiti."

"No," said Jim, dully.

"Better tell them what they want to know," said the stranger. "They're not the government people."

"Who are they then?"

"I don't know. I just sell them arms."

Then the man went away. Afterwards, Jim was not sure whether there had been anyone there or not.

He kept smelling things. A whiff of onions. An odour of coffee. Were they putting things just outside his door? He tried it once or twice, but it was always locked. If he lay flat on the floor, he could see a little way underneath the door, but there was no sign of any dish. Once, he thought he heard a dog bark, but since he woke a short while afterwards, it may have been a dream. Once, he jumped up and ran, straight into the wall, making his nose bleed.

When he was completely exhausted he was handed over to some new people and the torture began. Even in his distressful state, he realised what was happening to him. Prior to the successful republican revolution, the Yemen had been one of the last truly medieval societies in the civilised world. It had been ruled by a despotic leader, an absolute autocrat who still kept prisoners in dungeons, sometimes in fetters and chains, and tortured confessions out of his captives. The remains of this dark time had still not been completely swept away. The country was still in a state of civil war and the transition period had not yet passed by. Prisons were full and the

142

authorities had great difficulty in keeping complete control of punitive action. At a certain level self-styled vigilante groups were left very much to themselves and meted out, in the fervour of the changing times, their own justice. They had their own style of punishment and even their own prisons, especially in regions where officialdom was stretched and unable to maintain a strong presence.

It was into the hands of one of these groups that Jim had unfortunately fallen.

The prison consisted of a single hole in the rock face: a tunnel bored in the shape of a hook, some time during the six centuries between Christ and Mohammed. Those Moslem prisoners in the darkness of the hook's curve and terminus became perplexed regarding *gibla*, the direction of Mecca, the way to face in prayer. Stupefied by the lack of food, insufficient water and stale air heavy with the stink of human waste and gangrene, there was such a confusion amongst them when the call to prayer came; such a desperate shuffling and pushing; such a seemingly mindless urgency of movement in the confined space, that Jim believed a riot was taking place and he crouched against the rock wall with fear and hope vying for possession of his spirit. When it became obvious that a religious ceremony was taking place, he relaxed into disappointment.

New prisoners in the tunnel jail were always pushed to the rear, unless they held some political rank recognised and respected by the other inmates. Jim, on being cast within the rusty, iron-barred gate, was bundled and prodded, kicked and cursed, until he found himself in the pitch darkness of the rear of the tunnel, amongst a mass of bodies that heaved like a barrel full of frogs. Hemmed in on all sides by coughing, spitting, shapeless figures, his terror numbed him for some time. He fell asleep, and then woke in darkness to hear himself screaming. They struck him savagely, from all sides, inaccurately, about the head and shoulders, until he had ceased. He lapsed into complete silence, aware that his sanity was in danger of flying away from him like a bird vacating a cold nest.

Food consisted of bread and some unidentifiable vegetable mash, passed along from the entrance in buckets. Those at the rear had to make do with scraping the walls of the bucket with their fingernails and two mealtimes went by before Jim realised what the confusion was about. After that, he fought with the others for possession of a bucket and he found a new strength within himself. It was a dehumanising process.

Dreaming his life over, he had a strong sense of the past, but he always stopped just before he caught the plane to Aden. The rest was a painful memory, best left until he was more able to deal with it.

Alan squeezed the trigger of the Bren. Nothing happened. Dust came billowing across, engulfing him in its earth-borne clouds. Choking dust.

Sabalala pumped steadily away, into the dust-smoke with his SLR, emptying a clip of fifteen rounds.

"What's the matter?" he hissed.

"Bren's jammed," said Alan, helplessly.

The Fijian whipped off the magazine and pulled another one from his belt, clipping it in with one movement. Alan cocked the Bren and jerked the trigger. This time the LMG danced on its bipod, sending a full thirty rounds in the direction of the enemy. His hand touched the barrel as he went to change the mag again and he burned his fingers.

Sabalala gave him a nudge.

"Wait . . ."

They listened, hearing nothing, seeing nothing, in the thick rolls of dust thrown up by the Egyptian jeep.

"They've gone," said the Fijian, after a while. "I don't think they even got out – just threw a few live ones and carried on."

"There were eight of them. We must have hit someone."

"I don't think so. I couldn't see much – and you were too late."

The dust settled and they could see the dirt road below them, empty of all but tyre tracks. It wound between the rocks for a mile, then streaked out into the desert, blending with its neighbouring sands, before the perspective sharpened to a point.

"Hell, we could have . . ."

Sabalala said, "No. They had a cannon on the back. We're lucky they ran."

The Fijian suggested they wait for a while, in case of more movement on the road. A jeep often spearheaded a march.

The light was hard on Alan's eyes, burning with its brightness as well as its heat. It printed images on his brain. Images he did not know where to place. Surreal shapes and colours that *had* no place.

He looked at the Fijian. Sabalala's face was impassive. Such faces only belonged to temple idols. Sabalala was a statue. Sabalala was an ancient stone god. Alan suddenly had the comic impulse to give him mouth-to-mouth resuscitation – to breathe life into the Fijian carving. Then the thought frightened him with its homosexual implications and he flushed beneath his tan, as if others had heard his thoughts as spoken words.

"There's only two of us here," he said.

"What?" He fell under the scrutiny of the Fijian.

Now, he was embarrassed by the sound of the words. What had he said?

Sabalala picked up the discarded Bren magazine and poked around inside it with a stubby finger, moving the rounds. He swore in his own language. At least, to Alan it sounded like an obscenity.

"What's the matter?"

"The rims of the cases – no wonder it jammed. You've loaded it wrong. How many times? The rims must go to the front of the preceding round, not behind . . ."

"Did I load that one? Oh, shit, I'm sorry."

"It doesn't matter – they didn't stop. Next time the rims . . ."

"Yes, I know."

Every fourteenth day they let them out of the tunnel and sat them in circles in sunlight that robbed them of their sight. The prisoners were too blind to run, especially those from the rear of the jail. The contrast was almost a cruelty: fresh air, light, odours of the desert. These sharp, short reminders of the outside were worse than physical torture. One might see the act as a generous gesture, but to the prisoners the experience produced ambivalent feelings. Given just enough time outside to begin to appreciate what they were missing, the prisoners were thrown back into the foul darkness for another fourteen days.

These deprivations were such simple ones too: light and air. Not sex, strong drink, television, family, good food, cigars, or even freedom. Just light and air. Taken by all for granted. All but a tiny fraction of the human race.

Jim got used to the fleas, the stinking breath and faeces, the urine splashes on his clothes, mucus and vomit deposited on his feet. The world is a nice place without them, but when they are inevitable, persistent, you forget about them after a while. They are natural, and one good wash will restore the human body to its former *nice* condition. What was unnatural was the darkness which dirtied his mind. He never got used to waking up in blackness.

His second time outside brought him into contact with Hassan. Sitting down in the place to which he had been led, he observed a blurred figure before him, sheathed in a shifting frayed brilliance that defied precise contours.

"*Moya?*"

"*Aiwa.*" He nodded, holding out his hands for the cup. It was placed there and filled with water. He drank.

Suddenly, the figure was smaller than himself, down on its haunches. *A child*, he thought. He was aware that he was under scrutiny.

"You Inglish?"

"Yes."

"What you come here for?"

"To die, it seems."

There was a harsh, guttural laugh, but the sound was of youth.

"You not die yet. I am become doctor, *very* proud. My name Hassan."

Jim stared into the dark features surrounded by light.

"You're a water boy, not a doctor. How old are you?"

"I nine years. When I become man, then I become doctor. Nasser make me into doctor. First I must make money to bring to Cairo. Then I be doctor. First water boy, then doctor. Very proud."

"Well, Hassan, I can't wait that long. I think I'm going to die quite soon in there. You'll have to practise on someone else."

Gradually, as the day proceeded, the scene became more delineated and by evening Jim was able to observe the young boy in more detail. Hassan looked very much like any other street Arab. He wore a dirty vest, full of holes, and a pair of ex-army, ragged shorts, the crotch of which almost reached his knees. His thin brown face broke into a wide grin on seeing Jim's eyes on him and he immediately came and sat in front of the English prisoner.

"Ah, you see, mister! In your eyes – you see me at last."

"I see you. So, this is the great doctor, eh?"

"Very proud," said Hassan, bowing his head. Then, "You have baksheesh? For me to be a doctor?"

Jim showed him his empty pockets.

"Not here."

"Where? You tell Hassan."

"You won't be able to find it. I buried it. Buried treasure. Enough to make a hundred doctors of you."

"That much treasure?" The boy was dubious, gauging him for vestiges of the truth. He was nine years old on the outside only. On the inside, nine hundred years, especially when it came to money.

"The money is buried in the desert – near Lawdar, to the east. You know where that is?"

Jim had sent a message to Alan before he left England, to meet him at Lawdar. A merchant was holding money for him there.

"I know this place."

"Good, now all you have to do is find a way of getting me there."

The smile flashed on, like a lantern.

"Ahhh! There is no treasure. You wish to escape." He waved a bony little finger in Jim's face.

In spite of his predicament, Jim smiled back and ruffled the thick black hair of his new acquaintance.

"The sad thing is, the money's really there. At Lawdar. Not buried – you tumbled me there, you young rascal. It's in a kind of bank."

Hassan's face became serious.

"I think you play a game with me, because I am young boy – but I think bank is better than buried treasure. Bank is more real money." He looked towards the guards, who stood some distance away. "I help you escape," he whispered.

Sabalala was incensed.

"Lawdar? What the hell do you want to go there for?"

His slightly Australian accent always surprised Alan, when they hadn't been speaking for some time, and it always took him a few seconds to remember that the corporal wasn't an Arab, nor even an Englishman, but a Fijian recruited by way of the Australian army. Alan spoke no language but his own. Sabalala spoke three fluently, at least. Alan had officer status in the Radfan and operating areas, while Sabalala was a mere ranker, and a pretty lowly one at that. But there was no doubt who was boss.

"I've got to meet a friend there, at the end of the month."

Sabalala snorted, furiously. "Shit. I can't go *there*, man. I've already had orders to send you back. Your newspaper wants you back home."

"I don't work for them any more. I've resigned."

"Then you *got* to go. Unauthorised civilians aren't allowed up country. Hell, man, I've already put myself on the line, letting you fire weapons. You're supposed to be a noncombatant. I'd be up shit creek if anyone found out."

"I didn't say I wasn't grateful."

Sabalala stared at his feet.

"Well, I still can't help you. Not this time."

"That's okay. Now the desert's stopped trying to kill me and I've lost the touch of desert madness I had a while back, I'm fine. I'll make it."

"I'm sorry, you old bastard. You put me on the spot. I'd like to help . . ."

"It's okay. I said it was okay."

"Oh, fuck off then. What are you hanging around for?"

"Another bloody Fosters," said Alan, in an Australian accent.

The boy had dug a pit, covering it with cardboard, sand

148

glued to one side. The pit was deep and wide enough for a thin man to crouch inside, while the board covered the hole.

Jim had been in the jail five weeks. His strength had broken through that barrier which the stubborn, durable man keeps fortifying with hope, and he was deteriorating fast. One thing was sure, he kept telling himself, he would never go into an Arab city again.

The English spy, they had called him.

What was there to spy on? he had asked them.

That is what we want to know from you.

Then they beat him with rods to find the answer.

In the end, he was desperate to find an answer which they would accept. He would have confessed to anything, provided they accepted it and stopped beating him. *In order to escape more punishment*, he told himself between bouts of pain, *you have to find and accuse yourself of a credible, believable crime.* Many times he had screamed *Stop! stop! I want to confess*, but had been unable to go on because he did not know what to confess to. Until, in the end, probably disgusted with his lack of inventiveness and bored themselves with inflicting the blows, they fed him his lies bit by bit. It became a kind of game between them, with his captors teasingly offering a piece of information and Jim anxiously guessing the follow-up line. They would not give him his confession on a plate. He had to earn the content of his lies, using guile and intelligence. If he did not sound convincing – if the crime he pretended to have committed sounded hollow, they beat him all the harder and he soon learned the craft of storytelling and suspension of disbelief. He was never so glad to find crimes that they found abhorrent enough to put him in jail for, and would gladly have gone out and committed them all, if they had required proof of his confession. So long as they stopped beating him.

They threw him in the tunnel.

Now Hassan was to help him escape. The weals from the rods had not completely healed. Conditions in the tunnel had not helped in that respect. If he was caught again, they would beat him to death. He was sure of that. Yet, if he stayed, he would die a lingering death from dysentery or some respiratory disease. Lungs and bowels, the two most vulnerable organs when closely confined with one's own kind in insanitary conditions. Already there were traces of blood from both, in his spittle, in his excrement.

When the signal came from Hassan, all he had to do was roll backwards and drop into the pit, which the boy would cover. The guards counted the prisoners, but they were notoriously poor at arithmetic and would argue constantly over the figures. Besides, not all the inmates managed to get outside: the dying lay in the dark and awaited release. Thus, the guards never really knew how many charges they had on their hands and the counting was an exercise to satisfy the authorities.

Hassan and Jim had agreed to time the escape with sunset, when shadows played tricks with the eyes of the sentries.

Alan's tongue was like a fat, rough snake, filling his mouth. He had had no water for a day and a half and visions of iced lemonade were swimming before his eyes. Sabalala had left him, promising to return before nightfall. That was at noon yesterday. It was almost another nightfall.

All day he had lain in the shade of his camel, with his overcoat tightly buttoned at the neck. It was important not to let his sweat evaporate during the hot hours of daytime. Thirst is such an ugly pain, because it attacks both physical and mental processes. As the day progressed, Alan came to hate his camel, because it was *there*.

The beast sat, placidly studying the distant horizon through heavy-lidded eyes, caring nothing for the torment of its human master and easy in the fact that it had little to concern itself on the same score. Lying in the beast's shadow, its hot, musty smell added to the sensation of overpowering heat – a tangible thing that pressed upon Alan like a heavy, uncomfortable blanket. Its straw-dust coat was offensive to his nostrils and its pulsing body, slobbering mouth and clinkered hindquarters were infinitely distasteful. He hated the beast because it was there to hate and because it was his omnipresent companion.

As the approach of evening crawled towards him, Alan discerned a figure on the horizon and his heart gave a jump of hope. It was surely Sabalala? Almost instantly the terrible thirst left him and he stood up to get a better view. The distant traveller moved through a vertical river of heat waves: a distorted shape that rippled and shimmered, its details lost in air with visibility as imperfect as poorly fashioned glass.

He checked his watch. Sabalala had been away thirty hours and twenty minutes. That figure *had* to be the Fijian.

Alan coughed, the action tearing at his throat and causing him pain. His eyes were sore and his bones ached at every joint. Until the figure had appeared he had seriously considered cutting the camel somewhere and slaking his thirst on its blood. It was a drastic action, but his head was spinning and on the edge of delirium any idea was better than none. Whether he could have carried it out – how he actually proposed to cut the beast – had not formed part of his plan at that point. He just had some vague notion of sucking the liquid and easing the pain. In the back of his mind was the knowledge that Sabalala did not know of his predicament. Alan had only discovered the leak in the goatskin waterbag after the Fijian had left him. Perhaps the man would be in no hurry to return?

It had not been the desert this time. It was his own stupid fault. The goatskin had bounced against a sharp splinter in the camel saddle and the bag must have been leaking slowly all morning, dribbling down the camel's hind leg.

The rider's approach was infinitely slow. It was as if the figure were static, forming part of the landscape.

"Come on! Come on!" said Alan, growing impatient. Even if it were not Sabalala, the desert code provided for thirsty travellers, didn't it? He was beyond concern about the hostility of fierce tribesmen. In his waistband was a revolver which he *would* use. Kill a man for his water, if it were not offered, or withheld.

Near to Alan's foot a small brown rock moved, inching its way towards the camel's rear. It was a spider with a torso the size of an upturned cup. Alan savagely beat it to a pulp with his camel goad.

"There!" he said, with satisfaction, as if the spider was responsible both for his thirst and the slowness of the distant rider. The spider did not need to concern itself with thirst now. Perhaps it never had to? thought Alan, enviously. Some creatures did not drink. They absorbed moisture from the night air, or took it only as food. They did not sweat or piss – they were living husks of corn. Alan recalled that some humans survived without water in its sky-dropped form. The Kalahari Bushmen took their liquid intake from roots and the stomachs of the animals they killed.

"Everyone's better off than me," he cried, with a burst of self-pity. The camel stirred at the sound of his voice, its hump flopping to one side.

After darkness had fallen, Alan made a fire to direct the traveller. The stars came out – frustratingly distant chips of ice that tantalised, far beyond reach.

Everything seemed designed to torment him. Even the stars. The Milky Way. Milk! It looked so coolly inviting. Hateful.

The traveller arrived.

It was not Sabalala.

"*Moya?*" Alan croaked.

The hooded visitor held out a skin for him and he snatched it, gulping down three or four heavy swallows before it was taken back.

"*Tammam?*" said the man.

"*Aiwa.*" Alan gasped. "Good. *Tammam. Tammam.*"

The visitor moved to the fire and sat down. Alan felt sure he would be offered more water in a few moments. He cursed his own lack of manners in snatching the waterbag.

He sat down, opposite the man, who was poking the fire with a twig. In the light of the flames his hand seemed malformed. But then the thick sleeve of his ragged robe fell over the fingers again. The hood still hid his features like some sinister monk of a Gothic tale – an Edgar Allan Poe character.

The fire flared and Alan saw two eyes shine for a brief moment.

"You speak English?" asked Alan.

There was no perceptible movement from the figure.

"Do I know you? Have we met?"

Nothing. Not a nod, nor a shake of the head.

Alan began to get an uneasy feeling. Was this one of the

Wolves of the Radfan? Perhaps the offer of the water had been to put him off his guard?

"*Moya?*" asked Alan, again.

The man lifted his head, threw back his hood and then held out the skin. Alan gave a little cry and scuttled backward. He had drunk! He had already had a drink from the waterbag!

Having passed through a certain mountain village, into which he and Sabalala had been led by some guides with a warped sense of humour, he knew leprosy when he saw it.

He was sharing his fire with a leper!

Sharing a waterbag with a leper!

Oh Christ! Oh God!

The leper tossed him the waterbag and it hit the ground by his legs. He pulled out his revolver and pointed it at the repulsive creature by the fire.

I'd be doing him a favour.

"Put that damn gun away."

"Who . . .?"

"It's me . . ." Sabalala stepped into the light of the fire.

"What do you think you're doing?"

"The man's sick. I drank from his bag. Look at him!" Alan wiped his mouth on the arm of his sleeve. The gun became heavy and his hand was shaking furiously. His fingers felt locked to the grip. He lowered the weapon carefully and with difficulty. It was almost as if to draw it meant he had to use it, like a Gurkha with his knife, and his brain had accepted the first action as authority for the second. Luckily, he did not squeeze the trigger by instinct.

The gun safely in his lap, he said, "Aren't they supposed to warn people?"

"This is the desert," replied the Fijian, angrily. "What do you want? A bell – a sign? *Unclean!*"

He spoke rapidly in Arabic to the visitor who seemed unperturbed by Alan's dangerous antics.

Sabalala said, "He tells me it's not contagious – his kind. I don't think he's lying. I told him you were half out of your mind with thirst and he accepted that – said he'd seen it as soon as he came in and he had to snatch back the skin because you were drinking too fast."

"You don't *think* so?"

"That's right. I believe he's telling the truth. If you don't find that reassuring, I'm sorry, but killing him won't help you, even if he is lying."

"It's not good enough," shouted Alan.

"What do you want – sympathy?"

"No. I wanted fucking water, that's what I wanted. If you'd have come back sooner, this would never have happened. I've been waiting all day. All fucking day – going crazy – no water . . ." His stomach was hurting him now.

"You had no water?"

"That's what I said, no water. You deaf?"

"No, puzzled. You *had* water."

"I also had a comfortable life only a few short months ago, but that leaked away too . . ." He shook his wrist and gave out a cry of anguish.

"What's the matter?"

He gave the Fijian a helpless look.

"My watch has stopped, now . . ."

Jim and the boy had crossed the mountains on stolen camels. There had been no pursuit: at least, none of which they were aware. They had skirted Sana'a, the city growing like a dark red and white geometrical flower from its plateau: a bloom with cubic petals. Now they sat by the fire in the cold darkness, roasting a lizard. There was also a snake, which Hassan had caught, but even in his hunger Jim could not face it. The thought of snake made his stomach revolt. Lizard was bad enough.

Late in the night, they had visitors: a band of NLF guerrilla fighters who sat with them at their fire. Their leader seemed to be in two minds over what to do with them. He sat, his head swathed in a dusty cloth, and stared at Jim with penetrating black eyes.

"You are not an imperialist?" he said in his own tongue. "But you are English."

Jim replied carefully in Arabic. "I'm English, and I know you are fighting my people, but I'm not an imperialist. I'm just a traveller, who does not wish to recognise borders. This is a land without fences, so I'm sure you understand."

"You came here to fight?"

154

"No, I came to seek a friend. I have no wish to fight. Your cause is not mine. I don't wish to be involved in this issue."

"You are a coward, then?" The man's teeth showed for an instant.

"Not a coward, or why would I be here? I will defend myself, make no mistake about that – and my young friend here. But I have no desire to kill for the sake of it."

"You are a Moslem, perhaps? There are Europeans who are of the faith."

"No, I'm not even that. I'm not really anything."

The Arab pursed his lips, thoughtfully. Then his eyes rested on the boy.

"English. Not a Moslem. Not anything . . ."

Jim said, "I've read the Koran."

The Arab's head jerked up and he turned to smile at his grim-faced warriors.

"He has read the Koran." He looked at Jim again. "Tell me some."

"How about the fifth sura: 'In the Name of Allah, the Compassionate, the Merciful – It is the Merciful who has taught you the *Recital*. He created man and taught him articulate speech. The sun and the moon pursue their ordered course. The plants and the trees bow down in adoration.' "

"Merciful? You are clever, Englishman – to remember that particular line. You know *all* the Koran?"

"No. Do you?"

The Arab scratched his beard and shook his head. He still seemed uncertain, but Jim had definitely made an impression, he could see that.

Jim followed up his partial success.

" 'In the Name of Allah, the Compassionate, the Merciful, Say: I seek refuge in the Lord of Daybreak from the mischief of His creation; from the mischief of the night when she spreads her darkness; from the mischief of conjuring witches; from the mischief of the envier, when he envies.' "

The man held up his hand.

"Enough. We are leaving. Go quickly from this place, Englishman. We do not like you here."

They disappeared into the darkness, leaving Jim feeling as wet and limp as a rag in the rain.

"We'd better leave at dawn," he said to Hassan.

The boy nodded, clearly as shaken by the meeting as Jim had been himself. They huddled together at the fire.

To pass the time, Hassan told Jim his short history. He had been born in Taiz, in one of the backstreet hovels, the son of the third wife of a former *qāt* farmer who had lost his land. The father died of a heart attack, when Hassan was three years old, and his mother took him and his baby sister and travelled south, to beg on the streets of Aden.

They lived in a box constructed of biscuit tins filled with sand, down by the harbour. When his mother returned at night, with her two infants, they were covered in black bruises where she had pinched them to make them cry. With Moslems she did not need to draw attention to her plight: the Koran provides for beggars in its instructions to the faithful. But Europeans only parted with their money if shocked or moved or made to feel uncomfortable. Hassan's mother learned quickly that colonialists and tourists had to be persecuted into embarrassment by a persistent pleading accompanied by the wailing of a child. They would pay to make her go away.

At five years of age Hassan was selling fruit to the British troops on the beaches of Khormaksar, Conquest and Telegraph Bays. They would not let him into the more exclusive beach clubs, which catered for the officers and high-ranking civil servants, but the rankers' beaches were open to all and he even managed to slip into the Lido, the rankers' club, occasionally.

The fruit he purchased in the early morning, from Somali dhows over from Djibouti, and he tramped between the white bodies of the condescending British with his wares, until the last one left in the evening. They thought him bright because he knew the value of money at an age when their own children could hardly count to ten, but they laughed at his conviction that he was going to be a doctor some day. When he became too insistent with his wares, they swore at him in Arabic – the only words they had bothered to learn in his language – and the phrases were foul.

"Go fuck your mother. Your sister is a whore screwed by donkeys."

156

Had an Arab used the same words to an English child of that age they would have called him a pervert and beaten him senseless, but somehow they looked on Arabic as a meaning-less jumble of words and were insensible to their own immorality. Hassan bore the insults with tolerance, not knowing how else to deal with such people.

When he was six, he witnessed a shark attack on a middle-aged woman at the Lido. Grabbing a paddle from a nearby fisherman's canoe, he beat the shark with it, in the shallows, until it turned out to sea, taking half its victim with it. The remains were taken away in an ambulance and someone thrust an East African ten-shilling note in his hand. The head waiter, his old enemy, chased him from the Lido with the usual curses – not as bad as those used by the British, but more stinging because they came from the practised lips of one of his own kind.

At seven he saw a public execution – a case of adultery – and was confused by the festive air that surrounded that occasion.

At eight, the troubles began in the Protectorate. He saw a jeep full of soldiers blown to pieces, so that the metal parts of the vehicle and the limbs of the troops were intermingled on the sand. One of his young street friends lost a hand on finding a booby-trapped flashlight in the gutter, and a Somali informer was beaten to death with sticks on a rattan bed near to the cardboard on which he himself slept. The troops who used to buy his fruit often rough-handled him, searching him for weapons, and swore at him in their frustration at being open targets. A soldier shot a running Arab, who pushed past him in the street, and he heard the screams of the dying man as they took him away on a stretcher.

The violence grew. Arab killed soldier. Arab killed Arab. Soldier killed Arab. Horrible deaths, in fire and flame. Slow deaths. Instant deaths. He left Aden for the Yemen, returning to his birthplace at Taiz. The money he had saved to become a doctor was stolen from him by an uncle. He became a water boy at the jail. Then he met Jim.

"You've lived a hard life for a nine-year-old."

Hassan shrugged, and grinned.

"Fate, eh?"

The solemn nod.

Jim paused, looking up at the stars.

"Me too. Yet, I feel as if I've passed through an emotional darkness. The light is just showing through."

Hassan said, "I do not understand what you mean."

"Neither do I," replied the Englishman. "But I *feel* what I mean."

Three days after the great thirst, Alan was camping in the middle of a *wadi*. Sabalala had left him once again and he was making breakfast of flour cakes with a little of the water that the Fijian had left him. There was something wrong with the sky, but Alan was too intent on his own thoughts to pay it much attention.

He was thinking about the hill where he was to meet Jim, just outside Lawdar. He was glad that Jim had not suggested they meet in the town itself, because things were getting pretty dicey throughout South Arabia with the spread of Republicanism. It wasn't safe to enter any area where there were crowds.

His nose brought him back. The smell of burning filled the air and he saw that his flour cakes were black and crisp. The camel was making a terrible racket nearby.

"Damn!"

At that moment, something hit him on the shoulder. Then again. And again.

He looked up. The skies were black with pregnant clouds, bulging with water. They seemed almost low enough to touch. Heavy raindrops were splattering in the dust all around him. He looked across the *wadi* and he saw that he was in the centre – about quarter of a mile from each bank. Then the downpour came.

Never in his life had he experienced such rain. It came down like a wall of solid water, so that he could hardly breathe, and he swallowed it down by the mouthful, at first gratefully, then with some annoyance. His vision blurred, he could not see more than a foot in front of him. The camel was making lowing noises, which seemed to be getting fainter with each plaintive call. Soon his feet began to sink in the mud that was forming rapidly on the ground and he struggled to extract them as brown rivulets began snaking around his ankles.

Christ! A minute! It could only have been a minute and already the water was half an inch deep!

Leading the camel, he began walking swiftly in what he thought was the direction of the bank. Then, as the depth of the water increased, he broke into a run, the soles of his sandals like suction pads on the mud, sticking fast, holding him back. His thick coat became heavy, weighing him down. If only he had not burned the bloody cakes! He would have smelled the coming of the rain – a musty odour which was unmistakable.

"Help!" he screamed. "Somebody help me."

The camel cried out mournfully, too, its cries mingling with those of the man. Both knew they were in trouble and neither had any idea how to get out of it. They struggled forward, through the thickening sludge, the water up to the man's knees.

Alan could feel the soil being swept away from beneath his feet and it caused him to stumble, headlong, into the rushing torrent. He rose again, the rein still in his hand, splashing, bewildered by the direction of the flow. Surely, surely he should be running crosswise to it? Not following it?

Soon it was waist deep and he seemed no nearer to the bank. He was exhausted and sure he was going to drown. He recalled a similar experience on the East Anglian coast, as a boy, with the tide coming in faster than he could run. Two silver horns of water, closing round him, trapping him, keeping him from the safety of the beach. He would have died then had it not been for the boat moored offshore.

He sank deeper into the mud, feeling sharp rock incise his soles.

"Shut up, for Christ's sakes," he gargled at the mooning camel. "Please, please," his tone changed, as he prayed to a God he had long since abandoned.

When the water was chest high, the rain suddenly stopped. It continued to increase in depth, but at last he could see the bank. The flood had carried him off his feet for a few yards, but in towards the shore, and his fingers scrabbled for a hold on the crumbling soil. Eventually, he managed to pull

159

himself out, pulling the camel by the rein until it too was free of the rushing water. He lay there for a long time, thankful that he had not suffered the ignominy of drowning in the middle of a desert.

"Bloody perverse country," he gasped to his camel. "This is your bloody country – why didn't you warn me? First it tries to kill you with thirst, then it tries to drown you. You should have smelled the rain, you big bastard. You've got nostrils like caverns. What the hell do I feed you for, if you can't give me a simple warning?"

The camel, which had done its best, lifted its head and held itself aloof.

"Big bastard," repeated Alan, glad to be alive.

The sky was beginning to clear and the sun broke through the clouds in several places with brilliant shafts of light. Alan regained his feet and instinctively looked at his watch. It had started again.

Only, it was going backwards.

"Bloody technology," growled Alan. He took refuge in curses and verbally abusing his beast in times of stress. It kept him reasonably sane.

He began walking, letting the hot sun dry his clothes, knowing he was not far from Lawdar. The camel trailed on behind him. There were creatures all around, small and large, drinking from the puddles, taking little notice of the stranger in this time of plenty. At noon Alan came to a ridge and rested, looking down on the white mud-and-brick dwellings, the narrow streets, below him.

"Made it."

He looked down at himself, as he lay there. He was filthy from shoulder to toe. His beard and hair felt matted and his locks hung like clinkers from his head. His clothes were worn and ragged. His sandals were broken in two places. He was a wreck.

Yet, he was strangely happy.

He had made it to Lawdar, alone.

He was jubilant. God, if Sabalala could see him now! The Fijian had told him he would never make it. And here he was, against the odds. A three-day journey across country that hated him, through hills bristling with bandits, across stretches of sand like a blacksmith's forge, along river beds that flooded within minutes – and he had made it. The desert *must* have some respect for him now. He had made it to Lawdar, alone.

Jim and Hassan had been riding all day when they sighted Lawdar. It was decided between them that they should camp outside and enter during the evening when they could go in under cover of darkness. Jim had sent money to a merchant with whom his bank had done business at one time. He intended to collect this and buy more provisions, before meeting with Alan.

That evening, when camp had been established, Jim went up into the rocks to get a better sighting of the town; he saw a figure hunched by a rock: a man relieving himself. He squatted on his haunches himself, to get a better look at the man. A moment later, he knew it was Alan, beneath all the dirt and grime.

The sun drifted like a descending orange balloon, down behind the red hills, as he strolled towards his friend. The other man, adjusting his dress, did not notice his approach.

"*Salaam ali cum, Abu-al-Bundug!*" said Jim.

The other man started, visibly.

"Jesus, who the hell are you? What're you sneaking up like that for?"

"Don't you know me, Al?"

"Who – *Jim*? Is that you underneath there?"

"I wouldn't have recognised you either – you look like a bloody bandit, you bandit."

They shook hands and slapped each other on the arms the way men do when they are too shy to hug.

"Christ, it's *good* to see you, Jim. You said this hill and here we are – slap bang on top. You're two days early."

"So are you."

"Well – *I* came by fast camel. Listen, how did you know it was me, if you didn't recognise me?"

Jim smiled.

"You wiped your arse with your right hand. That's a Moslem's eating hand."

"Good job it was you, and not some red-neck tribesman –

161

I could've been wounded in a nasty place. Where are you camped?"

"Down the hill."

"I'll join you. I'll just go and get my bastard camel. He gets lonely if I leave him for too long. It's worse than being married . . ." He stopped. "Oh, by the way, Jim. I'm sorry . . ."

"Don't say any more at the moment. We'll talk about it later – and there's nothing to be sorry for. I'll see you at the bottom – and I've got a companion. An Arab boy by the name of Hassan. Okay?"

"Right."

The sun threw dark and light lanes across the wide expanse of wasteland as Alan joined Jim in his camp by a small overhang. A wild coffee tree, thirty feet tall, grew beside the overhang and they used the trunk to support their backs as they sat and talked, a little oblique from one another. Hassan found a better place, for him, down by the water where amongst the white rocks a *ban* tree grew, its thread-like leaves and pastel-pink blooms refreshed after the recent rain. He and Alan had taken an instant dislike to one another, which Jim had noticed straight away. There was little point in hiding things inside when the group had to cross the Rub al-Khali, the Empty Quarter, together. It was best if things were out in the open and they all knew where they stood.

"Bloody desert tried to drown me," said Alan.

"That's why I came out here. Sarah was worried about you. She thought you were going round the bend."

"Oh." Alan's voice took on a distant quality. "Well I'm not – going round the bend, that is. It did make me a little crazy for a while – I was sure it had it in for me. But then I seemed to get on top of it."

Jim thought: *yes, when it knew it had me in its power.*

Alan said, "How did you get up here? I heard they weren't letting anyone come up country now."

"Went round the coast to Mocha, by dhow. I had to give your pal Trevellian the slip. They caught me in Taiz. Threw me in jail. Young Hassan over there helped me escape. I promised him he would be a doctor."

"Bit of a wild promise, isn't it?"

162

"No. Not really." Jim lit up a Turkish cigarette, gulping down the smoke as he tried to sort out his thoughts. "So I came here for nothing. You didn't need me."

"I wouldn't say that. It'll be more fun with two of us. You remember I asked you to come before."

"What's all this about fighting? You didn't come here to take part in a war."

Alan shrugged. "One just sort of gets caught up in it. I got angry one day, when I was being shot at, and fired back. It's an easy thing to do."

Jim decided not to comment. It was pointless arguing with a man he might have to rely on in the desert.

"Well, now we've got to find the way home."

"That's easy – we just move south-west, down to Aden."

Jim explained patiently that the front door had been closed. Hassan had learned, the day before the jail break, that the last of the British had left Aden and the NLF had entered the streets in triumph. There was talk of it becoming a Marxist state now that the British presence had gone. They had been there for one and a quarter centuries and the fishing village that had become a large town wanted to wipe it clean of colonial rule. With the withdrawal of the British, the last of the sheiks who had held out against the Republicans were falling one by one. There was no Royalist help to be had in that direction. But there was still a British presence to the east, in Muscat and Oman. They had to make for those and leave by the back door.

"We have to strike north first," he said, "towards Dhufar. Once we're out of the village belt, we can head east."

"Suits me," said Alan. "Looks like I've exchanged one mother for another."

"I don't know what you mean."

"Sabalala – the Fijian. He mothered me. And now you're doing it. I don't need you people, you know. I can handle this by myself now. I've got the desert where I want it – underfoot."

"I'm sorry – I didn't mean it like that. What do *you* suggest we do?"

"I suggest we strike north, for Dhufar, and then east," Alan said, gravely.

They both laughed.

The two men continued exchanging information, occasionally twisting sideways from the trunk of the coffee tree, so that they could emphasise a point with a gesture of the hands. Finally, they came to the subject of Sarah. Alan became particularly evasive when Jim asked his friend what he intended to do.

Alan played sand through his fingers.

"I don't know – I thought I'd found a soul mate for a while. I mean, I felt bad about you, but, love and war you know – anyway, I'm not so keen now. I mean, I hardly know the woman. That sounds terrible, doesn't it? It looks like I've taken her away from you, just to prove that I could do it. But it wasn't like that – believe me. I felt – this is going to sound terribly old-fashioned – I felt bewitched by her. Then the spell wore off."

"I understand," Jim replied.

"Look, I . . ."

"No. I really *do* understand. I can't explain it to you yet, but I will some time. It's something that defies logic and I'm not sure you're ready for it yet."

Alan continued to apologise, but Jim was no longer listening. He was wondering about the future. Their immediate future. He had a presentiment that they were destined to experience something which, like that earlier incident, would alter the courses of their lives.

They broke off the conversation to eat a meal, during which Jim screwed his face into a look of distaste.

"What's the matter?" asked Alan, catching the look which was directed at him.

"You," answered Jim. "You're eating with your left hand."

Alan looked down at his palms and then nodded.

ALAN

The desert basked beneath the sun: a wide, green sea of undulating waves stretching into the distance. Here and there, a small outcrop of burnt sienna rock poked its way through the delicate plants. The first rain it had seen for seven years had caused an immediate change in the scenery and for a brief spell the desert had become a vast meadowland of weeds and wildflowers, with fragile stems and small leaves. It could not last long – a few days, perhaps, until the harsh sun burned the plants to a brown crispness. No doubt the fauna was eating as it had not done for several years. Over this green wilderness, as wide as the sky overhead, three figures made their way northwards.

They had gone into Lawdar under cover of darkness and using Hassan to make enquiries, had found the house of the merchant who was holding Jim's money. Alan noticed how nervous the old man was, as he quickly passed over the *riyals* without offering any hospitality, and he guessed that the political upheaval in the land was causing insecurity, especially amongst the wealthy class. For centuries they had been ruled by sheiks – some benign, some not – and now their autocratic rule was coming to an end. It was bound to cause anxiety amongst those who had something to lose.

Jim had paid the merchant generously for his part in banking the money and after purchasing guns and an extra pack camel from him, they left, to spend the night on the ridge above the town. They had awoken to the sound of the muezzins calling the faithful to prayer and had set off immediately afterwards. It was sensible to stay away from towns and villages if at all possible.

Alan wondered whether the fact that he had weaned Sarah away from Jim with mere letters still rankled with his friend. If it were him he would be hopping mad, but Jim was different. He seemed to accept these things far more calmly than other people. If Sarah could see either of them now, he thought, she would have a fit. Two sophisticated men-about-town reduced to shabby gypsies. Neither of them were a pretty sight.

In the heat of the daytime, there was little to do except sit hunched in the saddle and keep a wary eye out for Bedu. It was pleasant to have a green landscape for a change and not have to forage for *natsh* or *marikh* for camel fodder. How quickly the thousands of dormant seeds, scattered across the dust, had sprung to life! It was a small miracle to him that tiny brown kernels could survive a baking sun for years on end and suddenly, at the first touch of water, throw out roots and fresh green stems, leaves, flowers, as if they had been carefully nurtured by the loving hands of a gardener all that time.

Hassan, the boy, was obviously happy. Occasionally he broke out into excited chatter, which irritated Alan, but for the most part he seemed absorbed by his own dreams. The child was like those seeds, ready to bloom under the first shower of money. Alan thought Jim was being taken in by all that rubbish about the boy wanting to be a doctor. He was convinced it was just another Arab ploy to obtain money from the rich white men. Once the boy came in sight of some bazaar he would probably spend the lot on material goods: buy himself a portable radio and other useless items. Not that he blamed Hassan for that. Had he been raised in a dustbowl with barely enough to feed himself, he would have done the same. He just hoped Jim would not be too disappointed. His friend was too gullible – had too many ideals and trusted people too much.

Another thing Alan had difficulty in accepting was that Hassan knew little about the desert. To Alan, *Arab* and *nomad* were synonymous. How could you live right next door to something and not know anything about it? Granted the boy had been raised in a town, but he would have thought that natural curiosity would have had him learning about his environment. The previous day Alan had asked Hassan whether or not a particular root was good to eat.

"I eat meat and bread," Hassan had replied. "I know nothing about this thing. What do I know of such things?"

"You're an Arab, aren't you?"

Jim had intervened. "There are Arabs and Arabs," he had said. "Leave the boy alone. Would you expect a Londoner to tell you about Scottish wildlife? Eat the root – it's all right. I did my homework before I came here."

Alan was annoyed at Jim's intervention and threw the root away, saying he did not trust research done in a library and finished by quoting instances of people who thought they could classify edible fungi from books and had died through eating poisonous toadstools.

Hassan had retreated from this argument as soon as he was able, taking no sides. Alan had nothing but contempt for the boy. He was sure that, given the chance, the child would steal everything they had and run for it and he was determined to keep an eye on him. No doubt he fostered these arguments in the hope that the two Englishmen would come to a fight and kill each other. The little bastard would probably slit their throats while they slept, given half the chance.

He was sure that Hassan *did* know about desert survival, but was keeping the knowledge to himself. Again, he did not blame the boy. It was exactly what he would have done himself, in the same circumstances. Had he been a poor child without a future and two rich Arabs had come to his country and walked about as if they owned it, he would have taken them for all they were worth.

He was aware, as they travelled along, that Jim's eyes were constantly on his back. To distract himself from this thought, he spent his time gouging the dirt from beneath his fingernails, and from the creases in his hands, with a splinter of wood. Funny, at one time he would have detested grime, but here, where water was precious and washing a luxury, it almost seemed a sacrilege to be clean. He was quite happy with Arabian dirt, natural dirt. It was the filth in towns he abhorred. *That* kind of dirt came from human waste and pollution: grey dust that collected on railway carriage windows; sludge that found the corners of ledges. Who could be comfortable with that kind of dirt? Here, in the desert, he knew it was clean dirt: the result of rock erosion and disintegration of areas untouched by human foot. Nothing wrong with primal dirt. He had swallowed it in his food

167

without ill effects. Imagine doing that with a sandwich dropped in a London gutter! You would need fourteen injections in the stomach.

Mind you, he was careful not to touch the pi-dogs. The bastards were covered with ticks and lice, and slunk around like they spent their nights in town drains. He liked the Arab towns from a distance only: their sounds were poetry. The muezzins in the minarets; the rumble of wood carts; the lowing of the cattle. He liked to see the sun going down on them: the white walls fringed with rose tint, and the shadows stretching like cats awakening from a sleep. But when you got close to them, they were just hovels full of foul odours and streets crawling with urchins that pawed at your legs.

He wondered about Jim and the business he mentioned about being in jail. Should he delve any further or let things lie? Jim had always been a ganglion of insecurities and while the man was good at physical feats, he did not trust him to bear up under stress – mental stress. Why, even *he* had collapsed a little under the strain when he had been with Sabalala! Sarah's defection had obviously upset Jim, though he seemed to be doing his best to hide the fact. But Alan believed that it had brought them closer. Had given them something in common. It was a kind of bond, to have shared the same woman – to have been loved by the same person. *Shared* was perhaps the wrong word. Yet still the binding element was there. They were brothers in spirit, if not in flesh.

He wheeled his camel and came up alongside the man in question.

"What did you think of Sarah?" he asked. "As a person, I mean? I'm not prying into your physical experiences, God forbid. I'm interested in your assessment of her character . . ."

He saw Jim's lips tighten and he wondered what he had said that might have upset him. He decided that Jim must have thought he was about to criticise her and nothing could have been further from his mind. He decided to rectify the misapprehension.

He said, "She's a wonderful person, isn't she? You're privileged to have known her so well. Such a fine mind – I'm

168

full of admiration for her."

"I'm sure."

"No, really I am."

"I thought we'd talked all this out. You said you had been bewitched and then unbewitched and so we're all back to square one. She doesn't want me, she doesn't want you and neither of us want her, so everyone's happy at last."

"There's no need to get huffy. I didn't realise you still held a grudge."

Jim reined in his camel and stared at Alan, directly in the eyes. "Alan, listen to me, very carefully. I do not hold a grudge. I do not hold a grudge. Okay? End of conversation."

"Right. But I'd still like to know what you think of her. I thought she was pretty astute myself. The way she had a grasp of ambiguous subjects – looked beyond the obvious."

Jim prodded his camel forward again and Alan followed.

"Well," said Jim, after a moment's staring at the horizon ahead. "She certainly did that with me."

"Her letters were full of such enthusiasms. The search for knowledge – the interpretation of nature. Did you go walking often? She had a talented way of describing her walks in the country. A poetic gift . . ."

Jim said, "I've got a puzzle for you. What's the connection between Sarah and – Vivaldi, pomegranate blossom and Sergeant Troy?"

Alan thought very hard, then admitted, "I don't know. Does she like Vivaldi's music? And perhaps Thomas Hardy?"

"No. Nothing like that. It's to do with colours."

"Ah. Wait a minute – pomegranate blooms are red – bright scarlet – and Troy was a redcoat. Vivaldi I don't get."

"Vivaldi had red hair – they called him the Red Priest."

Alan nodded, then asked, "What's the connection with Sarah then?"

Jim had a wicked smile on his face.

"Well, let's go through them. Vivaldi's red hair attracted a woman and he lost his priesthood when he was discovered in a compromising situation with her. In some countries, pomegranate blooms, when worn in a girl's hair, signify willingness to make love. Troy's dashing red tunic attracted

169

Bathsheba to his bed – and there you have it. So you see, the colour red, and sex, are closely linked in all these cases."

Alan felt something dark stirring within him.

"And – Sarah?"

Jim smiled sweetly at him from his position in the saddle.

"Sarah always wore red panties when she wanted to screw. It was her signal. She had too fine a mind to suggest it outright . . ."

Alan allowed his mount to drop back a couple of paces and he stared at Jim's back, thinking he would like to put a knife somewhere on its broad expanse.

"You bastard," he said, quietly.

Jim turned and smiled grimly.

"The fact is, chum, she took us both for a ride. I don't believe it was entirely her fault, but I'm not going to sing her praises for you, just so's you can congratulate yourself on a conquest. Nothing happened between you. It all happened between us. I resented your interference then, but I think it should be dropped now. There's something far more power-ful at work, here, than a relationship between two people, or any weird triangular relationships. I don't know what it is yet, but I think we're going to find out quite soon – and when we do, I don't think it's going to matter what passed between Sarah and me – it's what lies behind all this that counts. Why we're here . . ."

Jim turned to face Alan, sitting back to front on his dromedary. For some reason Alan felt a little affronted by the posture. Was he being insulted again?

"It's all part of a game, Alan. The desert's playing with us, like pawns. Keep your eyes skinned for a white knight – he's going to knock us off the chessboard."

"You're crazy. What the hell are you talking about? Do you know what you're talking about?"

"Not exactly."

"Well the *simoom*'s not due yet. Let's wait until it comes before we start going gaga."

"Suit yourself."

Jim turned around in his saddle then and left Alan to his thoughts. Hassan had wandered a long way ahead and he had halted his camel, waiting for them to catch up.

170

They continued northward long after they had intended to turn east. Despite the recent rains, which admittedly might not have covered the whole area they were traversing at that time, the wells were almost dry, relinquishing only enough water for the three of them to reach the nearest watering place to the one at which they had stopped. Since the line of wells followed the slope of the land, from north to south, and the next parallel line was quite a distance away to the east, they were forced to go in one direction.

"Christ, we'll be in Saudi if we don't turn soon," grumbled Alan.

Jim nodded. "There's not much we can do about it – until we find a well with enough water to allow us to strike east."

They took a day's rest at a cave they discovered in the mountains, five days after leaving Lawdar. Jim took his rifle and climbed a ridge to look for gazelle, while Hassan and Alan did a few domestic chores round the camp. At noon, Alan looked up to see Jim walking along the narrow saddle-back of the ridge, beyond a line of chimneys cut in the igneous rock by past rainfall.

When Jim returned, close to evening, he had a wild goat around his shoulders, but he looked shaken. He tossed the goat on the ground beside the fire, where Hassan began to skin it.

"What's the matter?" asked Alan. "You don't look well – sun get to you? We can't afford to go down with heatstroke, you know."

Jim sat down beside him on the hard ground. The small creatures were beginning to stir on the rock-strewn floor of the high valley and the cave's interior began to darken with the dying sun.

"No, I'm not ill. At least I don't think so."

Shadows moved along the valley, filling its hollows with their blackness. Kites roosted for the night amongst the dark red crags of hook-like peaks, melting into the rock as the light faded around them. Somewhere in the hills a hyena crooned: a long, mournful note that carried its canine soul out into the wildernesses beyond its lair.

"Something happened to me up there, but I'm not sure what it was. How to explain it."

Alan's neck began to prickle as he got an uncomfortable feeling in the base of his skull. It was a feeling he knew from childhood, when his father insisted on telling him ghost stories before he went to sleep at night. He did not like it.

"Well? Are you going to tell me?"

Jim nodded towards the top of the ridge, just a dark line meeting a lesser darkness now.

"Up there – maybe it was the hunger – it pares away all those secondary thoughts. Up there I went through a kind of perception barrier. I've had it before, to a lesser degree, out in the desert. You know when you see a desert flower, or an emerald skink sliding through the sand, sometimes it seems as if you are experiencing the act of creation, rather than the result. You are catching the world in the making of its wonders – like being privy to an artist working on a painting, witnessing the mixing of the colours and the application of tone and texture.

"In England I hardly noticed the flowers – took them for granted. They were there, to be appreciated, but it's a surface appreciation – I saw them as complete forms. Out here, with endless days of sand and rock, gravel and stones, you appreciate any movement, or living plant that much more – you look into it, and beyond. It seems as if you can see every cell, tightly knitted to the others, and can see how they all fit into each other, to make the whole. When you're hungry for colour, thirsty for the fragrance of grass, eager for the sound of living things, you encapsulate any awakening of the senses within the moment – you hold it in your mind and take the time to give it the inspection it deserves. It seems to offer fresh values, better values than before. The very presence of life seems to enhance your own, make it something special in a spiritual sense.

"Living things *in* the desert – yet the desert itself has a life of its own. It has a will, formed from its vastness, from its emptiness, that impresses itself upon your spirit. *Place* has a soul, that makes itself evident when you drop your civilised shield and allow the primitive instincts to come forward. Up there, I felt that presence more strongly than I've ever felt it

172

before. The desert was not just *place* – it was – *alive*. It was aware of me."

Alan was fighting a growing terror within him at these words. Not that he believed a word of what he was being told, or even understood it, but it seemed that Jim was going crazy and he didn't know how he was going to deal with the situation. The most he could hope for was that it was temporary – a condition brought on by too much sun – and would evaporate with the telling of the story. His mind ran over the plants they had eaten over the last few days, but any hallucinogen would have affected them both, and Hassan, since they had all eaten of any harvest.

"You can't escape the desert's authority," Jim continued. "I realise that now. It sucks the old breath – the breath of civilised lands – from your lungs and replaces it with its own exhalations. The breath of place is breathed into your body, filling you with its spirit. Once here, you eat, drink and breathe the desert, until it owns you – you become part of it, sharing its respiration, its bodily fluids. You become drugged by its fumes and it possesses itself of you. It's a two-way process. It absorbs you and at the same time permeates your whole being with its own, until you're merely an animated part of itself. You move across its surface, but it controls you as surely as you control your own finger."

"You said you saw something," said Alan, anxious to get the story over with and out of the way if at all possible.

Jim rocked back on his heels. The smell of cooked meat was in the air now and Alan's stomach began to make urgent noises. They hadn't eaten meat for two days and he was sick of flour cakes.

"What I saw – out over the sands – was the desert's circular motion. It was barely perceptible – but it was there, like a faint whirlpool, a maelstrom. The Empty Quarter, to the east, was its centre."

"You saw this?"

"Perhaps *saw* is the wrong word? I *sensed* it. I told you about heightened perception. Well, I didn't see it with my *eye*, I determined it with an inner sight. Otherwise the movement would have been undetectable – if I hadn't allowed myself to drift . . ."

"Are you hungry?" said Alan. "I'm very hungry."

Jim looked up sharply.

"Of course I'm hungry. I'm bloody *starving*. Why do you think I went out to shoot the damn goat?"

"You went out to shoot a gazelle."

"Don't split hairs. If you don't like what I'm telling you, I can't help it. Maybe it was due to the sun and lack of water – I *still* felt it. It happened to me. That makes it worth repeating."

Alan was relieved. Jim sounded perfectly sane again. He wouldn't have to tie him to the back of his camel and lug him halfway across a continent, screaming and kicking.

"Okay, you've told me now. Can we eat?"

"I've finished. Let's join Hassan at the table."

The line of wells, their distances, and the yield of water from each of them, still forced the trio north. Jim told Alan he was experiencing a strong sense of being manipulated and Alan thought he was in for a new bout of mysticism and magic from his friend. He was relieved to find this was not the case. When he next came upon an attractive-looking plant, Alan tried to view it with new insight, fresh perspectives, but all he saw was a flower – quite pretty in its way, but nothing to startle his soul into revitalised revelations. He saw – a flower.

He wished now that he had held on to the box of dominoes. It was evident to him that Jim needed something to take his mind away from the dryness of the wells. Whenever his farmer father, who had taught him the game as a youngster, felt that life was getting on top of him, he would suggest a quiet game of dominoes. Public school had taught Alan a lot, but he never forgot his roots. His father was a simple man – not unintelligent, but uncomplicated – and he valued those things which his father held important. Dominoes was one of them. But Ali and Abdulla had pleaded with him to leave the box with them and he had not been able to refuse.

As they approached the oasis they saw that a caravan was camped at its edge. The tents of the occupants indicated that they were a wealthy group of nomads and Jim guessed that it was a sheik, probably on his way between a summer and winter palace.

"Surely they'd fly these days?" said Alan. "Or at the very least, use landrovers?"

"Depends how steeped they are in tradition," answered Jim. He wanted to ask Hassan's opinion, but the boy was at prayer.

"We've got to give it a try," he continued. "We need the water – and supplies if they'll let us have some. If they're hostile – well, we'll sort that out if it comes to it."

"We could send the boy in alone."

"He's not a *boy* in that sense. Anyway, they'd soon see he wasn't alone by the number of waterbags he was carrying. We'll all go in and hope for the best."

"Bully! Do you mind if I have an opinion, just as a participant you understand?"

Jim turned to face him.

"Well, what is it?"

Alan searched his mind for something to say. He had only argued out of sheer cussedness.

"We'll go in," he said at last.

Alan climbed on to his camel as Hassan completed his prayers. The sandflies that are to be found around most waterholes were feasting, drinking on his salty sweat, but he had not the energy to brush them off. The others were ready and he kicked his mount forward, wondering whether it was time to die.

Once, when he had been lying in the dark, in his room at the Red Sea Hotel, a flying rhino beetle hit the overhead fan with a sharp *crack* and was propelled by the blades like a cricket ball struck by a bat. The creature, hard as a bullet, had smacked into the side of his head with such force that he thought for a moment he had been shot. Lying there, in the dark, his hand immediately went up to find the hole in his temple, the blood. In the space of a moment a picture of the assassin came to him: a dark, fuzzy shadow on the balcony, arm through the open window, with the weapon in its hand.

Of course, it only took another moment to realise that he was not mortally wounded and he reached out, switching on the light. The beetle was on the white sheet: black, large and

175

buzzing its wings furiously, as it struggled to regain its feet. Squeamishly, Alan flicked it upright with the edge of his fingernail. It staggered a few paces on the white desert of starched cotton before launching itself heavily into the air again. Very soon it struck the fan a second time, was rocketed into the wall, and lay still, either stunned or dead.

Stupid things, Alan thought at the time. Why do they leave their natural environment and enter one totally strange to them? It was a sure way of finding death.

Yet, here he was, doing exactly that. He was flying into the fan.

The camel beneath him gave a start and seemed reluctant to continue. He kicked it hard, forcing it forward. What was the matter with the beast? They never seemed to have any reason for their capricious whims. Animals, other creatures and their ways, had always mystified him. He was much more at home with machines. Machines did what you told them to do. You turned the wheel of the car left and the machine followed obediently. It was that simple. You pulled on the left rein of a camel and it was likely to do anything, from a furious retreating dance, to bucking sideways sharply. There was no telling.

Those rhino beetles, for instance. Why *did* they fly into fans? They must feel the wind of the blades. What drew them into obvious danger? They were so predictable. He remembered his previous thought. *No*, they were unpredictable. Christ, they were both.

He had really thought he was dead that night. It was a strange feeling. You read that your life passes before you on the point of death. No pictures, no film shows had been visible to his eyes or brain. Just a terrible fear that filled his whole body. A wish to be somewhere else. Anywhere. At a party in Chelsea, or strolling along the banks of the Thames watching the rubbish float downstream. Anywhere but in a hotel bed in Aden with a bullet in the brain.

He wondered when he had caught his first fear of death. Certainly, it had not been in early childhood. At twelve he had been hit by a car as he ran out from behind a bus. He thought he had been killed that time too, but no fear flooded his body then. He had merely lain there, thinking how

176

strange it was to be looking up into the blue sky, with clouds surging through it. Then the face, like the Greek tragedy play mask he had made out of papier-mâché at school, coming between the clouds and his eyes.

"You stupid idiot!" said the face. Then, "Oh God, I've hit a child. Please, Christ, let him be alive."

The car had had a dented bumper, but after a few minutes Alan had got up and walked away, embarrassed by the attention and hoping his mother would not find out. Cars were like that, with him. They liked him. They recognised him for what he was: a creature at one with them, having an affinity with their machinated hearts.

When had his fear of death come then? What was the difference between the now-Alan and the then-Alan? He thought that somehow, the fear of death coincided with his discovery of women.

His first girlfriend had been Silvia, a nineteen-year-old who had told him from the start that her boyfriend was an army captain who was abroad and that she was going to marry him when he returned from his tour of duty. Nevertheless, Alan fell hopelessly in love with her. He thought the Alan dancing attendance on her would win her from her absent boyfriend. He was wrong, as he was always wrong about women. With another woman it might have been so, but with this one, who found romance in photographs of suntanned soldiers under foreign climes, it did not work. She allowed him to fall in love with her, then placed him gently aside.

The next one he met, some two years later, he had to leave for a while to attend a course in the north country. Absence to her was like wiping the slate clean. When he arrived home again she was with someone else and had difficulty in recalling past promises.

It had been the same story, several times, throughout his life. He had always used the wrong formula. Those who wanted him to cry, he was hard and mysterious with. Those who wanted to be dominated, he treated with tenderness, affection and broke down when they finally left him. Always the wrong Alan came forward. They left him. They all left him. He thought he would die not knowing what it was like

177

to be loved and his fear of death came.

The camel moved slowly forwards. Alan felt he was treading in the footsteps of kings. Perhaps those three kings that carried gifts to the infant Christ? What had happened to the gold? that's what he wanted to know. Joseph certainly wasn't a rich man afterwards. Maybe it was still buried under some floor in Bethlehem where a stable had once stood?

What if Christ were born today? How would the kings travel? In Cadillacs? Rolls-Royces? Bearing gifts of uranium, Chanel Number Five and gangland cement?

A pi-dog loped out of a ruined fort near the oasis, heading west. Its coat was bare in places, from the mange, and it had a heavy limp. It stopped, snapped at a fly, and then looked back at the fort before moving on again. When it saw the camels approaching, it turned again, went back to the fort and urinated at the base of an old palm before rubbing itself against the trunk.

Alan studied the palm. It was not exactly rooted in the earth, but at the same time it was not entirely out of the ground. The block of stone around which its roots were wrapped was crumbling to sand. Once the tree had reduced the block to dust with its tenacious, crushing grip, it would topple over, with nothing to support it. If it loosened its hold, it would fall anyway. Thus in clinging to life it brought itself nearer to death. The harder it held on, the quicker would be its end.

He had once seen a yew in a churchyard which the vicar told him was a thousand years old.

"Robin Hood probably used its branches for bows," he told the young Alan. He could have said that it had been used to hang outlaws from, when they stole the king's deer, but vicars tell children what they think they want to hear. The bow made from the tree, used to kill the deer, brought the robber of its branch back to itself to exact revenge. Trees are used to cycles: growing, shedding leaves to serve as humus for their seeds, themselves to grow again.

The bedraggled palm, with its dusty leaves, had probably come from a parent a thousand miles away. An Arab caravan had set out from Damascus, travelling south, carrying amongst other goods dates bound for the ports of the Indian

178

Ocean. The caravan master had eaten one, tossing the pip aside as he rested in the ruins of the fort, and urinating dogs and camels, and coffee slops, tea dregs, thrown outside the wall, had brought it to life. It was an abandoned orphan, scrubbing around for sustenance, merely to add to itself, its stature. If it could think, it would probably plan its eventual and inevitable fall to coincide with the passing of the caravan master, in order to take with it the man who had caused it to come to life in such a desolate, unwholesome place. Even trees, thought Alan, are entitled to a cyclic irony.

His camel had slowed its pace considerably. Did it know something he did not? Was there a rifle aimed at him at this very moment?

The finger squeezes and the mechanism of the gun, the levers, slides, ratchets and springs, begin the sequence, the procedure, which would end in the firing pin denting the base of the shell case, causing an explosion which would propel the bullet through an arc, beginning at the muzzle of the gun and ending at the target. It would draw a line, unperfected by any other instrument: a beautiful curve, between two points. At one end would be life, at the other end, death.

He was aware of someone speaking to him.

"What?"

"I think the reception committee is coming," said Jim.

They were surrounded by children of all ages, chattering in Arabic, but not begging. Soon an adult came and exchanged *salaams*. Jim spoke to him, briefly, in Arabic and he disappeared into a tent, to be replaced by a young man with a smooth face and intelligent eyes.

"My name is Sayid. My father asks that you should join us in his tent for tea," he said in perfect English.

Jim introduced his party. The man held the rein of his camel and began leading it towards the oasis. From his position in the saddle, Jim said, "You've been to Britain?"

"I was educated at the University of Kent," the young man replied. "Please, let's take the camel to water and then we can talk in comfort."

They did as they were asked, remaining silent until confronted by an old man wrapped in pure white cotton, whose teak-coloured face was so deeply lined the creases might have been sewn into the dry skin. He spoke to his son in rasping tones without smiling on the visitors. When he did look, at Alan, his eyes were like knives, trying to strip him to his bare soul. Between the host and his guests was a camel saddle covered with a sheepskin rug: a Bedu tradition.

Alan said, "Are we welcome?"

Sayid smiled. "Of course. Why should you not be?"

"Your father looks so fierce. He seems to hate me."

This brought a laugh and a translation, and then the old man grinned – an evil grin, Alan thought – revealing black and gold teeth inside the red, cavernous opening.

Jim said, "You must excuse the poor manners of my friend. The desert has not been kind to him . . ."

"Don't apologise for me," said Alan, in a furious whisper. Jim was insufferable at times. Why didn't he mind his own business?

This exchange was viewed with mild amusement on the part of the Arabs and Hassan spoke, for the first time, in Arabic. Alan did not understand what he said, exactly, but he saw Jim look embarrassed and uncomfortable and guessed it was not complimentary.

Little bastard, he thought, *I'll get you for that*.

There was more talk then, again in Arabic, between Jim and the old man. Alan felt completely left out of it. Everyone there could understand what was going on except him.

Then a cloth was raised from the carpet in front of them to reveal a spread of delicacies. The old man motioned for them to eat. Hassan left the tent at the same time.

"Where's he going?" asked Alan.

"It's Ramadan," replied Jim. "He'll eat after sunset with the others."

"He's not taken much notice of it up until now."

"I'm afraid he has. It's you who haven't taken much notice of him. Right hand only," he warned.

"I know, I know." He scanned the food in front of them. "Any sheeps' eyeballs?"

"If I find one, I'll save it for you," replied Jim.

Sayid said, "Do you wish to know what is in the dishes?"

"Yes please," answered Alan.

A catalogue followed. There was nothing terribly

180

unwholesome, and they were soon filling themselves.

The young Sayid told them that his father was not a sheik, but a merchant, and that he was pleased to be entertaining the two Christians at his table, since his son had told him much about the land from which they came.

"He doesn't disapprove of us?"

"Not entirely," was the reply.

Before they left the tent the old merchant whispered into his son's ear and the youth nodded gravely.

"My father asks that you join us tomorrow for a . . . I'm afraid to say," he smiled, "a rather barbaric game. An exhibition. Will you oblige him?"

They stared at the old man who smiled back with his top lip only.

Alan cleared his throat.

"Can we ask what this entails?"

"No. It's better that it's a surprise. You might not come otherwise."

"I see."

They of course had to agree and left the tent feeling victims of a confidence trick.

"Did you ever read *The Man Who Would Be King*?" asked Jim of Alan, when they were out of earshot.

"I know what you're thinking of – polo with a human head as a ball."

"Exactly."

"That was Afghanistan."

"Kafiristan."

"A long way from here."

They arrived at their camels to find that they had already been hobbled with short lengths of rope and there was nothing to do but sit and watch the world go by. The women, some doing their chores by the oasis, were wearing purdah, probably because the two Christians had arrived. They looked out at the strangers from behind blue masks and giggled amongst themselves.

Alan said, "What about that jousting game they play? Sabalala told me about it. *Jarid* it's called. They form armies and attack each other with spears."

Jim squinted at him.

"Real spears?"

"Well, sort of blunt wooden poles. No points on them, but I wouldn't be surprised if they bloody hurt."

"I know of a more dangerous one than that. They make a ridge out of sand and lay a rope along it, burying knives by their hilts on either side, so that the blades are upright."

Alan nodded. "Don't tell me. You have to walk along the rope, barefoot."

"While they beat you with sandbags attached to long cords."

"For God's sake, how did we get into this?"

"We didn't get much choice."

"Can't we make a run for it?"

"Too late for that. Besides, we've got to purchase some provisions from them. We're right down to the bottom of the larder. We'll just have to support each other in this. I'll have the rifles close by."

"You think it might come to that?"

"Better safe than sorry. I don't altogether trust that Sayid. If the buggers at Canterbury gave him a rough time, which they might have done, he'll be looking to take it out on us."

"That old man scares the hell out of me. He looks as though he's been conjured up in a pentangle. Evil-looking old bastard."

They passed the time by inspecting the ruined fort, which was little more than a wall of crumbling stone about a head high. Alan wondered about its history – whether any great battles had been fought within and without its walls. It stank now, of camel dung and human faeces. The people who had erected it would probably be horrified to learn that it had been reduced to becoming a toilet.

After dark, they heard the noise of feasting from the tents. Hassan had been invited to join some of the men – the drovers. It was a still, peaceful evening, with barely a breeze. The temperature had dropped and the two Englishmen sat huddled by a small fire. Laughter floated from the tents: they felt excluded, locked out.

Later, Sayid came to their fire and invited them to use one of the tents for the night. He said they would be alone and would be more comfortable under a roof. They accepted reluctantly, suspecting that they could be watched more easily if enclosed. He led them to the tent, which was covered in a soft, inviting carpet. They bade him good night and settled down in opposite corners, feeling somewhat awkward after spending so many nights out in the open. Perversely, it gave them a sense of insecurity. Neither of them felt like talking.

Alan lay staring at the darkness of the tent above him and wondered what they had in store for them the following morning. Whatever it was, he was determined to do his best. He wouldn't be shown up by a bunch of foreigners, not if he could help it!

Just then a terrible shrieking and wailing came from outside, near to the tent. He sat, bolt upright, to find himself staring across at where Jim lay, although he could not see him.

"Jim?"

"Yes – I hear it."

Alan was inclined to think that the whole desert could hear it.

"What the hell is it?"

"Sounds like a violin."

Alan was nonplussed.

Jim added, "It also sounds as if he's playing it with his left foot."

"Where the hell would they get a violin from?"

"A violin shop – Jesus, how would I know?"

At first the tune, if it could be called that, sounded wholly Arabic, but then something familiar began to filter through the awful din: a melody Alan knew well, from schooldays.

"Are you sure it's a violin?" he said. "Maybe they're torturing a pi-dog with red-hot irons? You know what that is – that tune? 'Greensleeves'. Bloody 'Greensleeves'. It's probably being played in our honour."

"Get some sleep, you'll need it tomorrow."

"Ha!"

The phantom violinist played 'Greensleeves' seventeen times in succession, in their honour, and left both men convinced that they were being worn down for their ordeal the following day. Alan decided that there was more to these bloody Arabs than he had previously thought. Their fore-fathers had obviously taken lessons from invading Spanish Inquisitors.

It was one morning when the pale dawn did not find their forms beneath its sky. Despite his anxiety, Alan had slept well. He lay with his hands behind his head listening to the sounds of activity in the camp outside. Pots were clanking and there was chatter mingling with the snorts of the camels.

"Are you awake?" he asked Jim.

"Yes."

Hassan brought them tea and bread. He seemed to be in a mood of suppressed excitement. The two men rose and ate and drank in silence in the cool interior of the tent. They were in no hurry. Any other time they would have regarded such a slow start to the day as a luxury, but this morning it had the air of condemnation about it. A locust which had found its way beneath the folds of the tent was regarding their breakfasting with apparent interest.

The two men went outside at last, carrying their rifles, but the preparations for the game were out of their sight, behind the wall of the fort. They sat outside the tent, waiting to be called, watching the women work. Hassan came to them.

"You slept well in the *house of hair*?" he said to Jim, using the Bedu name for tent.

"As well as can be expected," he replied.

"I have fed the camels."

"Good. Thank you."

"I have been with the drovers. Did you know they wash their hair in camel piss? It kills the lice. They told me this."

"Does it?"

"Yes. They told me – the women too." He wrinkled his nose. "I think I will not marry a Bedu girl. Everything is camel and goat – tent, clothes, sandals, everything. All made from goat hair and camel wool. To stink like goats and camels all your life . . ." He shook his head, wonderingly.

Alan said, "What the hell's he chattering about?"

"He's talking about the women."

"He's too young to be thinking of women," he said. "Much too young."

184

Jim smiled. "You'd be surprised. He's almost of marriage-able age."

"Well, I think childhood is too precious to tamper with so early."

Alan studied the black tents. The wind was blowing the sand in diaphanous veils over the aerodynamic shapes. They looked like huge black beetles, crawling across the sands, all heading in one direction. Monsters. The desert was full of suggestions of monsters. Nothing definite – just suggestions.

There was a shout from behind the wall and Hassan said eagerly, "They are ready."

The two men looked at one another and rose.

"Here we go," said Alan. "Don't forget your rifle."

They walked to the fort and turned the corner to be greeted by a loud cheer from the onlookers. The first thing Alan saw was the old man, sitting on his camel saddle as if he were an African king about to enjoy the spectacle of men in mortal combat. Then he saw the cricket stumps, complete with bails, out on the hardpacked earth.

Sayid, resplendent in full cricket whites, pads and bat, lifted his cap to them and called, "My father . . ." he indicated the merchant, beneath the shade of a palm ". . . has often heard stories from me about this barbaric game the English play. I promised him we would show him how it was performed."

"Good Lord," said Alan, involuntarily.

Jim laughed.

"This is supposed to be serious," said Alan. "I hope you can bowl."

"Not to save my life."

"Well, I'm not all that hot either," he said, bleakly. "This bastard is going to slaughter us. Look at him! He was probably opening bat at Canterbury. How humiliating. The British Empire is going out with a whimper. I can't bear it."

"Well, let's show them we don't go down easily."

Jim picked up the shiny new cricket ball from the ground and strode determinedly towards the wicket.

"Underarm or overarm?" he enquired politely of Sayid.

Alan groaned.

JIM

Since the caravan had replenished their supplies and the water at the oasis had been plentiful, they were at last able to turn eastwards, towards Oman.

They came out of a limestone area, and into a land of delicate volcanic-dust-grown plants. There were wide stretches of sandy basin broken by the occasional range of ragged hills. Here, the lava hung from rocks like frozen beards, and flat-topped trees provided shady rest stops in the valleys. Here were puff-cheeked snakes with red-ochre markings running through their pale, dusty-coloured lengths. Jim did not allow himself to be lulled into careless attitudes by this less hostile landscape: his eyes kept a constant check on the two necessities of life, the goatskin waterbag and the gun.

Of late, he had been having a recurring dream, wherein he lay dying from wounds, while Hassan hovered over his body like a shining angel, saying through his tears, "You not be sick. Not yet. I am not yet doctor. You wait for me to be doctor."

Jim always woke before the dying.

The dream, he was sure, was the result of stress. He felt that the group was being manipulated: that the desert, by withholding or granting its supplies of water, could turn them in any direction it wanted them to go. They were at the mercy of the watering places and their positions on the landscape.

Now the group was heading east, towards a well owned by the al-Kaffa, a notoriously aggressive tribe. He was uneasy because there was something about them which he failed to recall. Something he had heard or read. It worried him, constantly.

Then there was the stranger. The first time that Jim saw the figure it was a mere speck on the horizon. It was only when it moved that he knew it had life and he would have put it down to a stray camel, or a gazelle, had it not been for the fact that it stirred something within him – a sensation of disquiet – and he felt a shadow on his spirit.

Finally, they reached a long dark corridor of rock: volcanic cliffs which rose on either side with the vertical smoothness of obsidian. All along the faces of these cliffs were oblique striations, as fine as scratches on glass, as though some giant had carelessly scored them with his diamond ring as he dug between.

They entered and travelled along this gloomy passage and Jim's forebodings increased in the dimness of the corridor's unswerving length, until they came to its exit, beyond which lay a small basin with a remarkable feature: two rocks rose out of its centre, shaped like the tusks of an elephant.

Then he remembered. The well of the al-Kaffa mentioned in the hero's autobiography, where the man had *almost* encountered a group of three thieves, stealing the water without permission from its owners.

"We must leave here as soon as possible," he said to the others, as they camped beneath the tusks for the night. But the following morning, after drinking the water, Alan fell sick and became too ill to be moved. From his sickbed he remonstrated with Jim, saying that they should be on the move, and Jim wondered whether even his friend, less sensitive to atmospheres, was also feeling the oppression of this place.

"We can't go until you're better."

"I'm better. I really am," answered Alan, raising himself with obvious effort up on to his elbows, but after a moment he fell back. His face was the colour of dried pasta and his lips were cracked and breaking out into sores. He was in no condition to travel.

"I'm sick of the sight of sand and rock," moaned Alan. That's what's making me ill. It's driving me crazy, this land. He clutched at the dust with bony fingers. "Look at us. If we met in a London street we wouldn't recognise one another. Blistered faces – filthy dirty – these rags haven't seen water for two months. We look like a couple of *gamins*." He cast a weak but scornful glance at Hassan, who, if he understood, paid no attention to the ranting Englishman. The boy had

The boy had long since fallen into contempt of the companion of his friend and he did not bother to disguise it.

"We have to stay until – until you're fit," Jim said. "We have no choice." He looked around him. "We've had little choice all along. We were destined to end up here, in this desolate spot where there is no time."

Alan snorted. "What the hell's that supposed to mean? You're full of dramatic riddles, chum, and they irritate the hell out of me. All you do is stare out, over the desert. What do you expect to see?"

"It's not so much what I see as what I *feel*. Haven't you ever considered how this place has a timelessness to it? A hundred years ago – a thousand, a million – this looked just as it does now. There's nothing to mark the passage of time. This is the centre of the whirlpool – its heart. And it's unchanging. The wind blows, the sun beats, and the days pass without leaving any mark, any scars, to prove their passage. Time means nothing here. It *has* no meaning. We *all* exist at this moment."

Alan shook his head, wearily.

"Crazy. The sun's got to your brain at last. I thought you were the strong one – but I was wrong. Weak. You're as weak as I am. Whirlpool? This is the desert, man. Not the ocean."

"You wouldn't understand. I'm trying to explain but it just runs off you like rainwater. We don't own ourselves here. There's something more powerful. It has us and it's going to hold us, until . . ."

"Until what?"

"I don't know. I don't know how it's going to come out. Maybe we're never going to go home? Maybe we're not meant to?"

"Christ, you scare the pants off me with that spooky talk – "

"That's it. Spooks. Ghosts. Call them what you like. You meet them in places like this – the lonely marsh, the desolate moor, the desert – places where time has no meaning. Only they're not ghosts, do you see? They're just people, passing by each other at a crossroads in time. Time is marked by events. Nothing ever happens here, to leave any stain, and therefore time exists only within the moment, or not at all. A timelessness where everything exists at once. The wind blows the sand into different corners, but essentially this land is immutable. Why are you looking like that?"

He had changed tack so swiftly that it took Alan a while to answer.

"You know why. This kind of talk makes my head spin. I know you're more sensitive to atmospheres than I am, but I still think there's an element of *simoom* madness in it."

"Maybe. I don't know."

"Look – there're things happening in the world. Things going on all the time."

"But not *here*. Not here. Only we are here – and someone else."

"Someone else?" Alan raised his head a little from the sweat-soaked blanket that formed his pillow. He looked around the basin nervously. "Christ, you scare the pants off me. I . . ."

"Someone passed by this spot in his own time. Yet, if there is no time . . ."

Alan turned his head away. "I don't want to hear any more. I can feel my diarrhoea coming on again. It brings on my stomach trouble, that kind of talk. Scares the shit out of me. You should have been a witchdoctor, *shaman*, something like that – all your spooky talk."

They passed the rest of the day doing ordinary chores. Once or twice Jim saw Alan glance at his watch and shake his head. One of the saddles had come apart at a seam and Jim patiently sewed the leather back into place, making new holes where the old ones were torn. There was an intrinsic satisfaction to the work – an enjoyment in handling the soft, worn leather – which would have been denied him else-where. He liked using his hands. Even the laying of dried dung on dead shrubs to make a fire gave him an inner glow, because the task needed skill. Their matches were limited and one only could be expended for a single fire.

He could see some of this feeling coming out in Alan, though the other man would have denied it. He pretended to be disgusted at having to do manual work and grumbled the whole time – but Jim had noticed that the complaints were of

189

the kind that a mother makes when cooking her children's meal – there was a love beneath them that the worker did not wish to reveal. It was another way of expressing satisfaction.

Towards evening they made a fire in the shelter of the rocks, away from the wind. Alan was sitting up, his back against a hump of sand that Jim had made for him. He poked at the spitting fuel.

"Have you seen it?" he said quietly.

"What?" asked Jim.

"The fire – at the entrance to the corridor?"

"Yes."

"Who is it? One of the Wolves?"

"I don't know. I don't know who it is. I've seen him, from a distance. He was there before we entered the passage – way out in the desert. He seems to be following us."

"Maybe he's just coming to the well?"

"Maybe."

They both studied the distant red glow in the night. It was an eerie feeling, that they were so close to another human being. Somehow Jim looked on the basin as their own and the newcomer as an intruder. There was no comfort in the presence of a stranger. He could probably walk the distance in an hour, even at night, but he felt no inclination to do so. In fact his feelings revolted at the thought. He pulled his blanket closer round him, feeling the cold reaching deep inside him, into his bones. Hassan was already asleep, a small figure curled inside his bed on the soft sand.

"Can you use your rifle?" he asked Alan. "Are you fit enough?"

Alan was quiet for a moment. He had been humming to himself – some tuneless song from his schooldays.

"What the hell for?" he said, after a while.

"This well – it belongs to a tribe known as the al-Kaffa. They're not fond of strangers."

"And you think that buddy-boy out there is one of them? He won't attack us, surely? There's three of us. Three to one."

"Can you honestly see that stopping him? If he thinks he's in the right?"

Alan played with a twig, drawing in the dust by his hip.

190

He said, "I'm feeling a lot better. By tomorrow we should be able to move on. Early. What do you think?"

"I think that's a good idea."

A wind soughed softly along the surface of the sand. The desert had its own tuneless tunes; drew its own symbols in the sand. It held a thousand secrets locked in its breast, this harsh, forbidding land, and was relentless in the pursuit of its own kind of justice. It burned you, froze you, deprived you of sustenance. It sand-blasted your body and ate into your brain with its solitude and empty landscapes. It filled your mind with demons by day and night. It made promises it never kept, in the form of mirages. It was a bewitching liar – the land of *Fata Morgana*. When it wanted you, it could reach out, over the seas, and draw you to itself like a magnet draws an iron filing and locks it to itself. It gave of itself grudgingly and its parasites – the snakes, scorpions, hawks, spiders – were as cruel as itself in their efforts to survive.

What had happened to Sarah Ashcrofte, out in the desert? What subtleties of chicanery had been put to work on her civilised mind? It had taken her and twisted her, making of her an instrument.

Jim fell asleep with the image of her in his brain. But she had the blank face of a *jabal* and a body of sand that shifted, changing shape, as she walked towards him with her arms outstretched, welcoming him to her bed. He fought against her, but she overwhelmed him, burying his head in her breast, where he suffocated, slowly.

The following morning they rose early and ate their breakfast in silence. Then they set about loading the camels. Alan seemed to have recovered much of his strength, though his movements were slow and lethargic. The beasts were in a poor temper and he was having to contend with a camel that hindered him at every turn.

Hassan spoke to Jim as they worked.

"This man – out there. He will come now, you think? If he hurt my friend Jim, Hassan will kill him." The boy produced a broad-bladed *jambia* from beneath his shirt.

"No, Hassan," said Jim. "You must not kill anyone. What happens here is between us," he indicated Alan, "and this man. If something happens to me, you must run away. Go to

191

Cairo. Become a doctor. Do you understand?"

"I think about this." He pulled a strap tight on his mount, savagely, and the beast shifted its feet.

"No. There is no thinking to be done. Put the knife away. Promise me you will do as I say."

"I cannot."

"You *must*. I am your father now. You must do as I say."

"My father?" The boy's brown eyes were on his face, earnestly seeking something there.

"Do you promise?"

The youngster turned away.

"If you are my father, I must do as you say."

"Good."

Jim felt he had enough to cope with, without worrying about the boy. Inside, he was feeling terribly afraid – not of physical harm, that was a different kind of fear, but of himself. There was a Jim emerging that he had not known before: a cold, callous creature about to confront his destiny without emotion – that is, without the tender emotion that divides the gentle and meek from the hard and cruel. This new person felt detached from the old Jim, but dominant, as if a period of incubation had passed during which this personality had been protected while it grew, hard and unyielding in its nature. If he passed himself on the street, the old Jim would have shrank from the new; cowered against the wall.

Does a man ever know who he really is? The mild little man murders his loving wife; the tough, beer-swilling brute weeps like a baby at the death of the wife that nagged him almost insane. There are different people in us, for different circumstances. Some of them never come out, because they never need to. They are never called forth. If we live our entire lives in a suburban bungalow, doing accounts for a small firm of insurance brokers, we never meet the man inside us that, confronted by a rogue tiger, or impenetrable jungle that has to be crossed, or a sheer cliff-face that has to be climbed, does what is necessary.

The desert had changed Jim. Shown him another self. But, unlike Alan, he had expected that to happen. Now he knew, he was happy to return to the world of machines and clocks

192

and all those things he thought he hated.

Alan, too, had changed. Alan was more like the Desert Hero than Jim would, or could, ever be. Alan had crossed the desert from Sana'a to Lawdar on his own, and had survived. He had come to his own terms with the desert. Had now an understanding with it.

The difference between him and Alan was that he loved the desert, its people and its creatures: all that it stood for. But the desert did not wish to be loved. It responded best to a master: someone that treated it as a servile entity. Jim had too much affection for the desert and consequently it did not respect him. He felt integrated with it, an extension of it, and it disregarded him as it would some other part of itself: a kite or a pi-dog. It revealed its secrets to him, because he was close to it – but it would not treat him with respect.

Alan had tamed his environment: mastered it. He was in the mould of the Desert Hero: a man who held the desert in contempt and was consequently courted by it. Alan had brought the desert to heel, while Jim had adopted it.

Because he loved the desert, Jim would give it what it wanted, whatever the price to his soul. He was a sentimental man in close contact with the live earth.

Jim studied the wheeling of a kite above their camp: watched how the creature used the currents, the thermals, to conserve its energy. There was no flapping of the wings: merely a tilt occasionally, to direct it on to to a warmer current, or a streamlining as it prepared to stoop. Suddenly it dipped, down to an azure window in the rock: was framed by it for a second, before it drifted through the natural flying buttress and out of sight behind the *jabal*. The wind dry-rustled the grasses nearby and a lizard flattened itself to invisibility against the shadow of an ochre rock. There were messages in these sights and sounds, but he could not read them. Not yet.

He walked over to Alan.

"I think he's coming in," he said. "Listen."

There was an echoless padding, out in the sands.

Jim shouted to Hassan to stay by the camels.

"What's happening?" asked Alan, as Jim slid his rifle from his saddle.

193

"I don't know. Perhaps just talk – or maybe he'll come in shooting. I really don't know. We have to be prepared – expect the unexpected."

"What the hell does that mean?" growled Alan, taking out his own weapon. "Expect the unexpected? That's the sort of waffle you love, isn't it? Riddles and paradoxes that don't mean a thing. I'm just going to stand here and wait. If he gets hostile, whoever he is, *you* can do something about it. You're always telling me I have a penchant for violence. Let's see you handle it for a change . . ."

The padding on the crust of the sand increased its rate. Alan moved away from Jim, as if he wanted to be detached from the target area.

The rider was magnificent in his white, flowing robes and red-chequered headdress. No Arab would have dressed like that – not for a journey across the Great Sandy Desert. He came out of the sunrise, rippling in the wind, the rifle in the crook of his arm: poised, arrogant, every inch the public schoolboy hero. Jim could not see the aquiline nose, the sharp, blue eyes, at that distance, but he could imagine them. They would be regarding these ragged *gamins* in their camp by the well of the al-Kaffa, with disdain. Even the camel's stride was purposeful, as if it knew it was carrying one of the elite: a self-styled sultan, an English sheik. One of those who had written a place for himself in history. He *was* history.

"It was my duty, as a member of the al-Kaffa, to execute the thieves . . . it was a code by which I had chosen to live."

It was surely him. He was not real. He was the folk hero of *Boy's Own* comics; the swashbuckling, celluloid hero who lived to foster his legendary image. From his engraved saddle to his silver-embossed rifle, his image was designed to dazzle with its splendour: a figurehead behind which ordinary warriors could gather in confidence. The Bedu would not have followed one of their own as they followed him. Had he been an Arab, they would have known how he thought; would be familiar with his background; would identify with him too closely; would be hidebound by petty internal politics and jealousies, hampered by tradition.

194

He wheeled around the camp, crying out a name: using it as a battle shout.

The first shot went between Alan's legs, sending up a spurt of sand a foot behind him. He stood there, seemingly stupefied.

Again the rider cried out the name and that of the tribe that owned the well.

The second shot clipped Jim's boot. The attacker was playing with them. Alan loosed a shot, to no effect. The rider was moving fast, his robes flowing behind him like the wings of an avenging angel.

Then suddenly the unexpected happened. The man was obviously a skilled rider, but, perhaps in the excitement of the battle, he failed to see a pothole in the sand. One moment he was riding high in the saddle, every movement timed to precision, and the next he had lost control, was fighting to keep his beast on its feet.

The animal lurched heavily in full flight. Its front legs went down and it slewed along the surface of the dust on its knees. The rider dropped sideways, still clutching his weapon, and lay still.

Hassan ran forward, pulling his knife from its sheath.

Jim thought: *there's something wrong*. It should not be Hassan, it should be me, or Alan. Hassan was incidental. A peripheral figure.

The man on the ground levelled his weapon at the boy and then seemed to hesitate, as if he too knew that his target was not in the game: an extra piece thrown in, but of no importance.

A shot sounded and Hassan fell. Jim shouted. There was confusion for a moment. Then the boy examined his foot. The bullet had shattered a rock beneath his sole. He had merely stumbled.

No one moved. Stalemate.

Just then a young pack camel broke loose. The terrified animal careened around the men and the boy, bellowing. It loped over Hassan's prone body, leaving him untouched. Finally, it broke its circular run and charged out, into the desert.

It was Alan who broke the spell. He dropped on one knee

and fired. The bullet tore through the flapping robes of the attacker. It smacked into a patch of hard sand, beyond. Alan rolled sideways, expecting a return shot. None came. Instead there was laughter. Then a Bedu curse, in Arabic: "May you live in a city for the rest of your days." Not a weak curse, for a Bedu.

Jim was now the only one standing. An easy target. Yet the attacker did not fire. He suddenly realised why.

"His gun's jammed," he shouted.

The attacker went up on to one knee and was seen to be striking the bolt of his rifle with the heel of his hand.

Hassan was on his feet again. His *jambia* flashed in the sun. Thin little legs raced across the sand. He looked what he was: a child. A child, running it seemed, to greet a parent. A child with a toy in its hand.

Look what I've found, daddy.

A child who had taken the carving knife from the drawer and wanted to join the game.

Jim cried out, "Hassan!"

But the boy continued running, towards the kneeling figure.

Then the man sprang to his feet. The rifle went up to his shoulder.

"Not the boy," shouted Jim. "You want us."

Even at that distance he could see the frown. Then the jaw set.

"You bastard," he yelled, in English. "I know who you are . . ."

He began running then. Not for cover, but towards them. Jim saw what he was going to do. He wanted to reach the boy. Use him as a shield.

Hassan tripped in the same pothole that had downed the stranger's camel. But was on his feet again in an instant. His head was in the line of fire.

Jim stepped sideways smartly, paused, and squeezed the trigger. The running man stopped as if he'd hit a brick wall. He stayed on his feet and swatted at the air, brushing away a fly that was bothering him.

For a few moments he used his weapon like a walking stick, to steady his sagging body. He still had enough strength to swipe the boy aside, sending him sprawling in the dust.

Then he wiped his mouth on his sleeve and smiled when he saw the red streak on the white cloth.

Finally his legs seemed to fold in on themselves. The rifle fell sideways, silver mountings sparkling in the sunlight. Around the body, the robes fluttered, dipping themselves into the wound where the bullet had made its exit. After a few moments of profound stillness, a camel broke wind, noisily.

There was a storm coming, moving in from the north-east. The corpse was stretched out on the sands with the robes spread around it. It looked like a dead angel, fallen from the clouds. The dust formed itself into tawny veils, laying itself, sheet on sheet, over the dead man. As visibility dropped, rapidly, in the coming sandstorm, they saw a mound forming over the body.

Alan began to move forward, saying, "We must see if he's dead . . .", but the sandstorm increased in fury and it was all he could do to reach Hassan. The pair of them struggled back to where Jim was tethering the camels to one another.

The desert whipped at their faces, tore at their clothing and the volume of its wailing increased by the minute. It sound-ed, to Jim's ears, like the cry of a grieving woman. Alan gripped his arm, shouting above the howl of the wind.

"He called out the name of a dead man."

Jim nodded, dumbly.

"We saw him die," came the shout. But Jim was not sure whether his friend meant the death that had occurred a few minutes previously, or one that had occurred a long time ago, back in their childhood days, when they were ordinary people with ordinary lives.

Before they continued their journey eastwards, they looked for the body, but the sand had altered its expression and they were unsuccessful. The dead man's camel had also gone.

They reached the RAF base at Salalah without further incident.

It was there, surrounded by the comforts of civilisation, that they spoke about the man for the first time since the sandstorm had blown itself out. They were sitting in the bar, at the officers' mess, alone, at two o'clock in the morning.

"Who was he?" asked Alan.

Jim stared at his friend. "I have my own ideas – but I don't know that you'll find them acceptable."

Alan nodded. "No, I don't suppose I would, so I suppose they're best left unsaid. I suggest we say nothing to the authorities. It would only delay your flight and I doubt word of a missing Arab would reach this far."

Alan had also made up his own mind.

"You're not coming with us then?" asked Jim.

"I think I'll stay on here for a bit. Perhaps wander up to Kuwait – see what's happening in the oil world."

"Okay. Somehow I guessed you weren't ready to go home. If anyone had told me six months ago that you were destined to be an Arabian adventurer, I'd have laughed in their faces – but you're much more suited to the life than I am."

Alan took a sip of his drink. His blue eyes, startling in their tan setting, met Jim's again.

"And the boy? You said *us* a moment ago."

"Yes. I'm taking him with me."

"Good idea. You need someone to look after. Auntie Jim. You've been trying to mother me for the past few months. What about Madelaine?"

"I don't know. She's probably found somebody else now. I'll go and see her of course. We're not at each other's throats or anything like that."

"Good. Good. Well, let's shake hands here, properly. I don't want any of these RAF types to see me crying on your shoulder." He held out his hand, grinning.

Jim shook it gravely. He thought if anyone was likely to burst out into tears, it would be him.

"Look after yourself," he said.

"I intend to. When this is all over, watch out for the book."

The lights of the bar had been dimmed and the atmosphere was gloomy except for the glinting of the optics. Jim felt something stir within him: a disquiet at Alan's words. He was suddenly afraid for his friend.

"If I were you," he said, slowly. "I wouldn't mention that incident at the well. Let's keep it to ourselves."

Alan laughed. "Oh, it'll all have blown over by then. Besides. We were just defending ourselves. We had a right."

"Nevertheless . . ."

"All right. I'll think about it. Christ, you're a moody bastard these days." He slapped Jim on the shoulder. "You never used to be like this. You were the one with all the fun. The desert's changed you for the worse, my friend. Relax. Enjoy life."

It was Jim's turn to grin. "I intend to."

"And if you see Sarah, tell her it would have been wonderful, but I have a greater calling." He waved a hand in the air and they both drank solemnly.

On the flight home, with the vast empty quarter of the desert moving slowly below him, Jim asked himself the question, *why*? Had the desert really hated its hero and, thwarted of revenge by two young boys, recreated an incident from the past in order to obtain satisfaction? Or had it wanted to recall its own, to hold it for eternity, feeling that it had been robbed of the opportunity to pay reverence to its hero? He liked the second idea the best.

Then again, he admitted, it might all be in his own mind. Perhaps Alan was right? Maybe the man he had killed was an ordinary mortal, like himself, who just happened to be in the right place at the wrong time?

He looked at the boy, lying asleep, beside him. Perhaps some time in the future he would ask Hassan what he thought about it all. Whether the boy had felt any sense of preternatural atmosphere about the incident? He was too young, yet. Jim did not want to raise disturbing issues with the child – for that was what he was, a child still – when there was a strange land and strange people to cope with already. Hassan's experiences in an exotic country were about to start, not end. His adventures were just beginning.

The desert flowed beneath them, seemingly unending. Had they really crossed those stretches of sand and rock with pack animals? It seemed very unlikely, now that one was flying, hour after hour, over the same arid-looking land with its inhospitable scenery, its hostile environment. He settled back, to sleep himself.

The first thing Jim did, on arrival in the United Kingdom, was to visit the grave of the hero. It was still there. He had not altered the past. He noticed how unkempt the tomb was and he tidied it up a little, cutting down the nettles that had grown around the headstone, and scraping away the moss that had filled the lettering. The church and graveyard overlooked a valley, where the River Crouch wound its broad flat body. There were ghosts of warriors in that valley – Saxon and Viking – and apt company for the man.

So, the grave was a fact.

Did that mean that the man in the desert was an ordinary traveller? Or that a younger version of the hero occupied a natural grave in the sand?

Nothing was as neat as he would like it to be.

At first, he attempted to find Sarah.

She had left her house, almost immediately after Jim had gone to Aden. There was no forwarding address and all Jim's attempts to trace her whereabouts met with failure. Further investigation proved that her husband was missing, presumed dead, while out on operations in the Hadhramaut.

Maddie, although not wishing to live with Jim, was quite receptive to the idea that they see each other fairly often and she took a keen interest in Hassan: she was amazed at the hardships he had undergone in his short life and generally agreed to help Jim with the expenses of education.

"If he'd been our natural child, we would both have contributed," she said, "and I can tell you're very fond of the boy."

Jim still had hopes of getting back together with Maddie, but he was willing to admit to himself that they were dreams rather than probabilities. He did not try to explain to her what he could not explain to himself, and in any case, they would have sounded like fantastic excuses for what appeared to be the ordinary mid-life crisis of an over-imaginative man. He moved back, to his boyhood stamping grounds in Essex,

200

and found a job in a local clearance bank.

Shortly after Hassan had been settled in a school in Norfolk, Jim had a visit from a scholar from King's College, University of London. She explained who she was and said that she was writing a biography of the man believed to have been killed in an accident involving Jim and his friend Alan, when they had been schoolboys. The interview took place in Jim's new flat in Westcliff-on-Sea.

"I've tried to trace your friend," said the woman, who appeared to be about the same age as Jim himself, "but he seems to be abroad at the moment."

"He's in the desert – South-West Arabia," replied Jim, quietly.

"That's interesting." She scribbled a note on her pad. "What's he doing there?"

"You'll have to ask him that – when he returns." Jim paused. "You said 'believed' – believed to have been killed. What does that mean?"

The woman smiled.

"Oh, there've been a few rumours lately – nothing that's been substantiated, but one or two claims have been made."

"Can you tell me any more?"

She placed her hands in her lap and fixed her eyes on his face.

"It's been said that the man involved in the accident on the motorcycle was not . . ."

He interrupted. "Not the man you're writing about?"

"Yes. Those are the claims. As I said, it's nothing more than rumour at the moment. I'm trying to locate sources but these things are difficult – theories seem to drift in on the wind and when one attempts to find the originators, the trail goes cold."

"Are you the only one? Doing research I mean?"

"No, there's an investigative team of television reporters too. You'll probably get a visit from them. They're trying to find evidence proving that the man who died in the accident – well, that it was a case of mistaken identity."

"What do they say happened to the real man?"

She pursed her lips.

"There's a story going around that he was assassinated by British secret service agents – somewhere in the desert. It's true he was becoming an embarrassment to the government at the time – and there were others who wanted him out of the political scene of South-West Arabia. It's an unlikely story, don't you think? I mean, our government doesn't usually go in for that sort of thing. Does it?"

"It's a romantic story. It would mean he died in the desert that had helped him capture the imagination of people here."

"Quite – the desert that he loved."

"No." Jim spoke more sharply than he had intended. He softened his tone. "No, he didn't love the desert. He was its master. He used it, as one would use a slave, to further his own ambition – for his own purposes."

She smiled again, looking uncomfortable.

"Oh, come now . . ."

"Were there any other details?" he asked, brusquely. "About the assassination?"

"Plenty." She seemed put out by his abruptness. "That's the funny thing about these rumours that spring up many years after the death of some celebrity – there's nothing vague about them. Two secret service agents, with their Arab guide, were stationed at a well. When he rode in at dawn they were waiting for him.

"A report – which no one can seem to trace – apparently claims that he fired first and they returned fire in order to protect themselves. He was fatally wounded in the skirmish. A sandstorm was coming up, so, rather than attempt to carry the body back – not a very pleasant task anyway, under the circumstances – the two men left him buried by the sand, where he lay. The precise location is a mystery."

"And the other man – the one on the motorbike?"

"That's also uncertain. Obviously it would have to be someone who would not be missed. Someone who friends and relatives were not expecting to see again – perhaps about to emigrate? Something like that? They're even disputing the name – though it's a fairly common one – that the identification was a mistake, caused by disfigurement due to facial injuries. That whoever did the identification either made a mistake – or had reasons for falsifying the name. I'm sure we'll get to the truth one day, but it's a bit clouded at the moment. Some of those people I've wanted to interview are dead themselves."

Jim asked no more questions and allowed himself to be quizzed on the incident that had occurred during that early summer of his eventful life.

Five years after the interview Alan wrote to Jim saying he was coming home to Britain. He was going to write his book and, further, he was going to leave nothing out. Central to the work would be the incident at the well.

One quiet day in June, Jim received news that Alan had died in a motor accident. He was driving a hired car from the airport, along a winding English country lane, when the car went out of control and overturned. There were no witnesses, but a nearby cottager stated that he had heard the engine of another vehicle, which roared away, hidden by a high, dry-stone wall, immediately after the noise of the crash. He said it sounded like a motorcycle.